POLICE PROCEDURALS RESPECTED BY LAW ENFORCEMENT.™

"Usually it's hard for me to read cop books without picking them apart, but I read the entire Madison Knight series and I loved them all! The way Carolyn wrote Madison describes me and the way I work and even my personal life to a t."
—*Deputy Rebecca Hendrix, LeFlore County Sheriff's Department Poteau, Oklahoma, United States*

"Carolyn Arnold provides entertainment and accuracy."
—*Michael D. Scott, Patrolman (Ret.) Castroville, Texas, United States*

"For Police procedurals that are painstakingly researched and accurately portrayed look no further than Carolyn Arnold's works. The only way it gets more real than this is to leave the genre completely."
—*Zach Fortier, Police Officer (Ret.) Colorado, United States*

ALSO BY CAROLYN ARNOLD

Ties That Bind
Justified
Sacrifice
Found Innocent
Just Cause
Life Sentence
Eleven
Silent Graves
The Defenseless
Blue Baby
The Day Job is Murder
Vacation is Murder
Money is Murder
Politics is Murder
Family is Murder
Shopping is Murder
Christmas is Murder
Valentine's Day is Murder
Coffee is Murder
Assassination of a Dignitary
Hart's Choice

DEADLY IMPULSE

CAROLYN ARNOLD

HIBBERT
&
STILES
PUBLISHING INC.

Deadly Impulse (Book 6 in the Detective Madison Knight series)
Copyright © 2015 by Carolyn Arnold

Excerpt from *Eleven* (Book 1 in the Brandon Fisher FBI series) copyright ©
2011 by Carolyn Arnold

www.carolynarnold.net

2015 Hibbert & Stiles Publishing Inc. Edition

ISBN (e-book): 978-1-988064-36-9
ISBN (print): 978-1-988064-27-7

Chapter 1

Apparently not even a dead body could stop traffic.

Madison scanned the three-lane, westbound stream of cars. All of the drivers had somewhere to be. Even now, only a few braked to gawk at the investigation on the side of the road.

Squad cars with flashing lights cordoned off the right lane, and the officers were diverting traffic over. This was the busiest intersection in Stiles. With a population of about half a million, seventy-five thousand people passed through this section every hour. Shopping plazas with franchise restaurants and grocery stores occupied two of the four corners; the other two had health care buildings, including one of the city's three hospitals, the largest of which was on the northeast side of the intersection.

Peace Liberty Hospital sat on acres of land with chain-link fencing running its perimeter. It was outside that fence that the deceased had been found.

Cole Richards, the medical examiner, was working over the body as Crime Scene Unit investigators Cynthia Baxter and Mark Andrews were busy taking pictures and collecting anything that might be evidence.

Cynthia headed up the crime lab. She was also Madison's closest friend. Her strong genetics gave her the sexy librarian look, and she had wielded that power expertly over men until she got involved with Detective Lou Stanford of the Stiles PD. Now she was engaged. Three months had passed since the announcement, and Madison still hardly believed it some days.

Mark was the only man on the forensics team and the youngest of its four members. Both elements served to make him the target of blame and teasing. All in good fun, of course, even if he might not think so at times. He had long, dark hair that he tied back into a ponytail at the nape of his neck. His hairstyle and other mannerisms had most of his colleagues curious about his sexual preference. To date, it remained an enigma.

Madison lowered her sunglasses and took in the scene. It was midday and mid-July, and the sun was beating down with nondiscriminatory heat.

The deceased was an elderly woman, her identity unknown and age estimated to be in her late sixties or early seventies. She had a short cut of gray hair and wore a T-shirt and a skirt. She sat in a wheelchair on the side of the road, her head dipped to her chest at an unnatural angle. That position alone would disclose to anyone paying enough attention that she was dead.

It was a sad state when people were too preoccupied with their busy lives to notice an elderly woman on the side of the road like that. As it was, people would have passed in good quantity before the jogger who had found her had come along.

His name was Erik Marsh, and he was sitting in the back of a squad car providing his statement to the officers who had arrived first on scene. She and Terry would talk to him shortly. The people who found a body were always the first suspects.

The woman's chair was on the grass beside the sidewalk, placing her closer to the fence than the road. Based on her thin arms and frail frame, she would have needed help to get there. A wooden board strapped to the back of the chair read, PUT AN END TO ABORTION.

"Protesters in this area are not uncommon, but what makes an older lady come out and sit in the hot sun with a sign strapped to her?" She asked the rhetorical question of her partner, ruminating on what brought the woman to this point.

Her partner, Terry Grant, was three years younger than she was and her total opposite. He loved running, and his hair was always perfect—rarely were one of his blond hairs out of place. Madison, on the other hand, hated mornings, so she stuck with a wake-up-and-wear-it cut. While she had a hard time making commitments, Terry was married to his sweetheart of just over five years. Annabelle was pregnant with their first child and due any day.

Madison continued. "Not to mention, why would she get involved in such an issue? Her child-birthing days are behind her."

"She could have faced this issue earlier in life, or maybe a family member had? She could have been trying to keep things the way they used to be."

"When was abortion legalized?"

"In most states, 1973. That would make her somewhere in her late twenties, early thirties, if she faced the issue herself." Terry pulled his phone out and poised a finger over the screen. Despite Madison's desire that he take notes on a lined pad, like other cops, he was adamant about embracing technology. His hardheaded determination was paying off, though, as his texting speed was improving.

"There's no way she came alone. Someone must've brought her here. But was she dead when they dropped her off, or did she die sitting in this heat? My grandmother always wore a hat on a hot day." She paced a few steps and brainstormed aloud. "I don't think this woman chose to come here."

"Good deduction," Cole Richards stated matter-of-factly.

It was the only way Richards talked to her these days. Madison's friendship with him used to be one based upon mutual respect, but things had changed when she questioned his ruling on a prior case. From there, she had dug into his personal past. If she could go back and change things she would.

Richards continued. "Her forearms show bruising to indicate she was in a struggle, but the cause of death still needs to be determined."

Madison's gaze fell to the woman's wrists, marred in hues of purple. Heat surged through her, the fire of adrenaline blending with rage.

Richards's dark skin pinched around his eyes as he squinted

in the bright sun. "Based on the coloring of the contusions, they happened around the time of death."

"And when was that?"

"I estimate time of death between twelve and eighteen hours ago. Her body is in full rigor."

"You can't narrow it down any more than that?" Madison asked.

Richards shook his head. "Liver temp will be off given the heat. I'll know more once I get her back to the morgue and conduct a full autopsy."

"When will that be?"

He shrugged. "I'll let you know."

Madison nodded. "So you don't think she died here?" She hoped his answer would instill some faith in humanity. Surely if she'd been here for that length of time, someone would have seen her before Marsh.

"Again, I'll let you know."

"What about lividity? Doesn't it tell you anything?" Terry asked.

Lividity was the settlement, or pooling, of blood in the body after death. If it showed in the woman's buttocks and the backs of her thighs, she would have died in a sitting position. But that would've only told them she'd died in her chair, not her actual location.

"I'll let you know once I conduct the autopsy. As for *where* she died, I will leave that up to you to determine." Richards signaled for his assistant, Milo, to come with the stretcher and body bag. Sadness always soured Madison's gut when the black plastic came out, ready to wrap the dead in its dark cocoon.

She turned to face the road. "Protesters against abortion are nothing new around here, but I have a hard time accepting that she was a regular. Why would a woman her age get involved with such a controversial issue?"

"No idea. All I care about is finding out what happened to this poor woman." He put his phone away, seemingly done with taking notes.

Madison watched as the woman was sealed inside the bag. Memories of her grandmother rushed back and made her more determined to figure out all that happened to this woman. Her grandmother had been the greatest influence and supporter in Madison's life. She had died of brain tumor a couple of years ago and had left everything to Madison, overlooking Madison's mother and causing the already-existing rift between them to grow. Madison had turned down marriage and children for law enforcement, and that didn't sit well with her mother.

Madison gestured to the twentysomething man dressed in spandex who was talking with an officer and running a hand through his hair. "First, we'll speak to Marsh over there. After that, we'll show her picture to hospital personnel and see if they recognize her. If she was a regular protester or a patient, maybe we'll get an ID."

Terry opened his mouth to speak, but before he could get any words out, Cynthia called over. "Maddy," she said, holding up the protest sign in her gloved hands. "You might want to see this."

Madison and Terry stepped closer to the chair, and she followed the direction of Cynthia's pointing finger. There was an imprint on the wheelchair: PROPERTY OF PEACE LIBERTY HOSPITAL.

"We found it when we removed the sign," Cynthia said. "It looks like there is a serial number on it, too. VG235. The hospital does loan out chairs, and I bet they track it and match it to patients by those numbers."

Madison's heart sped up. Maybe this case would be an easy one to solve. In the least, having an ID was a good start. "Have Marsh brought in. We'll get to him soon."

Chapter 2

"The serial number VG235 was assigned to Elaine Bush." Jackie, the nurse behind the emergency room desk, looked over the glasses perched on her nose.

"We're going to need her address," Madison said, just as a page went out over the intercom. It was in hospital code, but Madison understood every word. A patient was missing from the psychiatric ward.

Jackie listened to the announcement and then asked, "Do you have a warrant?"

Madison was aware of the blood heating in her veins. She swore she could sense every cell as it moved through her. Her earlobes warmed, too. She didn't have the patience for a nurse on a power trip. Terry stood beside Madison, quietly letting her take the lead.

The nurse accompanying Jackie kept glancing over. She had registered several patients in the time they had asked a few questions. The scowl on her face indicated she wasn't too impressed having to handle the workload by herself. The waiting room was full to capacity with people of all ages, sporting all sorts of injuries.

Jackie must have sensed her coworker's attitude. She quickly glanced over at her and shrugged. She looked back at Madison. "I don't understand why you need—"

"Elaine Bush's body was found outside of your hospital an hour ago," Madison said.

"Help me! He's going to die." A woman in her thirties ran to the counter, dragging a man behind her. Blood poured out of a head wound.

Madison averted her eyes but not before she noticed the rebar projecting from his skull. And…all that blood.

The bile rose in her throat, and her legs became unsteady. She set her hands on the counter for balance. Her head was spinning slightly.

"Here." A nurse ran over, placed the man in a wheelchair, and carted him off. This left behind the hysterical woman, tears streaming down her face, her arms flailing in wild arcs. A second nurse at the desk calmed the woman down enough to obtain her insurance information.

When Madison looked back at Jackie, she tilted her head to the right. She wasn't fazed by what had just transpired. Of course, for an ER nurse, she had probably seen similar, or even worse, before.

Jackie's eyes drifted to Madison's hands. "You don't like blood, do you?"

Madison lifted them from the counter.

"You're a cop and you don't like blood?" Jackie chuckled. "How do you—"

"Never mind me. The woman in the wheelchair didn't die of natural causes." It might have been a push on the facts, but it was justifiable. The woman had bruising on her wrists. There had clearly been a struggle. The circumstances were strange, at best.

The grin on Jackie's face melted. She touched her neck, which had turned blotchy from nerves, a telltale sign for some people. "You're telling me she was murdered?"

"It hasn't been ruled out." Madison held eye contact. The pause allowed the smells of the hospital to permeate her sinuses— antiseptic cleaner and the fragrance of flowers, the smell of sickness and death. To think life was also brought into the world in this place…

"All right. One minute." Jackie pushed her glasses up her nose and put her attention back to the computer monitor. "Miss Bush lives at— That's odd."

"What?" Madison asked.

"There's a note on her file. The wheelchair, VG235, must have been reassigned. She ended up with another one."

"What do you mean? I don't understand."

Jackie drew her eyes from the monitor to meet Madison's. "According to Elaine's record, when they went to get her chair upon checkout, it wasn't there."

"It wasn't there? You're telling me it disappeared? It seems a lot goes missing around here," Madison said, remembering the announcement over the speakers.

Jackie's eyes glazed over in brief confusion, and then she pointed to the ceiling. "You understood the code."

Madison nodded.

"I don't know what else to tell you about the chair. It's missing as far as we're concerned."

"Well, we found it along with a dead woman."

Jackie's blotchy skin was now a bright red. "From my end, there's no way to know who she was if the chair had been missing." Her words came out low, in an almost apologetic tone.

"We're going to need Elaine Bush's number," Madison said. They needed to confirm, without a doubt, that Elaine wasn't the one in the chair.

"Certainly."

The other nurse glared over at Jackie. "Watch what you're doing," she said.

"Keri, a woman is dead."

"Still." The other nurse shook her head and went back to another patient.

"Here you go." Jackie handed Madison a piece of paper with Bush's phone number scribbled on it.

Madison dialed it immediately. After three rings, a woman answered, identifying herself as Elaine Bush. After confirming some information with the woman, Madison hung up the phone.

She stepped away from the counter, gesturing for Terry to come with her. "The woman in that chair was not Elaine Bush."

"So we find out who she was."

She nodded. "Unfortunately, it's not going to be quite that simple. I'd wager she didn't die where she was found, all things considered."

"You want to make a bet?" There was a spark in Terry's eyes. It wouldn't be the first time they made bets during an investigation. The regular was twenty dollars. While she'd like to claim she won the majority of the time, it wasn't necessarily an honest assessment. But she wasn't in the mood.

"No, I don't want to make a bet. I want to find a killer."

"Come on, I could use the extra money with the baby coming."

She sighed. "Fine."

"The regular amount?"

"Sure, why not?"

"You say the lady died elsewhere, and I say she died where she was found." He extended his hand to seal the wager with a shake. She complied, and he was all business when he pulled his hand back. "Let's go to the abortion clinic, see if they recognize the woman. You didn't actually think it would be as easy as providing them a chair number and getting an ID, did you?"

"I had hoped."

"Zip-a-dee-doo-dah, zip-a-dee-ay. My, oh my…" A man in a white hospital gown was skipping down the hall, a few orderlies chasing after him.

"It seems they found their missing psych patient." Apparently, Terry had understood the code, as well.

Madison rolled her eyes at his obvious statement. "Nothing escapes your grasp, does it?" She headed toward the elevator, hiding her smirk.

Chapter 3

"How does a wheelchair just go missing?" Madison asked Terry as they shared an elevator up two floors to the abortion clinic.

"I can only imagine the traffic going through this place in a day. It might not be as hard as you think."

"A hospital employee wouldn't stand out pushing one."

"Like I said, Maddy, I don't think anyone would. You saw how crowded that waiting room was and the number of people who were being helped by the other nurse at the desk."

Her phone vibrated, notifying her of a text message. It was from Cynthia. Richards booked the autopsy for first thing the next morning. Madison shared this information with Terry, and although he nodded, his eyes seemed distant—a common occurrence these days.

Doctors had told Terry and Annabelle that their baby could be born with spina bifida, but they strived to stay positive.

"Are you thinking about the baby?" Madison asked.

"I'm thinking of *him*, yes." He gave her a slick smile. Despite ultrasounds not revealing the baby's sex, Terry was convinced it was a boy.

"How is Annabelle these days?"

"She's excited, nervous. She wants him out." He laughed, but the expression quickly deflated.

"Good. And I bet." Madison was thirty-five and didn't have a mothering bone in her body. If she thought pregnancy through to birth—all the bodily fluids and the blood—it made her squeamish and just sealed the fact she would likely never have a family.

"So if you get to ask about my life…" he teased.

"Oh, no, you don't. My relationship with Matthews is off the table."

"Matthews? Sounds rather formal and cold."

Troy Matthews was head of SWAT for Stiles PD. She'd known him for years, but it wasn't until a recent case that their friendship had turned into something more. Despite her initial resistance, some things cannot be stopped. The draw she had to him was one such thing. He was an alpha male and, as such, attracted women in droves. He was into working out and ripped. But he was serious-minded and interested solely in her—or so he kept trying to convince her.

Madison took a deep breath thinking back to last night—their bodies entangled, moving together… She had to wish the images from her mind. At least for right now. They were on a case.

"I can tell by the flush of your cheeks, things are heating up."

"Oh, shut up." She punched him in the shoulder and then smirked. Her relationship with Terry would never change. He was like the younger brother she'd never had.

"By the way, you're looking good these days," he added.

She narrowed her eyes, tempted to punch him again.

"What?" He lifted his shoulders, hands palms out toward her. "I just noticed. I thought women liked this type of acknowledgment."

But she wasn't "most women." She wasn't worried about what men thought of her. After being betrayed by her fiancé in her early twenties, she'd been somewhat bitter for the better part of a decade now. It didn't help that he—Toby Sovereign—was also a detective and currently working with Stiles PD. The greatest tragedy was how she held what he had done to her against all men who had entered her life—up until now. She still dated, of course, but she never allowed anyone to get too close. No, her heart was hers and hers alone. With that state of mind, though, the loneliness was also hers alone. She had both Cynthia and Terry to thank for helping her to see that life was too short to sit around and mope. Even Troy deserved some of the credit.

"You must be working out," Terry said, breaking her train of thought. "Does Troy have you on a program?" Terry snickered, evidently amused with his innuendo.

"Would you just—"

The elevator dinged, interrupting as it announced their arrival on the second floor.

She stepped out first. Not that she'd admit it to Terry, master of the treadmill, who ran ten miles every morning, but she *was* exercising. And eating healthier. Before her shifts, she'd walk Hershey, her chocolate lab, at a brisk pace for an hour. Thanks to the obedience classes she was able to fit in every other Saturday, he was a pleasure to walk. She had started with one block and kept building herself up.

She hated to concede that the new lifestyle had anything to do with Matthews—Troy. She still slipped sometimes, but it was beginning to get easier to refer to him by first name. She was doomed. Whenever she sensed the trepidation setting in, the hesitancy over accepting their relationship, she'd blurt out *Matthews* to establish focus again.

But life had taken her through a lot in recent months. She had almost died at the hands of the Russian Mafia and came close to being raped by one of them, too. Faced with the muzzle of a revolver to her head, she had promised herself that she would forgive past hurts and try to love again with a full heart. The latter was really tough. It equated to vulnerability, the very thing she always did her best to avoid.

The elevator started to close, and Terry was still in it. She stuck her hand out to hold back the doors. "Are you coming?"

"Yeah. I guess so."

There was a small waiting area in the clinic with three patients waiting for their turn. One woman was by herself. The other two had someone with them—one a man, the other seemingly a female friend.

Madison and Terry approached the front counter. The blond receptionist's smile faded when Madison held up her badge.

Then she brought up a photograph of the dead woman on her phone and extended it to the nurse. "Do you recognize this woman?"

She leaned forward and squinted as if she needed glasses but refused to wear them. "I do."

"Do you know her name?"

"No. Sorry." She sat back in her chair and Madison noted her name tag: MARY ELLEN.

Mary Ellen had just looked at the picture of a dead woman she recognized, and there was no evidence that the news shook her.

"She was found outside the hospital perimeter."

"Someone killed her? That's why you're here?" Tears beaded in her eyes as if everything was just sinking in.

"You knew her, but you don't know her name?" Madison was struck by the conflicting responses and emotion. First, no reaction, and now she seemed distraught. But Madison could relate to how the woman was feeling. Not that she ever cried at a crime scene. It was bad enough that she hated the sight of blood and had vomited in front of Troy Matthews once because of it. But there had been exceptional circumstances.

"I pass the protesters on the way home in the evening," Mary Ellen replied, "and I have seen her out there before."

"Was she normally in a wheelchair?"

Mary Ellen shook her head. "Even though I work in here and she stands against abortion, she was inspiring. Here was this delicate, gray-haired woman, standing tall for what she believed in."

"She was out there on a daily basis?" Terry asked.

"Come to think of it, she hasn't been out there in some time."

Madison glanced at Terry. It was likely that whoever left the woman outside the hospital knew that she protested abortion.

"'Some time'?" Madison prompted for a precise answer.

"A couple months, I think."

"Was she ill? Did she have an operation?"

"I'm sorry, I don't know."

"Did you happen to notice the sign she held?" Madison asked.

"Yeah, it said, 'Put an end to abortion.' Simple and direct."

"A wood sign, painted lettering?" Terry inquired.

"Yes." Mary Ellen's eyes squeezed shut and then opened again. "What does that have to do with anything?"

"She was found with that sign strapped to the back of a wheelchair," Madison said. She thanked Mary Ellen for her insights, and after they spoke to some other nurses, Madison and Terry headed back for the elevator. It was apparent they were missing key aspects to this case already. No ID on the woman. No apparent motive. Was she disposed of because the family couldn't afford burial? Had her death been an argument taken too far? It likely wasn't elder abuse, as Richards had said the bruising happened around the time of death. She factored in, as well, that it was possible the person who left her there was the one who found her. Remorse could have set in afterward.

"We need to see what Marsh has to say," she said. Part of her expected Terry to defend the man's innocence, how he probably just happened upon the older woman. "You have nothing to say?"

"Nope. I agree with you."

"You what?" Terry was rarely in quick agreement, and while it was an obvious next step to what was before them, he'd been overly accommodating since her recent situation with the Russians. In some ways, she'd rather he go back to his regular, snappy nature that had her defending herself at most intervals along an investigation.

Chapter 4

Officer Ranson, who operated the front desk for Stiles PD, smiled at Madison. Her hair was dyed a dark maroon, and was, in Madison's opinion, a win compared to the deep purple from last week.

"I'm looking for Erik Marsh," she said. "He was brought in regarding my case—"

"She means *our* case," Terry corrected.

Ranson's gaze went from Terry to Madison, a smile on her face. "He's in interrogation room three."

"Detective Knight." It was her boss, Sergeant Winston. "What's the latest on the new case?"

Madison wondered if he babysat his other detectives the way he did her. Every time she turned around, he was requesting an update. He was about talk; she was about action.

"We're just about to question Erik Marsh," Madison said.

"Let's go to my office." Winston stepped away, motioning for her and Terry to follow him.

She felt like she was being summoned to the principal's office. "Sarge, can we do this another time?"

"Another time that is convenient for you?"

"Preferably, yes."

Winston shook his head. "You'll never change."

She wanted to say *likewise* but managed to hold the word back. Things were better between them since Chief McAlexandar stepped down, but it seemed like the puppet strings still stretched from the man's retirement.

The new police chief, Andrea Fletcher, wasn't hands-on. Beyond her appointment to office, Madison wouldn't even know of her existence. But there was a reason Fletcher didn't get involved the way McAlexandar had. He had been pocketing money from the Russians and had used his position as chief to keep the police out of their business. As soon as Madison had the irrefutable proof of this, McAlexandar would be facing prosecution.

While Madison had a part in locking away the head of the Mafia, Dimitre Petrov, his reach extended from behind bars. Dimitre's defense attorney, Bryan Lexan, was killed shortly after Dimitre was sentenced to life. Madison had no doubt the former police chief hid discriminatory evidence in the case, and it went cold. All of that had been the better part of five years ago, but a few months ago, Madison had found some restitution. Her hardheaded determination to finally close the investigation resulted in her being captured by the Russians and a subsequent string of murders. The sad part was even though she knew the identity of the assassin—Constantine Romanov—justice hadn't yet been served. Constantine had managed to escape custody and was probably back in Russia.

As for at least a couple victims, Madison felt their blood was on McAlexandar's hands. He may not have been the one to pull the trigger, but he had provided the necessary information to lead Dimitre's man to the right place at the right time. In prior cases, he had made evidence disappear for the Russians, and to top it off, he was in direct contact with Dimitre. The latter was corroborated by live testimony from the former warden at Dimitre's prison, who was too afraid to go on record. But one thing was sure: there was no reason for McAlexandar to be communicating with Dimitre unless they had evil intentions.

So Madison managed what was within her control. She had Dimitre transferred from "Club Med" to a real prison, one where he'd have to start his relationships from scratch. Everyone was bought where he was before. But her control, her reach, only seemed to be getting her so far. Surely McAlexandar, a cog in the wheel, would be easier to bring down than a Russian assassin would. She'd have to give the matter some thought.

"On the count of three, pull the trigger."

The quick flashback made goose bumps raise the hairs on her arms. As she pulled herself back to the present, she aligned eyes with Terry.

"Let's get this over with," she said, and she and Terry entered the sergeant's office.

Winston sat behind his desk. As usual, it was heaped with paperwork. Next to one pile was a mug with ring stains and some coffee inside. The lack of steam told Madison the beverage was cold by this point. She shuddered to think how bitter it would be now. Fresh brew from the bull pen was strong enough to disintegrate a spoon.

The sergeant clasped his hands together on the desk. "Tell me where you are with the case."

"We were about to speak with the man who found her, Erik Marsh," Madison said. She somehow resisted rolling her eyes. Her boss was preoccupied with every tiny step in a case.

"What are you thinking so far?" The sarge's gaze went to Terry.

Terry glanced at Madison and then answered. "It's still early. Whether she died by intentional or accidental means still needs to be determined by Richards."

"I understand that she had bruising on her arms. That shows she was defending herself."

"Yes," Madison chimed in. "On her wrists. But the bruises didn't kill her." Madison rose. "We've got to speak to Marsh. Now."

Her hurry held no impact on the sergeant. Neither did her cold response. His eyes skimmed over her and went back to Terry, who was still seated.

Terry continued. "It seems possible that a loved one got into an altercation with her, but the wheelchair she was in was definitely stolen from the hospital."

"Maybe a family member dropped her off to save funeral expenses?" Winston theorized.

"It's possible but doesn't explain the bruising," Madison began. "Sarge, we need to speak to Marsh. We don't even know who this woman is yet."

Winston brushed them off with his hand. They were almost out the door when he called out. "Keep me informed, Knight."

CHAPTER 5

"WHAT IS UP WITH THAT MAN? You'd think he'd be less controlling with McAlexandar gone," she said as they walked down the hall. Her strides were long, her earlobes heated from anger.

"He's got a new boss now. Something tells me he might not be adjusting to it as well as we are," Terry said.

"Isn't that too bad." Madison smirked. She loved having a woman at the top. It might still be a man's world, but a revolution had begun. She stopped outside interrogation room three. "Let me do the talking."

"Of course. You're so good at it."

"Hardy har."

"That's my line."

Her smile disappeared as she reviewed the background report an officer had pulled on Erik Marsh. "Just great. He doesn't have a mark on his record." She sighed and stepped into the room. Strong-smelling perspiration slapped her in the face. Erik Marsh must've put in quite a workout before finding the deceased.

"Can I go now?" he asked right away.

Madison slid into a chair across from him. "I'm Detective Knight, and this"—she indicated Terry with a slight bob of her head—"is my partner, Detective Grant. We have some questions for you first."

Confusion showed in Marsh's eyes. "I told everything I know to an officer already."

"We have reason to believe that the woman might have died of natural causes." If he believed that's what they thought, it might draw him out more.

"If she died from natural causes, why are detectives investigating her death?"

He was smart, she'd give him that. "A body found under these circumstances needs to be investigated, regardless of the cause of death." She let that sit there for a few seconds. "Did you ever see that woman before today?"

"No."

"You're sure?"

"I swear."

Terry walked behind him, jingling the change in his pocket. It was a method he used to throw suspects off and distract them in the hopes of making them slip up.

Marsh looked over a shoulder at Terry. He stopped the jingling for a second.

"Like I told that cop, I just found her like that. I was on my midday jog. People usually pay attention to me. I don't know, I have good energy, I guess. But she didn't look at me and her head was at an odd angle. I could tell something wasn't right."

"After you saw her, what did you do?" Madison asked.

An exasperated exhale. "I went over to her. She was dead. I called nine-one-one."

"And you waited for officers to arrive?"

He nodded.

"Then what did you do?"

"Like I said, I've been through all this. I need a shower, lady—detective." He corrected himself under her watchful eye. "I never saw her before in my life. I wish I could still say that."

"You said the first thing you noticed about her was the tilt of her head?"

"Yes. Can I go now?"

"One more question: where were you last night until the wee hours this morning?"

His cheeks puffed and he blew out the air. "Last night, I had a beer with a friend, over at his place. In the wee hours I would have been sleeping next to my wife."

Madison asked for his friend's name and made a note of his alibi. But without anything substantive to hold him any longer, Madison had Terry show Erik out. Terry returned to the room.

"What are you thinking?" Terry asked.

"I think that she was placed in that chair after death, but not long after."

"Based on?"

"Richards estimated that she had died likely between twelve and eighteen hours prior. She was in full rigor."

"Right. It's twelve hours to set, twelve in, and twelve to come out."

"Rigor starts setting in between two to six hours after death. We found her at noon."

"Okay. So, the time of death would be between six last night and midnight."

"That's quite the time span, but she was likely placed in the wheelchair within a couple hours of death…for her neck to settle forward," Madison said.

"Richards will be able to confirm the position she died in with lividity."

"We're looking for someone who took that chair anytime from eight last night until two this morning."

"Not that this helps us. A hospital is a somewhat public place, Maddy. People can come and go. Do you really think those nurses would notice someone leaving with the chair? They could just think they were taking it out to help someone from their car."

She hated to admit that he had a point.

"What do you suggest for our next step?" Terry asked.

Her gaze caught the clock: 4:00 PM. "Call Erik's friend, confirm what Erik told us. Then your next step will be to speak with the picketers."

"Me? And what are you going to be doing?" He crossed his arms.

"I have an appointment."

"But you're in the middle of a case."

His statement would normally make her think twice about leaving, but this time she waved a hand over her head on her way to the door. "Tell me how you make out."

He mumbled something. She wasn't going to let it deter her. When she was held captive by the Russians, she had also promised to take care of herself if she survived the whole ordeal. That included seeing a psychiatrist.

Chapter 6

ALL TERRY WANTED TO DO was go home to Annabelle. With the baby due any day, it was taking a lot out of her, rallying her fears to the forefront, reawakening the possibility that their son could be born with spina bifida. He did his best to placate her, telling her everything would be all right until he went hoarse. But it didn't seem his words were getting through. She had this image in her mind of everything going sideways, and her viewpoint made him face the possible reality that their son wouldn't be born healthy.

Terry wasn't worried about changes to his own life. He was concerned with the quality of his son's, the tribulations he'd undergo, the teasing he'd receive from other children. He'd never fit in, no matter how marvelous he was. His peers would see only his disability.

Every parent wanted to bring a child into the world and have them be loved by everyone. But, sadly, humanity hadn't evolved to the level of accepting differences, despite the claims to the contrary. Instead of embracing uniqueness, those who were different were persecuted.

He parked at the curb. The scene had been cleared and the protesters had already moved in. There were six of them—four women and two men. They stopped jostling their signs when he walked toward them.

Badge held up, he said, "Stiles PD. I have some questions."

A brunette came closer to him, distinguishing herself as the leader. "My name's Janis. We stand in defense of saving lives."

She waved her sign up and down, antagonizing the rest to follow her lead.

They must have thought he was there to remove them from the city's property. He could have shown them a photo of the dead woman, but he'd try things another way first. "Are you familiar with an older woman who protested here?"

The chanting stopped, and the rest of the crowd gathered closer behind Janis.

"Faye!" This came from a man standing in the back. He was well over six feet tall with a scrawny frame and greasy hair. He wore jean shorts and a white T-shirt with an image of a fetus encased in a heart. Above the graphic was CHOOSE LIFE.

"We all knew her," Janis said.

Maybe he'd be home to Annabelle sooner than he thought. "Do you know her last name?"

Janis was shaking her head. "We are friends here for a shared purpose, but we don't get into one another's business."

"Did Faye protest on a regular basis?" He remembered what the nurse had said but wanted to hear if Janis's answer matched.

"She did, but we haven't seen her in a while. We have talked about her and thought that maybe she had died. Wait a minute—" her gaze drifted to his badge "—something did happen to her, didn't it?"

"That's what I'm trying to find out. A woman was found dead here this morning. Her identity still needs to be confirmed." It was time to bring out the photograph. He extended it to Janis.

She hesitated, then took it and looked at the image. "Oh my God." Her sign slipped to the ground. She covered her mouth and spun to face the group.

The guy with the printed T-shirt analyzed Terry, his gaze taking him in from his shoes to his eyes.

"Is there something I can help you with?" Terry asked.

The guy shook his head. "I'm just in shock."

"What's your name?"

"Craig."

"Well, Craig, how well did you know Faye?"

Craig's face scrunched up in disgust. "I don't have a grandma fetish, if that's what you mean."

"Yet, it's funny how you went right there." No reaction. Terry's implication soared right over the guy's head. Craig wasn't too bright.

Terry's mind slipped to thoughts of his son again. His boy would be brilliant. God, he couldn't wait to meet the little fella. Sometimes it was hard to reel in the emotions while eagerly anticipating his arrival into the world. He could already see him graduating high school, even college, and falling in love and getting married. His envisioning always stopped there. Beyond that, he and Annabelle would probably be in a nursing home having *their* diapers changed. Why was life such a circle?

He mentally shook himself back to the investigation. "Did family drop her off? Did she walk? Did she take public transportation?"

"She walked, I think."

"She must not have lived too far away, then?" It was a reach. It was possible she took public transportation to one of the plazas across the street and walked from there.

"Not sure, but I think so."

"Think so, what? She walked or lived close-by?" Terry asked to clarify.

"Both."

Janis rejoined them. Her cheeks were stained with tears as she handed the photo back to Terry. "Faye walked. She loved getting fresh air. That's what she said anyway."

Terry nodded. "One more question. Do any of you know why Faye protested?"

Janis was chewing on her bottom lip. "I do."

CHAPTER 7

PH.D. TABITHA CONNOR GESTURED TOWARD the sofa. She was the perfect image of a psychiatrist with her straight posture, chignon, and thin frame. Her eyes were intelligent, too—knowing.

After Madison was freed of the Russians, she had been ordered by her superiors to see a shrink. Her resistance hadn't mattered. The fact that shrinks were for other people, not her, hadn't mattered. Dr. Connor had refused to be manipulated, even by the former chief.

But somewhere along the line, things had changed. Madison now came to see Dr. Connor willingly. It was at the urging of a few people, including her younger sister, Chelsea. For being six years her junior, Chelsea was like a surrogate mother. They got along better than Madison did with their mother.

Madison settled onto the sofa in Dr. Connor's office, the one she now found comforting and familiar. She grabbed a throw pillow and placed it on her lap. She pinched one corner.

"The last time you were here we talked about these events you continue to experience," Dr. Connor said.

Dr. Connor called flashbacks and nightmares *events* as opposed to *episodes* because she found the terminology friendlier.

"Have you experienced any more since your last visit?" Dr. Connor's pen was poised over her notepad.

Madison's natural inclination was to refuse acknowledging what had happened earlier in the day, how the brief recollection had hit her out of nowhere, how it had affected her viscerally. Maybe it was brought on by the fact that she was coming here this afternoon. She remained hesitant about speaking her feelings out loud, even to Dr. Connor. She might not be a stranger anymore, but she was another individual. And verbalizing emotions made them real. They were easier to ignore when they remained unsaid.

"I sense that you did have an event."

"I did," Madison said.

"Do you want to talk about it?"

"I have a choice?" She attempted to smile but wasn't sure it showed.

"You always have a choice, Madison. But I assume you continue coming here for a reason."

And they both were aware of what that reason was: being held hostage by members of the Russian Mafia, having a revolver pressed to her temple, and almost being raped three months ago. The whole thing had changed her perceptions of life, of herself, and of her limitations. And it brought up a lot of unresolved anger.

Before all this, she had been strong-willed, determined, and unstoppable. Now, she was at the mercy of flashbacks that would catapult her back in time at any given moment. And they were so clear they encompassed all five senses. She heard the Russians' voices. She felt the pressure of the gun's barrel against her head. She smelled and tasted her own blood.

"Madison?"

She slowly lifted her eyes to meet the doctor's. "I had a brief event this afternoon." She paused to build her strength. "It went back to when Anatolli had the revolver to my head."

"Ah, yes, Russian roulette?" she confirmed.

"Yes, without the Russian part." Her saliva thickened to paste.

"We simply call it roulette when we play. The Russian part would be redundant." Sergey paces the room. She catches the flicker in his eyes. "Anatolli's going to pull the trigger. If you live, we will take our time with you. If you die..." He shrugs. "Well, I suppose, game over."

Both men laugh.

The chills came over her in a flash. She rubbed her arms, the hairs standing on end.

Dr. Connor scribbled something in her notebook. "And how did this make you feel?"

"Cold."

"Did you just have another event?"

Madison shook her head.

Dr. Connor angled her head to the left. "This only works if you're honest with me."

The doctor held the eye contact. Madison looked away first.

"Yes," she admitted.

"Share with me."

Madison slid her hands up and down her arms vigorously as she explained. The movement sounded like two sheets of sandpaper rubbing together. "This afternoon, it was, 'On the count of three, pull the trigger.'" Her heart palpitated.

"What is it about those words that strike you?"

Dr. Connor was all about hidden messages and subtext. They had discussed this before. According to her, emotions came up when they were ready to be addressed.

Madison took a guess. "I was given to the count of three to live?"

Dr. Connor uncrossed her legs but remained settled with her back against her chair. "Are you sure that's all?"

"I think so."

"Countdowns can also represent goals needing to be achieved or things to be accomplished. Look beyond the obvious, Madison. Could it be the pressure you place on yourself to have all the answers? To solve every murder brought your way? What were you dealing with when this memory arose?"

Madison gave the question consideration. "I was thinking about Constantine Romanov."

The man who almost raped and killed me…

"What about Constantine?"

The rage firing through her system was unavoidable. It came without invitation; it came without hesitation. It was raw, instinctual. "I was trying to solve that cold case for years, and I finally had the man behind that murder and several others." She paused. Emotion was churning through her and changing its face so quickly it was hard to adjust from one moment to the next. Guilt and remorse were trying to bury themselves deep in her soul. "If I had just let it go…"

Dr. Connor gave it a few beats, letting Madison's words hang before she spoke. "You still blame yourself."

Madison blinked back the tears. If therapy was supposed to be good for her, why did she always feel worse when she left? Stranger still was that she kept returning.

"Of course, I do. I had him. He was in custody." Madison paused, daring Connor to object, to interject that she hadn't been the one guarding the man's hospital room when he'd escaped. "This is all on me, but so help me God, that man will pay for what he did." The anger was back, superseding any sadness or self-flagellation. She looked Dr. Connor in the eye. "I swear to you as long as Constantine Romanov roams this planet as a free man, I will never rest. I will be his stalker, his shadow, his bump in the night. If it's the last thing I do, he will pay for his crimes."

"Including what he did to you?"

Madison couldn't bring herself to answer. All those lives lost because she had kept prying. But what other choice did she have? She needed to find out who was behind the murders and make them stop.

"You are always concerned about other people, Maddy. Constantine almost raped you, and he would have succeeded if—"

"But he didn't, did he?" she challenged, wishing she could just forget it all.

Chapter 8

Madison had left Dr. Connor's office angry and determined. And full of self-doubt. Did she even possess the ability to take down Constantine? He could be anywhere in the world. She had no doubt he was laughing over her incompetence.

She had considered showing up at Terry's house to ask how he had made out with the protesters, but she needed some time alone. Instead, she had left him a voice mail, picked up a bottle of wine, and headed home.

There were three things she could rely on to improve her mood—a glass of red, Hershey's fur, and a Hershey's *bar*. The wine was on the coffee table in front of her. Her chocolate lab was on the couch beside her. The bar was already in her stomach.

She rubbed Hershey's head, her mind far away.

From Dr. Connor's office to home, Madison had recalled the age-old advice to dig two graves when setting out for revenge. It was a warning pulled from the recesses of her mind. What it meant was unmistakable, but she was inclined to ignore the advice.

Constantine probably existed under an alias, but she would find him. Or it might be easier to let him come to her. It had worked before.

In the dim light coming through the windows, she makes out his silhouette on her couch.

"How nice of you to join me, Detective. I've been waiting all night."

She reaches to her waist and draws her gun.

"I wouldn't do that if I were you." He turns on the light on the side table next to him, leaving Madison's eyes to adjust to the brightness. When they do, she sees that Constantine is holding Hershey under his right arm. *"We've been waiting for you. Why don't you put the gun down?"* He puts his hands on both sides of the dog's head, staring down into his eyes. *"Cute dog you have here. But I've never seen the purpose of dogs. It would only take one twist and your little hush puppy would be in doggie heaven."*

Her heart raced. Her breathing was shallow. She sank her fingers into Hershey's fur as the flashback hurtled forward at lightning speed.

Constantine finds the base of her shirt and rips the material up her torso until she lies exposed, her breasts screened off only by her bra.

Her stomach roils as his hands wrap around her and unclasp her bra. "I should just strangle you with this."

Shivers trickled through her, shaking her frame.

She hated what he had done to her. He might not have raped her body, but he had violated her, nonetheless. He had left her powerless and waiting. He would surely be sent back to kill her, but she refused to live looking over her shoulder. She would not allow the Russians to wield that much control. It was bad enough the memories haunted her as waking nightmares.

Madison rubbed Hershey's head again and then leaned over to kiss him. She barely escaped the slip of his tongue and she laughed. *Oh, to be a dog.* They had no concerns. Every second was the dawn of a new adventure. When they were tired, they slept. When they were hungry, they ate. When they wanted to play, they played. It was such a simple existence.

She gulped down a mouthful of wine and set the glass back on the table.

It had happened right here, three months ago.

If not for her quick maneuver and trigger finger, things would have ended differently. She swallowed. She wanted to forget all of it but kept remembering—the humiliation, the vulnerability, the regret. She should have shot him to kill, but she had wanted him to pay for his crimes. She had been naive. If a man like that walked away, he disappeared into the wind.

She got up from the sofa and went to her desk. Her apartment was compact and open concept. The front door opened to the kitchen on the left, a small dining table to the right, and the living space behind both. Her office—in the loosest sense of the word—was a desk and a dated computer set up to the side of her living room. But she did have Internet access.

As she sat down, her wine in one hand, she didn't know what she was going to do, but she had to draw the man to her somehow. It must have been the haze from the alcohol or her stubborn nature that made her feel she had to *do* something. She didn't need to do anything. She knew this in her soul. Constantine would be back without any effort on her part. He was on the No-Fly List, but that wouldn't stop him from returning to the States. The Russians wouldn't be satisfied with his freedom. Her investigation into Lexan's death had upended their organization.

Her landline rang. She jumped, her wine sloshing over the lip of the glass.

"Shit." She licked her fingers and put the glass down. She didn't really care about leaving a wine stain on the top of the desk. It was a cheap find at a department store.

"Who is it?" she answered the phone. For this line to ring, it meant someone was downstairs and wanted up.

"Terry."

She hit the button that unlocked the front door, and a couple of minutes later, Terry was in her apartment.

"How did you make out with the protesters? I left you a voice mail," she said.

"I'm here, aren't I?" He brushed past her, moving farther into her place. "Drinking alone, are we?" He must have noticed the wineglass.

"Don't change the subject. What did you find out? Did they know her?"

"You know it's not good to drink alone. Some would say only alcoholics drink a—"

"Terry, so help me God." She closed the door and then turned to him.

He was smirking. Good old Terry, who lived to bug her. He really was like the brother she never had.

He laughed, and she followed his gaze to the bottle on the counter.

"Do you want some? If you do, I won't be drinking alone anymore."

He dismissed her with a wave of his hand. "I'm not staying long. I just came by to let you know I have a first name. Faye."

"And that's all?"

"Wow, Terry, that's awesome. Good work," he mocked.

She narrowed her eyes at him.

"Fine. Be all serious. You know how we were trying to figure out why a woman her age would protest abortion. I have the answer. But I also wanted to let you know that Erik's alibi has been verified."

"All right, now you're killing me."

"Her sister was going to have an abortion, but she didn't. Apparently she'd been a teen when she got pregnant."

"There must be quite the age difference between Faye and her sister. You had mentioned abortion became legal in '73."

He nodded. "Well, in this case, Faye's parents demanded her sister have an abortion, rather than shipping her off and giving the kid up for adoption."

"They were worried about their reputations," Madison guessed aloud.

"Most likely. But Faye's sister ran away and raised the child on her own. She didn't resurface for years."

Madison nodded, understanding perfectly. "Faye's sister and her child were precious to Faye so she protested for them."

"And to make it even more personal," Terry added, "Faye wasn't able to have children."

Chapter 9

I can't move my wrists. The smell of blood is up my nose, in my mouth. The shadows looming in the corners shift and transform.

Anatolli emerges, holding a revolver.

My heart is beating like a piston, and my breath is labored as I struggle against the restraints.

He's coming closer and there's nothing I can do.

My head is locked in place, the clasp around my neck limiting my range of motion.

He's pulling on my hair, yanking it so hard my vision goes to pinpricks of red with flashes of white.

"You are going to die." His spittle mists my face, and he lowers to look me in the eye. But it is no longer Anatolli. It's Constantine.

Madison jolted awake and bounded from her bed. Hershey let out a startled bark. He must have been dreaming, too. Madison hoped he'd been running through a field or eating a bone—something peaceful.

"Sorry, buddy."

Hershey stretched out, worming his way to the edge of the mattress.

She rubbed his fur, waiting for her heartbeat to calm down. "It was a nightmare, that's all."

Was that all? It was so vivid. Her visceral reactions to the images were so real. She knew these men were dead, but Constantine was still alive, out there somewhere. And the simple fact remained that she had upset the Russians and there would be consequences.

Really, it was surprising that they had let her live as long as they had. Dimitre Petrov must have derived more pleasure from toying with and manipulating her than killing her.

She sat down on her bed, reality hitting her. The Russians would have tired of playing games. When they came for her next, they would be coming to kill her. Oddly, she found herself hoping they'd torture her first so she could find a window to escape. And if she got the chance, she'd shoot to kill this time.

Her breathing slowed. But would that be enough? The Russians would just substitute Constantine's face for that of another hired killer—plenty volunteered their services for blood money.

And while Constantine was likely out of the country, this left her with another ally of the Russians—the former police chief, Patrick McAlexandar. The fact that he had relinquished his post at the police department and was staying out of the media spotlight these days did little to change her opinion of his guilt.

Chapter 10

RICHARDS WAS AT HIS DESK writing notes into a journal but stood when they approached. "First things first. Lividity shows that the deceased—"

"We know her first name is Faye now." She hated referring to the murdered as *victims* or *bodies* unless there was no other option.

"The *deceased* didn't die in the chair. Lividity starts twenty minutes to three hours after death. The blood pools show she died lying on her side, but rigor set in when she was in the chair."

His attachment to using the word *deceased* confirmed their relationship still hadn't returned to what it had once been.

"And the cause of death?" Madison asked.

"A heart attack. Now, it is possible that certain drugs could have brought it on. I will be requesting a tox panel to see if any of them can be detected. Once we have her ID, we can look at what medications she took and see if any of them interacted. You know I don't like to play with hypothetical scenarios—that is all your influence—" there was the hint of a smile on his face "—but combining the heart attack with the bruising on her wrists, I wonder if the struggle didn't bring it on."

"Did you find any other evidence that she may have been abused?"

"Besides the bruising that I believe ties into her death, no. It seems she was otherwise healthy and well nourished."

Madison's gaze drifted across the room to the small woman's frame on the steel slab.

Richards walked over and wheeled the remains into a freezer slot.

Despite all the bodies Madison had seen over her ten years as a cop, it never became easier. There was a fine line between human emotion and objectivity, and it took a lot of willpower to have the latter. It was her training and hardheaded determination to find justice and provide peace to those left behind that kept her going—to make sure the victims' lives were acknowledged, honored, and respected.

Richards crossed his arms. "The sad part is that death is preventable with most heart attacks."

"Assuming the struggle brought on the attack, she was left to die," Terry said. "The other person might not have necessarily meant to kill her. They were fighting, she dropped due to the chest pain, the person panics."

"It doesn't explain why she was placed in a wheelchair and taken to where the protesters hung out," she said, glancing at Richards, then back to Terry. "There has to be a reason for that. I wonder if abortion tied into the altercation. Someone she loved might have been pregnant and thinking about having an abortion. We already know how adamant and dead set against it she was because of her sister. It's possible whoever is behind this knew that, too. And for someone believing in a woman's right to choose, those kinds of conversations often get heated pretty fast. But to the point of leaving her to die?"

"The person would have had to leave her to get the wheelchair. You can't premeditate a heart attack," Terry said.

Madison conceded with a nod. With rigor setting in about two hours after death, someone had had enough time to get the chair and return to Faye. It led Madison to another theory. "They must've made a conscious decision to get the wheelchair, put her in it, and then wheel her into position."

Richards exhaled a deep breath. He obviously would have preferred that they take their hypothesizing outside the morgue.

Terry continued as if he either hadn't noticed or didn't care. "I think so, too. The fact that the chair was missing from the hospital tells us it wasn't signed out; someone simply took it. Do you think they intended to kill her if the heart attack hadn't happened?"

Madison shrugged. "We have no way to know that yet."

"Either way, the person left Faye's dead body and then came back after getting the chair," Terry began. "That takes some balls."

"Or stupidity," she said.

"Where do you think the altercation took place?" Terry asked.

"I'm assuming Faye's house. That'd be the only safe place, really, to leave her dead body without fear of someone discovering it."

"The other protesters said she lived near the hospital."

"You're just telling me this now?" Madison crossed her arms. "Did you look up the name Faye in the system? You could narrow the search parameters to show homeowners by that name in a certain radius of the hospital."

"No, I—"

"We'll have to do that as soon as we leave here." She paused for a second. Typically this level of incompetence would send her spinning, but Terry was under a lot of pressure. She could see it, so she let it go this time. "So what makes someone confront an older lady about abortion? Assuming, of course, that's what happened."

"No idea. And why not just leave? Someone would find her— Faye—eventually," Terry said.

"There would still be an investigation. Along that line, I'd guess wherever she died would show more signs of struggle. We need to find where she lived."

Richards cleared his throat. "I might be able to help with that. The victim—*Faye*," he said to appease her, as given away by the softness in his features, "had a hip replacement. And from what I can tell it was relatively recent. There—"

"The nurse from the clinic mentioned not seeing her for a while. She must have been healing from the surgery," Madison surmised. Richards's gaze hardened at her for her interruption. "Sorry."

"I was going to say that there is a serial number on the hip replacement, and that should lead us to her full name and address."

Depending on timing, that may eliminate the need to conduct the database search. "When do you expect to know more?" Madison asked.

"I'd say within the hour. I made the call upon discovery."

She nodded. Thank God for Richards's competency. How could she have ever doubted his ability, his thoroughness? As that worry lifted, something else settled into the pit of her gut, though: someone had let Faye die.

CHAPTER 11

TERRY WAS GETTING A COFFEE from the bull pen and Madison was at her desk, waiting to hear back on the ID connected to the serial number. She glanced over her shoulder—no sign of Terry—and she brought up Constantine Romanov's file on her computer and stared at his face. Her heart raced at the image—this time from rage. This man had taken so many lives, probably more than they would ever be aware of. While they didn't know for sure, she felt pretty certain that he would have returned to his homeland. And if she was right, that meant he'd be reporting to the head of the Russian Mafia—Roman Petrov, Dimitre's father. And he was a bigger son of a bitch than his son was. His hands were stained red, and his banks were full of blood money.

"Hey there, Bulldog."

She smirked, flicked the monitor off, and turned in the direction of the male voice that was becoming so familiar to her. Troy Matthews stood beside her desk. His green eyes were piercing as he gazed straight into hers. If he had a superpower, it would be his ability to read minds. He wasn't smiling, but he rarely smiled. It was just his nature. Getting him to show the expression at all was a challenge for her, but every once in a while she was victorious in her efforts.

"You know how I feel about that nickname," she said.

"The other one isn't appropriate for work."

"Would you cut it out?" What he alluded to wasn't a nickname per se, it was a description: *Sexy*. "Your nicknames need some work."

"Oh." He placed a hand on his chest, feigning insult. "I don't have to call you that if you don't want me to."

She narrowed her eyes. "You know I like that one." And there it was. She couldn't carry on a conversation with the guy for a minute before she found herself swept up in his charm. Where had her strong, independent spirit gone? She grappled to establish a commanding presence. "I'm working on a case. What's up?"

He angled to see her screen. "Top secret I see, and as for the *what's up*, it's probably another loaded conversation not suitable for work." There was a slight curve to his lips.

She rose to her feet. He didn't back up, and they were pressed chest to chest with only about an inch—if that—between them. "You have to stop doing this."

"Turning you on?" he whispered, lowering his head until their brows were nearly touching.

Modesty wasn't one of the man's qualities, but that served to make him even more irresistible.

He placed his hands on her arms, the span of them wrapping around her biceps. Under his touch, she was vulnerable, delicate, female. She rarely experienced those three things, yet he was able to merge them together. It was a heady rush.

"Are you ready for tomorrow night?" he asked.

She wanted to forget about tomorrow night. There was a charity event for fallen officers in the line of duty, and it would consist of a four-course dinner and dancing. It was being held in the ballroom of a ritzy hotel where marble floors and arched ceilings came standard. Any cop with a sense of responsibility toward his brethren, which was every one, would be there, or at least would have purchased tickets. In place of the badges and uniforms would be tuxedos and gowns. The thought of wearing a dress swirled nausea deep in her gut. She did her best to avoid occasions that required formal attire.

"I don't have anything to wear." A lie, but if it was based on preference, then she didn't have a suitable thing in her wardrobe.

"You're going to stand me up?" He stepped away from her and

moved behind her. "Not a chance. Nope. I'm not allowing it."

He had bought the tickets the second they had become available. She had, too, but not with any intention of actually attending. She'd given her tickets to Leland King, a top reporter for the *Stiles Times*. She had told the man to take a date.

She glanced over her shoulder at Troy, ready to defend her position, but found their faces were next to touching. Again. Damn, the man was smooth. In his maneuvering, he had also positioned himself near the nape of her neck. His breath was whirling a heat storm against her skin, and her gaze traced from his mystical eyes to his lips, then back up.

"Are you going to say no? To me?" he asked.

Again with the confidence… If he were any other man, she'd slam the proverbial door in his face. But Troy Matthews had the ability to both empower and weaken her. He lifted her up and grounded her. He possessed her, yet encouraged her independence.

She sighed. "I'll go."

Troy came around in front of her again. "I'm glad that's settled. Besides, it will give you a chance to get to know Chief Fletcher."

"And why would I—"

He held a finger to her lips to silence her. Again, any other guy would have gotten his finger broken.

He continued. "I know you didn't get along with McAlexandar. He was a chauvinist pig. Fletcher is a woman," he said.

"Thanks, I hadn't noticed," she said, shaking her head. "But it seems you did." She raised an eyebrow at him.

"Someone sounds jealous, but trust me, there's nothing to worry about."

With his statement, she was reminded of how far she'd come. For years, she had allowed and encouraged open relationships. It wasn't because she wanted the man she was seeing to shack up with other women, but it guarded her heart. No promises made. No promises broken. But with all she had been through, she had changed. Toby may have broken her heart, but that didn't mean every man after him *was* him. And as the saying goes, *what doesn't kill you makes you stronger.*

"That's not what I meant," she said, trying to back out of him thinking she was jealous.

There was the subtlest smile on his lips. She watched it dissipate before it was fully born.

"The way you talk about her, it sounds like you know her quite well."

"I'm not going to say I don't." And there was the wall he would erect from time to time.

She changed the subject from the chief. "Why are so excited about this gala, anyway?"

"It's in honor of fallen heroes. Why wouldn't I be?" The light in his eyes betrayed him.

"What if I said I'm not buying it?"

He raised his arms in surrender. "All right, you got me. It's getting you into a dress"—he leaned in, his breath hot on her cheek—"so afterward, I can get you out of it." He waited until the timing was perfect to tease her. Then he pulled back. Turning to walk away, he said, "I'll pick you up at seven."

"No," she said, "I'll meet you there." She had to take back *some* of her power.

"You got it." He waved and was off.

Now…to resume regular breathing. Being next to the man was a rush. It was a miracle she didn't pass out when they made love. *Made love?* God, he had not only gotten physically beneath her skin, but he had managed to entwine her heart somehow.

"I see lover boy stopped by." Terry dropped into his chair and slurped coffee from his mug.

She narrowed her eyes at him as she took a seat. "Terry."

"What?"

"Don't you have a case to work on?"

He shrugged, letting his focus drift from her to a file on his desk.

While Terry went back to work, her mind dwelled on Troy. He had said he was excited because of the event's purpose. The part about getting her into a dress was a diversion. Why did he really want her to go with him? Unfortunately, there was only one way to find out. And it involved a gown, makeup, and jewelry.

Chapter 12

Cynthia came up behind Terry and leaned over him, her gaze on Madison. "Did you hear that? It sounded an awful lot like wedding bells." She straightened. "I saw you and Mr. Hot Stuff over here. Be careful, or the two of you will set the place on fire."

"Cyn, we've been through this." Madison established eye contact. As best friends, they'd had this conversation a number of times. The relationship between her and Troy was just for fun. Yes, they had made a commitment to remain monogamous, but beyond that, she retained her freedom and independence. Wedding bells were definitely not something she anticipated— or wanted—anytime soon, if ever. There were times she was shocked she even took the leap of the C-word. *Commitment.*

"If the wedding bells belong to anyone, it's you," Madison said.

Cynthia lit up, her grin touching her eyes. "True."

"So are you here just to harass me or do you have something insightful to offer?" Madison teased.

Cynthia scoffed, pretending to be offended. The grin turned into a bitter scowl, and a hand went to a hip. "She's always business, isn't she?"

"That's Maddy," Terry said.

"I hope she never changes. And, yes, in answer to your question, Madison, I do have news for you."

"You have the full ID on Faye?" Madison asked, wondering if Richards had passed this information along to Cynthia.

"Nope. Well, not that I've heard anyway."

"So what is it?"

Cynthia smirked at Terry. "This girl's never going to learn patience, either, huh?"

"I'd say if it were going to happen, it would have by now," he said.

"You and me both."

Madison clasped her hands on her desk. Inside, she was pulsating. "Cynthia?"

"There was a lot of 'evidence' in the area where Faye was found. What pieces are significant will be determined as the case moves along."

"And at the speed we're going, the case has already been locked away in storage and marked *cold*," Madison said.

"Seriously?"

Being told, in effect, to check her patience again was too much. Her determination flared to life.

Faye likely had family out there looking for her who had no idea what had happened to her. Their job—*her* job—was to find who had taken her away from them. She was also responsible for bringing peace to Faye's loved ones by determining what truly happened. Madison may not be able to reverse time and undo what had occurred, but it was within her power to provide closure.

"Someone's grandmother is dead, Cynthia. She was found yesterday morning. It's been about twenty-four hours since we found her. Whatever you can tell us would be helpful." She toned down the harshness of the last sentence, gauging Cynthia's reaction through her body language. And it wasn't favorable.

Her brow lowered, her lips set in a straight line, and her nostrils were flaring a bit. Cynthia crossed her arms. "Don't talk to me like that. You're making this about *your* grandmother, but you have no right."

Madison sensed Terry watching her, but her eyes never left Cynthia's. Seconds later, Cynthia's face softened, her expression turning into more of a grimace. Remorse lapped over Madison. "You're right, I shouldn't have talked to you like—"

"You are under a lot of stress—"

"But it's not a good reason," Madison finished Cynthia's sentence. She was thankful for a friend like Cynthia, one who understood her complicated moods, her stubbornness, and determination. "I won't interrupt again. Please. Go ahead."

Cynthia bobbed her head. "Of the items we found, the only thing providing DNA was a cigarette butt found on a public sidewalk. It could be anyone's."

Madison decided to be optimistic. "Once we get a suspect, it might help us."

Cynthia smiled and glanced at Terry. "So she *can* be positive."

"Actually, I have been more so lately," Madison voiced in her defense.

"Uh-huh." Cynthia laughed.

Madison's cell phone rang then, the ID showing it was Richards. She quickly accepted the call. "Tell me you have a full name and address."

Richards never missed a beat in responding, and she hung up while on the move. She glanced behind her to see Terry jogging to catch up. And she smiled at Cynthia.

The woman's name was Faye Duncan, and they had an address.

CHAPTER 13

MADISON MAY HAVE REACTED ON IMPULSE, running off in glee over the fact that they had the victim's full name. The implication of having it, though, came afterward and slammed into her—hard. An identity meant notifying next of kin. She hated doing that as much as she hated the sight of blood.

Terry had looked up Faye Duncan's basic information in the car. The woman had outlived two husbands and left behind her only sister, Della Carpenter. Della would have been the one pregnant as a teen. She also lived in Stiles.

Officers were sent to Faye's house to watch over it while Madison and Terry headed to speak to Della.

Maybe she could persuade Terry to provide notice even though he had given it the last time. Uniformed officers could do it in a detective's stead, but that wouldn't be a smart decision. Clues could be gleaned from delivery of the news.

She had to look at this from the standpoint that they were bringing closure to Faye's family. Then she'd be able to manage it better, she told herself. But that reasoning hadn't worked yet.

"So, Terry, I guess it's your turn." He'd know what she was alluding to, and she was hoping that his memory was failing him or that his preoccupation with his baby would make him agree without thinking about it.

He glanced over at her from the passenger seat. His right arm was braced on the window ledge. He had the window down, and the breeze teased his blond hair. "Not a chance, Maddy."

She grumbled as she pulled the department car into Della

Carpenter's driveway. Her house was a gray-brick bungalow. The fragrance of freshly cut grass tickled Madison's sinuses and she almost sneezed.

A brunette woman was already standing at the front door.

According to the file, Della was ten years younger than Faye's sixty-eight. If this was Della, she must have dyed her hair.

"Can I help you?" The woman's voice wavered, full of fear and curiosity.

Madison flashed her badge. "Are you Della Carpenter?"

"Yes." Della gripped at the front of her shirt, bunching up the fabric in the middle of her chest. "What is it?"

"Can we come in for a moment?" Madison's heart sank as Della reached for the railing to steady herself.

Based on Della's reaction, Madison guessed at least one death notification had been served to her in the past. Her heart squeezed. It only made delivering the news that much harder.

Terry went to Della, threaded her arm through his, and guided her inside the house. He helped her to a sofa chair in the living area left of the entry. Madison and Terry sat across from her on a couch.

Della's eyes were full of tears when she looked up at them. "I know why you're here." Emotion fractured her words. "My husband—" she paused, holding a hand to her neck "—died in a car accident, and the police came then, too." She stopped there, her gaze taking them in, drifting over their clothing. "You're not police officers, though. No uniforms. Are you detectives?"

"Yes." Madison nodded along with the verbal response and formally introduced herself and Terry.

Della's chin quivered. "This means someone was killed, doesn't it?"

Madison's heart hammered. It was these moments of truth she detested most. The ones where she couldn't ease the news she had to deliver.

"We are here regarding your sister, Faye Duncan. Her body was found—"

Della gasped, her hand snapping up to cover her mouth.

Her frame shook and tears poured in a steady stream down her cheeks.

Madison gave it a couple of seconds. "She was found yesterday morning on the property outside Peace Liberty Hospital."

The older woman continued to hold her hand over her mouth. Her eyes were wide and her lashes soaked with unshed tears.

"She died of a heart attack, but we have reason to believe—"

Della took a deep breath and sniffled loudly. "Do you think someone caused it?"

"Her body was moved after she died."

Della's face blanched. "You said you found her yesterday. Why wasn't I told then?" She pulled a tissue from a nearby box and blew her nose.

"She was left without ID." Madison gave Della a few seconds to assimilate that information. "Do you know of anyone who could have done this to her?"

Della shook her head. "She was loved by everyone who met her. She was active in the community and stood up for what she believed."

"Active in the community?" Terry asked.

"Well, she protested abortion. That's all I meant by that. You said she was found outside the hospital. That's where the protests happened. Did one of those people do this to her?"

"It's too early to say." Madison didn't want to disclose the fact that nothing there led to that suspicion. In fact, background reports showed the other protesters were clean.

"But she was found there."

"She was." It was time for Madison to elaborate. "Your sister was also found strapped into a wheelchair." Verbalizing *your sister* gave Madison's chest a burning ache. She couldn't imagine handling the news of Chelsea's death. The truth was that she wouldn't handle it; she'd lose it.

"A wheelchair? That doesn't make sense. Sure, she had one just after her surgery, but she didn't like using it. She let me take her for a few walks in it only because she missed the fresh air. That was three months ago. Up until the hip replacement, she was as healthy as an ox. She even hated to have in-home care. Said it made her feel like an invalid."

Madison glanced at Terry. "Do you know which service she used?"

"I sure do." Della rose to her feet, swaying mildly, and took a few seconds to right her balance before leaving the room. Seconds later, she came back with a business card and extended it to Madison. "I kept this in case I needed to contact them. I never did, though, and I'm horrible about cleaning the front of my fridge. That's where I had it. I have food flyers from years ago still up there."

Madison read the card: HEAVEN'S CARE. WE'RE HERE FOR YOU.

She flipped to the back, but it was blank. She passed the card to Terry.

"When did she last use the service?" he asked.

"I'm not sure. Probably as soon as she could get rid of them."

Maybe they weren't as close as Madison had thought, but then again, she and Chelsea didn't know all the details of each other's lives.

"How did you feel about the nurses from there?" Madison was thinking one could have lost his or her patience with Faye and things could have progressed from there. Even if the service wasn't working with Faye at the time of her death, there was nothing to say that a nurse who had a problem with Faye hadn't returned.

"They were fine, I guess. Faye never mentioned any issues. You don't think they—" Della waved her hand in the air, seemingly not having the strength to verbalize the accusation.

"It's too early to know." That's what Madison said, but inside, she was lit aflame because they had a lead. "Would you happen to have access to your sister's house?"

"Of course I do." Tears seeped from her eyes, flowing freely down her cheeks. "Zoe's going to be so upset."

"Who is Zoe?" Madison asked.

"She's my granddaughter, Faye's great-niece."

Chapter 14

MADISON AND TERRY LEFT DELLA after she'd insisted she would be okay. She had called her daughter, Kimberly Bell, while they were there, and she was set to arrive within the half hour. So they were headed to Faye Duncan's, house keys in hand. Cynthia and Mark from the crime lab were meeting them there.

"As soon as we take a look at her place, you and I will go over to Heaven's Care to see if we can talk to the nurse who worked with Faye," Madison said. "It's sad to think that the person she trusted to take care of her might be involved with this."

"You seem to be forgetting that Faye only used them for a short time period after her operation—three months ago."

"You think they might not be involved because of that? There's nothing to say the person didn't return after their employment had ended."

Terry rubbed the back of his neck. "It's too early to tell."

That was her partner, willing to hide behind the lack of firm evidence as an excuse for not hypothesizing. She let her gut lead her, though, and right now it was pointing to the in-home care service.

"Let's make a bet. I'll say a nurse is behind Faye's death," Madison said. "I'll give you a chance to make your money back. Double or nothing."

"We don't know where she even died yet."

"You're in denial. Are you in or not?"

"Fine."

There was no handshake to seal this bet, and his face had gone sullen.

This wasn't like him. Especially not when a wager was in play. "Are you all right?" she asked.

"I'm all right, but it's Annabelle. She's having a hard time staying positive."

"And she's looking to you for help with that?"

Terry glared at her.

Madison cracked a smile. "I couldn't help it. Someone said earlier today I wasn't—"

"I know, Maddy," he said in a softened tone.

She was never good at the sentimental conversations, the ones that drew out feelings and emotions, but she had come a long way. She still had more to go, of course, and right now, she had two options: continue this discussion or divert. The old Madison would have diverted. Why bare raw emotion? Yet, if her friendship with Cynthia had taught her one thing, it was to be more emotionally available.

She steadied her breath, considering her words before she spoke. "I'm sure you are a great comfort to her, Terry. She's lucky to have your support."

He glanced at her, pressing his chin to his shoulder. His eyes assessed hers. "You're not just saying that?"

"No, I'm not. You were there for me when I went through what I did."

"Sometimes it didn't feel like it. I was moody and temperamental."

"That part is all forgotten." And it was. It had been rough immediately following her rescue. Things between them had come to verbal blows. He threatened to get a new partner, and a part of her would have let him. But all that had been months ago, and as Dr. Connor had helped her realize, Terry had been undergoing a lot of stress in his own life, too.

"Forgotten? Nice of you, Madison, but—"

"No *buts*. You stood up for me. You defended me with Blake." Blake Golden was an ex-boyfriend who turned out to be another defense attorney on the Russians' payroll.

"I guess I did." Their eyes locked. "Look back at the road, please." Terry pointed out the windshield.

She smiled at him first. "You're such a wimp." She pulled around a slow-moving sedan and netted the result she was going for. Terry reached for the dash to steady his fears, and she laughed.

FAYE DUNCAN'S HOUSE WAS A single-story rancher with beige siding. The shutters on the front windows and the front door were teal. It told Madison that Faye had spunk, if the protesting at her age wasn't enough to prove that fact. And as noted by the protesters, Faye really had lived close to the hospital.

Cynthia and Mark were unloading the forensics van when she and Terry pulled into the driveway behind them.

Madison gave a generic greeting while moving toward the house. Determination energized her stride, taking her to the front door quickly. Faye had two locks—one built into the knob and a dead bolt. She guessed correctly as to which key went in which lock and had the knob unlocked in no time. With the dead bolt, there was nothing to do.

Madison cracked the door open and tucked her head inside the house. "The twist lock built into the handle was the only one locked," she tossed back to her colleagues.

Terry stood immediately behind her. Cynthia and Mark were at the base of the front stairs.

"So the perp got her into the chair and pulled the door locked behind him," Terry said.

"That's assuming she died here." Madison was trying not to get excited. "As for going out the front, there's a flaw. There's no wheelchair ramp, and I can't imagine them taking Faye's dead body down those stairs."

"True, and her neighbors would notice," Terry reasoned.

He had a point, but she was confident they'd discover an explanation.

Madison and Terry did a quick sweep of the property before Cynthia and Mark entered the home. And there had definitely been a struggle in the kitchen. One smashed mug on the floor. A second one remained intact on the counter. The electric kettle remained full, and a teapot was awaiting water that never came.

Cynthia took pictures of the scene. Then, gloved, Cynthia lifted the lid on the pot to find two tea bags inside.

So Faye had gotten as far as starting the tea, but from the time the person had entered the home until Faye entered the kitchen, things had taken a turn for the worse… Plus, it was now clear that the perp was someone Faye had known and trusted. Tea was offered to *guests*, not intruders.

Madison paced through the area. The kitchen had a square layout with the sink facing an outside wall with a window overlooking a patio. A counter separated the scullery area from the dining space, where there was a table for four.

"What are you thinking, Maddy?" Terry came up next to her, his phone out and his finger hovering over the screen.

She glanced at what he had already noted and pointed to it. "The same thing you're thinking."

"She knew her attacker."

"Exactly. But what makes someone kill an old lady?" Madison asked.

"What makes someone kill, *period*?"

She nodded, giving the rhetorical question to Terry. He had a point. Expanding on that, thinking of a world without murder was a foreign concept, and Madison suspected that's all it would remain—a concept. There would always be someone who sought bloodshed as the solution to a problem, as being a justifiable action or reaction.

But why Faye Duncan?

The hypotheticals fired. There was a heated argument that had turned physical. The bruises on Faye's wrists proved that much. What if the person hadn't intended to go that far, and when Faye had her heart attack, the person panicked as Terry suggested earlier? The person could have a past record. Maybe they didn't want to go back to prison. She shared this with Terry.

"It's possible, but it's the mentality of a hit-and-run driver,"

Terry said.

"There's no excuse for—"

Terry held up his hand to silence her, and she glared at him but remained quiet.

He continued. "There's that moment when one must choose between fight and flight."

"You're thinking it's as simple as them choosing flight? Then why the wheelchair? They could have just left her in the house."

"Has anyone taken responsibility for or even reported her death, other than the jogger? I'd say the perp chose flight. But it doesn't necessarily mean the person had a record."

She watched him peck RECORD and then spoke. "Okay, let's say this person was an average citizen with no record. Things got out of hand, they freaked out thinking that they killed her. Maybe calling nine-one-one didn't even occur to them." The defense was ludicrous. Regardless of the fight-or-flight response, if someone didn't have anything to hide they would have dialed 911. She shared her reasoning with Terry and expanded on the thought. "Whoever did this to Faye had something to protect."

"You mean their butt?"

A smirk tugged at her lips. Leave it to Terry to verbalize it without any hint of profanity. He detested foul language more than a priest on Sunday. It was how she felt about spoken clichés. "You mean, their ass? Yes. But maybe it's even more than that."

"Like what?"

She shook her head. "That, I don't know yet."

"And since when do you try to justify a crime?"

His question rendered her mute for a few seconds. The judge within found her guilty—she had just run through the possibilities while trying to assign reason. Some might perceive that as justification. But her drive had always been to obtain justice for victims, not justify the killer's actions.

Now, she'd be lying if she said she never thought of exacting revenge. The stark truth was that inside every human mind lives a killer. If she were to take that ill-fated shot again, Constantine would be rotting six feet under. As the thoughts fired, she realized Terry was staring at her.

"I'm not justifying whoever did this at all," she said.

He remained silent, his gaze fixed on her.

"Would you cut that out? I'm fine."

Terry pressed his lips. "You're *fine*? I never doubted that you were. But most of us prefer to be better than *fine*."

She used to say *fine* a lot right after everything had happened, and now it seemed to be back. An awkward silence fell between them, and Madison glanced over at Cynthia. She was staring back at her and Madison wondered how much she had overheard.

Madison gloved up and slid the patio door open. She really needed some fresh air. Just as she began to step outside, she stopped. The door had been unlocked.

She exited onto the deck, which was only about a foot and a half from the ground. There was one low step straight ahead. To her left and next to the deck was the end of the paved driveway.

Madison looked around. There was also a high fence that would've afforded Faye complete privacy. Enough that the perp could have brought the wheelchair inside the fence, taken it up onto the deck, wheeled it into the house, loaded up Faye, and managed to roll the chair down the single step and sweep right down the paved walkway from the deck to the drive.

Madison surveyed the space again, this time on a more detailed level. Faye had a nice little oasis set up out here. Flower baskets hung from wrought iron brackets placed on the fence, and potted plants added color to the small deck. An electric water fountain resembling a creek with rocks was situated next to a glass-top table with two chairs. One was nestled up to the table and one was pulled back.

Had someone been sitting there recently?

She bit her lip, thinking. Maybe she was trying to see something when there wasn't anything to see. Faye had lived alone.

She studied the chair's design. It was low and angled back. She looked at the other end of the deck where there was another chair. That one was higher off the ground. Three chairs, one woman.

And Faye had recently had hip surgery. She would've given preference to the latter chair. So who sat on the one that was pulled out? Was it their perp?

She tapped first on the window over the sink and then on the patio door to get everyone's attention.

Madison filled them in on her observations. Terry watched her, uncertainty lingering in his eyes. She knew she had left him in the house, wondering about her stability.

"Detective Knight?" Mark was in the garden that was off to the side of the deck. His gloved hand held tweezers and a clear evidence bag. Inside was a cigarette butt.

Cynthia paused from dusting the patio door for prints and looked at Madison. "There's nothing in the house to indicate that Faye smoked. Maybe the one from the crime scene wasn't a coincidence."

Chapter 15

It had been a month since Heaven's Care worked for Faye Duncan. But it didn't mean that whoever was behind her death didn't work there. In fact, Madison had forty dollars in favor of someone there being responsible. They would have been familiar with her house, and Faye would have trusted them and wouldn't have hesitated to make tea for them. Accepting that someone in health care may have caused the old lady's death chilled Madison. Nurses were in such a position to help people—to save lives, not take them.

The Heaven's Care office was located downtown in a business district that catered mostly to lawyers, accountants, and other of that professional ilk. The company was housed in a century-old house that was large by modern-day standards.

A woman greeted them with a smile and chipper "hello" when they graced the doorway of Heaven's Care's second-floor suite. The space didn't speak of catering to the public, as it resembled a home office more than anything. Madison figured it existed for the sake of a business card. The address legitimized them more than a service run out of a home. It was also likely that the government was a factor, given they were in the health care profession.

"We're detectives with Stiles PD." Madison pointed to her badge, which hung from a length of silver chain and nestled against her chest.

The police presence didn't seem to faze the woman. Her facial features remained relaxed, placid. There was a pleasant gleam in her eyes. "What can I do for you?"

"We'd like to speak with whoever was Faye Duncan's nurse," Madison said.

"She was a sweetheart." Her gaze drifted between them. "Wait a minute… Did something happen to her?"

Was *a sweetheart? Past tense?*

"You tell us," Madison said.

"When I said *was* a sweetheart—" she swallowed audibly "—I meant when I worked… Did something happen to her?" The woman turned to Terry.

"What's your name?" Terry asked.

"Jody Marsh."

Madison tried not to react. Marsh was the surname of the man who had found Faye Duncan. He had claimed never to have seen her before. The two of them could have worked together, or out of love for Jody, he "found" Faye's body.

"Is there something you should be telling us, Mrs. Marsh?" Madison asked.

"No… I don't think so."

"You are married to Erik Marsh. Am I right?"

"Yeah, I—" Jody's legs buckled and she reached for a corner of the desk. She slinked along the edge, bracing against it for support. She dropped into the chair. "Erik told me that he found— Oh my God. I had no idea it was…" She raked her fingers through her hair as she leaned forward, facing the surface of her desk.

Her nails were clear-polished but had a yellowish tinge to them. That, combined with the subtle scent of nicotine, confirmed Jody was a smoker.

"When was the last time you saw Faye Duncan?" Madison was talking to Jody's hair. If she stared long enough, maybe it would prompt the woman to lift her head.

Seconds later, it worked. Jody sat back, caressing her stomach. "The last time I was there was a month ago. I can get you the exact date." She made a movement toward a filing cabinet.

"In a minute. Are you sure you didn't pop in for a visit after that?" Terry asked.

Jody nodded. "I had thought about it, but as nice as Faye was, she was set in her ways. As far as she was concerned, she didn't need a nurse and she resented my existence—at least in that capacity."

"She knew you in another capacity?" Madison asked.

"I need to watch the words I use. I just meant that she couldn't see past the fact that I was there to take care of her. She hated what I represented. But she's not—wasn't—the only patient who claims to have everything under control when they don't."

Madison could relate to Faye. It wasn't easy to admit needing help. "What about your husband? Would he have ever met her?"

"No, I don't see why."

Based on what she was saying, Erik's testimony that he'd never seen Faye before seemed truthful.

"Did anyone besides yourself work for Faye?" Madison asked.

Jody shook her head.

"You said that Miss Duncan was 'set in her ways,'" Terry said.

"You probably know that she protested abortion up until her surgery?"

Madison nodded.

"I always figured she'd go back after she healed," Jody said.

"Did she ever tell you why she protested?" They knew the answer from Faye's fellow protesters, but Madison was gauging Jody's knowledge.

"No. As I said, she resented me for what I represented. She didn't speak to me as she would other people. She saw me as an inconvenience." The last word was tinged with sadness.

"You were around when she had visitors?" Madison asked, picking up on the "as she would other people" comment.

"Not so much *visitors*, but her sister and great-niece would come over."

"Everyone speaks to family differently." But relatives were usually treated worse than friends or strangers…

"You wouldn't say that if you saw her with Zoe. That's Faye's great-niece. The two of them had such a strong bond. It was magical watching them in a room together."

Madison recalled how Della had mentioned how much the death would impact the girl. Madison didn't know how old she was, though, and made a mental note to check into it. Della was going to contact her family to provide notice, but it would still be prudent for Madison and Terry to pay Zoe a visit, depending on her age.

"I see that you smoke." Madison pointed to Jody's fingernails.

Jody withdrew her hands, lowering them beneath the desk. "It's a habit I can't seem to shake."

"There was a cigarette found next to Miss Duncan's body and on her property."

"She was found near Peace Liberty Hospital, right? That's what Erik told me. It's not because I was there. Well, I'd have no reason to go that way, and I don't like to toss the butts just anywhere," Jody rambled.

"You never would have smoked at Miss Duncan's and tossed one into the grass or garden?" Terry asked. "You're sure of that?"

"Faye's property? I'm most certainly sure. I wasn't to smoke anywhere near or around her. She detested the habit. Said it was dirty and self-destructive. I respected her enough to hold off until after my shift. I'd light up in my car. And by then, well, I was shaking for one."

"You never took a break during the day?" Madison asked.

"No, Faye never would have tolerated it. She made that clear from day one. As I said, she was set in her ways. She knew what she wanted and didn't want, what she liked and didn't like. She asked if I smoked the first time we met, and she made it clear that if I even smelled like a cigarette, my employment would be over—not just with her but altogether. She must not have realized that I own the company."

Madison had heard enough. Whoever had smoked that cigarette in Faye's backyard had done so after she was dead. Faye and Jody clearly hadn't been close, but the latter had respect for the older woman. The cigarette butt still had the potential to disprove her story, of course, and the truth of that matter would lie in the forensic findings.

"Would you be willing to provide us with a DNA sample?" Madison asked.

"I have nothing to hide, but I also know my rights. I won't without a warrant. Sorry."

"Will you at least tell us where you were between six o'clock Wednesday night and two o'clock Thursday morning?"

"I was at home watching TV and then went to bed with Erik."

Chapter 16

"She seemed pretty upset to be involved in Faye's death," Terry said from the passenger seat as they left Heaven's Care. "Did you want to pay me now or later?"

Madison maneuvered the department sedan around a slow-moving vehicle and cut Terry a sly sideways look. "It's too early to say for sure. Husband and wife are each other's alibis. That doesn't sound off to you?"

"They say they were together for the wee hours of the night. I'm in bed with my wife at that time, too. Wait a minute. You don't have the money, do you? My son's almost here."

"Terry, if anyone owes money, it's you. Faye died in her home. You said she passed away outside the hospital."

"But then you upped the bet." He held up his hands. "Fine. Back to business. You're telling me you still suspect her? I should have known better. You believe all are guilty until proven innocent."

She preferred to consider herself diligent.

"Let's just wait and see where the evidence takes us." She wished she could simply follow her gut, but her second-guessing nature wouldn't allow for the leniency. And what harm did it do to view the woman as a suspect until she was cleared? None. She owed Faye Duncan as much—to investigate without prejudice, to push until justice was achieved. "I also say we get a warrant for Jody's DNA."

"Well, it's not going to line up. She didn't do it," Terry mumbled.

Madison glowered at him, but the expression met with the

back of his head. He was facing the window. She flicked a glance at the clock on the dash: 1:30 PM. They had left Cynthia and Mark at Faye's house with the instruction to thoroughly scour the place. Madison wanted to know everyone who came in and out of the house in the last few months. It was apparent Cynthia still didn't have anything to report or she would have called. It didn't mean evidence wasn't necessarily there; it just may not have been processed yet.

In regard to prints, Madison suspected there would have been quite a few pulled. They would be run against databases back in the lab after all the evidence was collected. And even then, there might not be anything to go on. Madison didn't hold a strong conviction that their perp had a record. While most criminals didn't progress from law-abiding citizen to murderer by skipping the in-between steps and less serious charges, it was altogether possible. Either they weren't caught before or the situation with Faye had escalated and resulted in a negligent homicide. The disposal of the body was another issue.

Her cell rang, and she passed it to Terry.

"If it's the sarge, I'll hold the phone to your ear," he said.

"And since when are you afraid to talk to him?"

"I'm not afraid to—"

It rang again.

"Can you answer that?"

"Hello, this is Madison's phone."

She found his greeting humorous but, in light of the case, kept her amusement from showing.

His eyes trailed over to her. "It's Cynthia."

"Put her on speaker."

"Maddy, Mark and I are wrapping up at the house. Anything it's going to give us, we've collected."

"That was record time."

"Well, the only place showing a struggle was the kitchen. Nothing in her home office was disturbed. All the prints have been lifted, the photographs taken."

"What about her prescriptions?"

"I called them in to Richards and none of them would have brought on the heart attack. Canvassing officers stopped by looking for you, by the way. I said I'd pass on the message. Of course, the detailed reports will be available for you back at the station."

"All right. Keep me posted."

"Keep *us* posted," Terry corrected.

As much as they were a team, her instinct was to go about life solo, responsible only for her actions and, by extension, not allowing others in. Despite her efforts to change, her old habits were still sticking.

"Anything else?" Madison asked Cynthia.

"That's it for now. I'll let you know once anything useful comes back."

"Let me know. Period. I'll decide if it's useful."

"Yes, Maddy." Cynthia's laugh came through before the line went dead.

Terry handed Madison's phone back to her and turned to face the window again. Apparently, he wasn't chatty today, which was surprising after the way he had pried into her *fine* at Faye's house earlier. But right now, Faye Duncan required her attention. The sad part was that the leads were drying out and the suspect pool was nil unless she still considered Jody Marsh.

Marsh had expressed Faye's hatred over smoking. As Madison had assumed before, Faye had likely been dead when the person—the killer, probably—had a cigarette in the backyard. Had they been sitting there to calm their nerves or to wait for the perfect time to wheel Faye to the hospital perimeter? And with all that sitting around, why not use that time to clean up after the scuffle? Why leave the broken cup on the floor? The perp didn't seem to be concerned about leaving trace evidence behind.

Madison slammed her palm against the steering wheel. "Our killer can't have a record," she concluded.

Terry's eyes went from her hand to her eyes. "And what did the car do to—" His cell phone rang, cutting off his sentence. He answered immediately. "Really? Are you sure… Okay, give me five minutes… Hang in there." He hung up and reached over for the lights. "How fast can you drive this thing?"

"What is—"

"Annabelle's in labor."

Chapter 17

Terry dismissed the laws of the road in favor of getting Annabelle to the hospital faster. And to think he gave Madison a hard time about her driving. He was tearing through Stiles like a professional race car driver.

"Oh!" Annabelle was in the passenger seat, her legs stretched out and feet pressed against the floor. Her right hand gripped the armrest, and her left curled around her belly. "Please…ooh!"

"I'm moving as fast I can."

His wife touched his arm. "Please…slow d—" Her eyes enlarged. She gritted her teeth, and seemed to be bearing down.

He eased the pressure on the gas, if only a little bit. He needed to get her and the baby safely to the hospital, but a car accident would do the opposite.

He slowed their speed even more. He reached the next intersection on a yellow light. He hadn't seen the color change, so that meant the red light was coming. He applied the brakes.

"What are you do— Ouch!" She held on to her belly with both hands. "This baby is coming."

Women were difficult to please, especially pregnant ones. Add labor into the mix and it made for a volatile combination.

"Move this car or so help me God." She bit down and winced, her breath wheezing out between clenched teeth. "Terry!"

He looked left, then right, then checked his mirrors. He repeated the sequence. Traffic was light. There was one car on the left, a few behind them, and a few ahead. The light was still yellow.

He glanced over at Annabelle. God, she looked like she was in a lot of pain.

"Here goes." He slammed his foot down on the gas pedal, and the car lunged forward so hard he feared the engine might drop.

The light was a solid red by the time they sailed underneath it.

A couple in a car facing them were flailing their arms, and based on their wide-open mouths, they were yelling. He could only imagine that they were calling him an idiot—or worse.

Fifteen minutes to the hospital from this point. He had to make it in five or the little guy might be born in the front seat.

He pulled under the overhang for the ER in closer to eight minutes. He jumped out and went around to her door, yelling at a male nurse who was puffing away on a cigarette. "Go get a wheelchair! She's in labor!"

The man reacted swiftly, squashing out his smoke in an outdoor ashtray and hurrying inside. He returned soon after with the wheelchair, and he and Terry helped Annabelle into it.

"Congratulations." The male nurse patted Terry on the back but stopped outside the automatic doors. He seemed ready to pick up where he had left off.

The nurses behind the desk were the same ones as the day before. Terry signaled for Jackie to come over, but another female nurse intercepted.

"How far apart are the contractions?" she asked. His mind went blank.

"They've been off and on..." Annabelle replied amid gushes of breath. "Mostly on."

"All right. We'll get you into a room and keep an eye on you. Has your water broken?"

Annabelle gritted her teeth and shook her head.

The nurse wheeled Annabelle off as Terry tried to keep up. For the last nine months, his primary concern was his son's health. He had skipped right over delivery to when he'd be holding his baby in his arms. If Annabelle knew, she'd say it was easy for him to forget about the birthing process. The thought made him smile. Annabelle's sassiness was just one of the many things he loved about the woman. And now she was going to bring their child into the world—a true miracle and gift that no amount of gratitude could ever come close to compensating for.

They maneuvered down the crowded hallways, and he nearly bumped straight into a blonde. Her arms went out toward him to counter her balance, but she had shoved to the left just in time. Her coffee-bean eyes slid to meet his as she went past.

"Congratulations," she said and then smiled.

"Thank—"

The blonde was out of sight, having blended into the crowd.

Terry turned around, sidestepped to avoid another collision, and was thrilled when the nurse turned into a room. Not long from now he'd be a father.

CHAPTER 18

EVERYTHING SEEMED OUT OF HER control. For one, the case. They had an ID for Faye but were still at a dead end. They had the scene of the crime, but the motivation needed for someone to let the elderly woman die and dispose of her body wasn't there. She was hardheaded, set in her ways. She had stood up for what she believed in and no doubt would have created disagreements with those around her. Assuming she was opinionated for all her sixty-eight years, why did it only catch up with her now? Had she debated with the wrong person? The perp would've had to disagree with her to the point that he or she was willing to let her die and then cover up her death.

Another aspect outside of Madison's control was timing. The forensic findings needed to be processed, and now Terry's wife was in labor. Madison was a blend of excited and scared for them. In both cases—business and personal—all she could do was wait.

It was midafternoon, and she headed back to the station.

"Hey, Maddy," Officer Ranson said when Madison came in the main door. Madison's timing always seemed to have her arriving when Ranson was between calls.

Madison nodded and rushed through to her desk. She needed to read the officers' reports from their canvassing efforts, or at least those that had already come back. But before that, she'd dig into Zoe Bell and find out more about her. If she piqued Madison's curiosity, the next step would be to visit her.

She took a chance on the coffee from the bull pen, momentarily cursing her lack of forethought to pick up a Starbucks on the way to the station. The coffee now sat on her desk, the top of it a fine film. She sniffed it. It smelled *okay*. But she set it aside in favor of bringing up the information on Zoe Bell.

The DMV photo showed a striking female, aged twenty-one. Her hair was blond and her eyes were so gray and bright that they were silver. While most people didn't photograph well in license photos—Madison had never had one she was proud of—there were exceptions. Zoe Bell was one of them. She was model-beautiful even with a straight face.

The record noted she was five feet and seven inches, one hundred and ten pounds, didn't need glasses, and lived on Pine Street. That was only a few blocks over from Faye Duncan's house. Madison wondered if it was a choice based on their close relationship or if it had just happened that way.

There were no marks on Zoe's driving record, and Madison switched over to the criminal database. Nothing there, either. From what Madison could tell, Zoe was squeaky-clean. But no one was that perfect.

Madison leaned back in her chair, cradling the mug of muddy brew, her eyes fixed on the screen and the image of Zoe Bell. About a minute later, Madison set the cup back on her desk, still not brave enough to take a sip, and she questioned why she had even bothered getting the coffee.

Next, she searched Zoe's address in the database. No one else came back a match. That meant Zoe lived alone. So what did Zoe do for work?

Another query revealed Angels Incorporated had employed Zoe Bell for the past two years. The position noted was manager.

Impressive—at least at face value. But what was Angels Incorporated, and what exactly did they do? The address on file for the company was in a residential neighborhood. Maybe they were a dot-com. She was certainly in the right age to prove herself useful and current.

Madison brought up a search engine and typed in *Angels Incorporated*. No results. It wasn't an Internet-based business if they didn't even have a website—a rarity in today's world.

She scribbled down the company's and Zoe's addresses on a piece of paper and tucked it into her pocket. She'd try Zoe at home first.

CHAPTER 19

THE CERULEAN SKY WAS MUTED by tufts of thick cloud cover that threatened rain. The warm air and subtle breeze were replaced by stillness and humidity as Madison drove to Zoe Bell's house, debating whether to follow up with Terry or not. But if there had been news, surely he would have called. She decided it best to leave it for now and stop by the hospital after her shift. Hopefully by then she'd have a little boy to welcome into the world. Add to that a *healthy* little boy.

She pulled into Zoe's driveway. The house was in an older neighborhood, crafted before the modern day cookie-cutter builds. Zoe's was a two-story red brick dotted with many front windows. A welcome mat at the front door read, IF YOU FORGOT THE WINE, GO HOME. Madison smiled but then reminded herself Zoe was a potential suspect.

The doorbell was a standard chime and loud enough for Zoe to have heard if she was home, but Madison strained to listen and could hear no movement inside the house. She stepped back and looked up at the structure. All the curtains were opened. What had started out as an ordinary day for Zoe had taken such a turn. Madison figured she must be at Della's mourning Faye's death.

Madison hated what she had to do, but she was without choice. She would head over to Della's and talk to the two women together. She'd probably speak to Kimberly, Della's daughter, as well. While she hated to interfere with their grieving, this was a murder investigation and timing was crucial.

A few minutes later, she was knocking on Della's door. There weren't any cars in the driveway, and Della answered. A tissue was bunched up in one hand, and her eyes were bloodshot, her face puffy.

"What are you doing here, Detective?"

"Grandma, you should have let me get the door." Zoe walked into the foyer and passed a steaming mug to Della. It smelled like olive oil.

"Thank you, sweetie." Della blew on the hot liquid but never took a sip.

Zoe wrapped an arm around her grandmother, eyeing Madison with suspicion.

Madison held up her badge. "Detective Knight."

"I still don't understand." Zoe passed a look to Della. "Why are you here? Have you found out who did this to my great-aunt?"

Madison studied the girl's face, one she wanted to find guilty but couldn't. Zoe's gray eyes were even more stunning in person, like peering into liquid metal. Her features were placid, softened by grief, and the way her frame sagged from sorrow was innocent and genuine. Her eyes testified to the shock she was feeling, and Madison could only imagine how the girl would be once the full news sank in.

Zoe was waiting for a response to her question.

"Unfortunately, we haven't yet," Madison said.

There was confusion in both Zoe's and Della's expressions. Madison would need to provide something by way of explanation for her visit, and it couldn't be the truth. After coming face-to-face with Zoe, what had driven Madison to meet her no longer seemed relevant.

Madison tilted her chin up and addressed Della. "I just came by to see if you needed anything."

"No, I'm fine. Well, I will be, I guess." Della's voice trembled.

"Was your daughter able to make it over?" Madison asked, remembering both that Kimberly had been coming over earlier and that there was no car in the drive.

"My mother had to go to the hospital. She volunteers

there. She's always given standing by one's word the utmost importance," Zoe said. Based on the edge to her tone, Zoe didn't seem to understand her mother's position given the situation.

"Your grandmother said you and your great-aunt were close. I'm sorry for your loss."

Zoe bit her bottom lip as tears welled in her eyes. One fell, and she swiped at it.

"Zoe, do you know anyone—"

"Anyone who would have done this to her?" She shook her head. No longer meeting Madison's eyes, she added, "I haven't a clue why anyone would."

"What about the in-home nurse, Jody Marsh? What did you think of her?"

"I met her once. She was pleasant, especially given the way my great-aunt treated her as such an inconvenience."

Della reached for her granddaughter's hand. "You know what she was like, Zoe. Very independent."

"Yeah." Back to Madison. "I can't imagine someone doing this to her, of all people. Yes, she spoke her mind, but she called it how it was. Those qualities made her that much more special."

A lawn mower rumbled to life in a neighbor's yard. They'd better hurry if they didn't want to get poured on partway through cutting the grass.

"Do you mind if I step inside for a minute?" Madison asked.

Both women backed up in invitation, and Madison walked across the threshold. Della shut the door behind her.

They sat in the living area where she and Terry had been earlier in the day. Grief clung to the air like thick gauze.

"What was your relationship with your great-aunt?" Madison gently prodded.

"She was a friend, really. She was a lot smarter than other people my age." There was the hint of a smile on her lips as she seemed to get caught up in memories. "I could talk to her about anything." Zoe's face was pale, and she rubbed her stomach.

"What did you talk about?"

"What *didn't* we talk about would be a better question. She was such an open-minded woman."

"Some thought she was set in her ways. You even said she spoke her mind," Madison said.

Zoe giggled. It cut like broken glass in the grief-filled room. "Yes, she did. And yes, she was. But trust me, she had modern views, too. Like she accepted people's sexual preferences, whatever they were."

Faye Duncan had indeed been a woman of contradiction. She had made her stand against abortion known. She even took it further than most by protesting outside the hospital. She wasn't satisfied to hang back and express her opinion in private.

"You work at Angels Incorporated?"

"That's right. But what does this have to do with anything?"

Zoe's blank stare made Madison question why it mattered, but Madison trudged forward. "You're a manager there?"

"Are you suspecting my granddaughter of something?" Della asked.

There was nothing more to say at this point. Until she knew more about Angels Incorporated there was no reason to question its legitimacy. But why had Zoe responded the way she had?

She glanced at a clock on the wall. It was just after four. She'd leave here, scribble down some notes, and get over to the hospital to check on Terry and Annabelle.

CHAPTER 20

MADISON PICKED UP HERSHEY FROM the kennel and dropped him off at home before catching up with Cynthia in the lab.

"I can't believe Terry's gonna be a dad," Madison said as she walked with Cynthia through the station's hallways.

"You've had nine months to prepare."

"I guess, but a lot has happened in that time."

Cynthia looked over at her. "You can say that again." There were a few seconds of silence before Cynthia continued. "How are you, by the way?"

"Me? I'm fine."

There was that blasted word again.

"You realize that's how you respond when anyone asks that question… For most people, the default is *good* or *great*. And for those who are sickly happy, it's *awesome* or *super*."

Madison recognized Cynthia's efforts to bury her psychobabble beneath humor. "I know what you're trying to do."

"And what's that?" She flashed a guilty grin.

"You are attempting to lighten what you're actually saying. You think I'm damaged."

A full-fledged smile spread across her face. "Well, that's obvious."

"Hey!"

"Knight."

Crap. Sergeant Winston. And based on the volume and the sound of his steps, he wasn't far behind them.

"Oh God." The expression left her lips without thought.

"You know I can hear you? I'm right here," he added.

Madison stopped walking, and so did Cynthia.

"What is it, Sarge?" Madison asked.

"What is it always, Knight? What is the latest with the old lady case?"

Moments like this reconfirmed why they bashed heads so much. Winston's underlying discrimination against women was bad enough. But to refer to the investigation as "the old lady case," that was the intolerable line.

"Her name was Faye Duncan. She was sixty-eight. But let's say I worry about the case and you worry about your desk? The last time I looked, you had a lot of paperwork."

"Why I never." Winston straightened his back, his belly pushing out farther. "You realize that I am your boss, right? That comments like that can get you suspended. Utter disrespect, Knight."

Cynthia's face registered sheer terror. Madison pulled out her car keys and handed them to her. "I'll meet up with you in a second."

There was a thank-you enclosed in Cynthia's eyes.

Madison aligned her gaze with Winston's. "Whoever let Miss Duncan die and moved her body was close to her."

"You're certain of that?"

She wasn't dignifying his question with an answer. If she weren't certain, she wouldn't have said it. "There are no key suspects at this time."

"Sounds like you're off to a fast start with this one."

It was a dig. He knew how she felt about every case, how they became personal, tattooed into her flesh, as it were, and embedded in her heart. Her desire with every case that involved death was to wrap it up quickly, bring the responsible party to justice, and obtain closure for the family.

There was no winning in her current situation, though. If she shot her mouth off again, Winston wouldn't tolerate it, and Madison couldn't stay around him much longer without risking just that. She turned to leave.

"I assume you would have come to me with these updates?"

Updates? All I have is the victim's name.

"You can assume that." She kept her back to him. A pulse tapped beneath her skin from his earlier mention that she wasn't making quick progress with the investigation. It was one thing to be aware of it and another to have it pointed out.

As the station's doors closed behind her, she wished it meant the job was being left behind, too. But she knew herself better than that. She'd go to the hospital for Terry, Annabelle, and their son. She'd smile and share in their celebration. Yet, in the back of her mind, she'd be working the case.

Madison angled the stuffed bear Cynthia had insisted she buy. "Are you sure this was necessary?"

"Yes." Cynthia held a floral arrangement in a vase.

They had stopped at a store on the way to the hospital only when Cynthia had become adamant that they couldn't show up empty-handed. The nurse who had directed them to the Grants' room told them the baby hadn't arrived yet and that they were to keep their visit brief.

Madison's heart was beating fast. Until now, she hadn't thought about how Terry's becoming a father might change their relationship. It seemed like a silly thing for her to start thinking about, but it had to change the dynamics of their partnership.

Terry had always been one to put his family first, even when it was Annabelle and their two beagles, Todd and Bailey. His dogs were like his children. He worked hard but always knew when to stop for the day. He succeeded in severing the tie between business and personal, something Madison wasn't sure she'd ever figure out. Heck, she was even involved with a colleague from work. Talk about a direct link between both worlds.

"Here we are. Are you ready to go in?" Cynthia bobbed her head toward the door numbered 311.

"Of course."

Annabelle's bed was at an angle so she was somewhere between lying down and sitting. Her cheeks were tear-streaked and blotchy. Terry got up from where he was sitting at the end of the bed.

"Hey guys," he said.

"I got you this." Madison held up the bear, fending off the inevitable vulnerability that came with such personal moments. She smiled at him, and then her eyes drifted to Annabelle.

Terry took the bear from her. "Wow, thanks, Maddy, but I stopped playing with stuffed toys when I was about five."

Madison laughed to ease her discomfort. Even though she had experience around babies—Chelsea had three children—it never got easier for her.

Terry playfully slanted the bear side to side, but there was stress in his eyes.

Cynthia was now next to Annabelle asking how she was doing. Annabelle was nodding her head and rubbing her stomach in response.

Madison almost said the meaningless words, *So no little guy yet?* Small talk was a sure sign as to how uncomfortable she was feeling.

"Her contractions have slowed down a lot," Terry said.

Not that Madison was an expert on birth, but she knew that wasn't a good thing. She went to Annabelle, took her hand, and squeezed it. She wished she knew what to say at that moment, but any offering she could think of seemed blasé and unfounded. She couldn't promise a healthy baby. She couldn't know that everything would be okay. The truth was, she had no idea whether it would be or not. One fact remained: They would need to wait to find out.

Annabelle wiped the corner of her eyes. Disappointment and heartbreak were etched in her irises. "I just want this little guy out of me."

Terry rushed to Annabelle's side. "Daniel's coming, baby."

Daniel? Madison finally knew the name. Terry just kept saying he was having a son.

Annabelle smiled at Madison. "He's so certain it's a boy."

"Because it is." He caressed his wife's forehead, smoothing her hair back.

The tenderness Madison witnessed at that moment had her seeing Terry the husband, not her partner. Madison glanced at Cynthia, who had this doe-eyed look of wonderment on her face. Leave it to a former party girl turned fiancée to get mushy over the love shown between a husband and wife. This was exactly why Madison's inclination was to run far away from any relationship that threatened to take her independence. To become that attached to another living being was just asking for something bad to happen.

A doctor in a white coat came into the room, flipping pages on a chart he held. "Mr. and Mrs. Grant." He paused to smile politely at Terry and Annabelle. He acknowledged Madison and Cynthia but gave an indication with his eye contact that they best leave the room.

"They can stay," Annabelle said. She must have seen the doctor's look.

"Very well. The baby's head hasn't dropped yet. I suggest you go home, get some rest—"

"Go home?" Annabelle struggled to straighten up, but Terry coaxed her to stay still.

"Yes. Trust me, Mrs. Grant. I've been doing this a long time. Your baby isn't coming tonight. But it won't be long."

"Won't be long? That's easy for you to say."

Terry put a hand on his wife's shoulder and squeezed. "Thank you, Doctor."

"Terry, how can you be okay with this? I want Daniel out now!" Annabelle cried out.

The doctor left as smoothly as he had arrived.

"What are you smiling about?" Annabelle asked Terry. She was scowling.

"That's the first time you called him Daniel."

Her expression softened, and Terry leaned over his wife and tapped a kiss to her brow. "I love you."

"I love you, too."

Madison was trying to catch Cynthia's eye. It was time to

go. But Cynthia's gaze was glazed over. What was going on in Madison's world? She needed a drink.

"Cyn?" Madison said. It seemed like an effort for her friend to wrest her eyes from Terry and Annabelle. "Why don't we head out?"

Terry straightened, and both he and Annabelle looked at her. "Thank you for coming, Maddy," he said. "And Cynthia."

"Of course." Madison smiled, then nibbled on her lip. She knew that look on his face. It was written in his eyes. He realized how hard it was for her to let down her walls and open up to the emotional side of life.

In the hallway, Cynthia put her arm around Madison's waist. "Drinks? They're on me."

"I love the way your brain works."

CHAPTER 21

MADISON AND CYNTHIA HEADED TO one of their favorite drinking spots—Cracker Jack. It was a popular watering hole near downtown that had good music and dim lighting. They catered to the crowd who liked to get out to a bar without the clubbing scene—also known as thirtysomethings and up. Not that Madison had ever favored nightclubs. The thought of strangers bumping up against her, strange men taking liberties with their hands while "dancing"… None of it appealed to her.

They walked through the bar and sat down in a booth. Cynthia immediately grabbed the drink menu. Madison didn't need to look. She'd stick with red wine.

"That was pretty intense," Cynthia said from behind her menu.

That was one way of putting it. All the built-up energy to welcome Terry and Annabelle's baby into the world, only to have it crash down around them with disappointment.

"I'm never having children," Madison said.

Cynthia peered over her menu at her. "Like that's a surprise. But you know what they say. Never say—"

"Don't even finish that one. In my case—in *this* case—it's the truth. I don't get babies."

Cynthia shook with laughter. "You don't *get* babies? What is there to *get*? Besides, don't you have three nieces? You know how to handle children."

"Oh no, there's a big difference between being an aunt and being a moth—"

"Maddy? I thought that was you." Troy was standing by the

table and shuffled Madison over so he could sit beside her.

Her cheeks heated. God, she hoped he hadn't heard what she and Cynthia had been discussing. The topic of children was a conversation she didn't want to have, period, let alone have overheard by Troy.

Madison turned toward him, and he flung an arm around her. "What are you do—"

"Excuse us, Cynthia," Troy said.

Cynthia smirked. "Sure. No problem."

Madison looked from her friend to Troy. "No problem? What are you—"

Then his mouth was pressed to hers. She wanted to protest and push him away, but she didn't have the resolve or the fortitude. God, he was all-encompassing. The way he took her, the hunger, the possession. But her friend was across the table... Madison put her hands on his chest and tore her lips from his.

"You can't tell me you didn't like that." His green eyes were piercing through Madison's brown ones. Held captive by his gaze, it seemed there was no one else around them, and her heart was racing. Damn him.

She managed to extricate herself from his stare to look at Cynthia, who was grinning as if she had lost her mind. Madison fired her a glare.

"Don't let me interrupt your evening." Troy took his arm back, establishing eye contact with Madison again as he slid out of the booth.

"You don't have to leave," Cynthia said.

"Well, I'm here with some of the guys from the station." He jacked his thumb toward the four men at the bar. Madison recognized them from his SWAT unit. How she and Cynthia had missed them when they came in, Madison didn't know. "See you tomorrow night, Maddy."

And with that, he was gone, off to the other corner of the room, where he stood next to one of his beefed-up colleagues. She found herself wondering what they talked about in their free time. How many bench presses they could each do? The best meal replacements and protein drinks?

Troy didn't give her another glance after he'd reached his friends. God, that man was irresistible. He respected her independence but fed her carnal hunger. He was the only man who she allowed to tell her how things were, too. There was usually no question to his statements. They were conclusions based on a confidence that would cross over to cockiness in anyone else. He had some secret trick that tempered what he said to make her want to comply, and she liked it.

Wow. Cynthia mouthed the word and dropped the menu to the table.

"Don't say a thing."

"The guy comes over here and kisses you like that and I'm not allowed to say anything? Yeah, right."

Where was a waitress in this bar? Maybe something a little harder than wine would fit the spot. As if sensing Madison's silent pleading, Stacey, a bottle-blond waitress with the stature of Betty Boop, came over for their orders.

"What will you ladies have tonight?"

"I'm looking for something to hit me hard but that goes down smooth," Madison said, and she caught Cynthia's eye. After what had just happened with Troy, red wine wasn't going to cut it anymore.

"You're thinking a shot?" Stacey's pen was poised over her notepad.

"Yeah."

"A shot?" Cynthia repeated Stacey's question.

"Yes." Madison remained adamant. It was rare for her to drink shots, but sometimes a girl had to do what a girl had to do.

"All right. Sweet or sour?" Stacey asked.

"No tequila, if that's what's your asking."

Stacey smiled. "Sweet, then?"

"Sure."

Stacey turned to Cynthia. "Two of those?"

"Okay," Cynthia said.

"Two of what exactly?" Madison asked.

"Do you trust me?" Stacey let her eyes go back and forth between the two of them and then rested on Madison.

"Fine, why not?"

"Excellent. I'll be right back."

"Actually, Stacey, why don't you make it four? Two each," Cynthia said.

Stacey pointed her pen at Cynthia. "I love the way you think. And the way you drink. Give me two minutes."

"What is up with you?" Cynthia asked.

"Me? You're the one who just ordered us two drinks each when we have no idea what they are."

"Sometimes you have to live on the edge."

Wasn't she already doing that by being involved with Troy Matthews? She looked back at him, and one of the guys from the team was slapping him on the back. The four of them erupted in laughter. Probably over something only they would find amusing.

"Earth to Madison," Cynthia said.

Busted.

Madison turned to face Cynthia. "I'm going to have to end things."

"Excuse me? Are you crazy? The guy's hot, and he's crazy about you. Plus, he gives you space. Although just a few minutes ago…"

"Don't even start."

Cynthia giggled. "It's good to see you finally involved with someone as complicated as you are."

"I'm complicated?"

"That really isn't a question, is it? You have a wall around you, Maddy. It's starting to come down, but part of it still stands strong."

Where were their drinks?

"I know you've been through a lot," her friend went on, "and have been hurt by love before."

"You make me sound so pathetic."

"You are not pathetic. You are wary and on guard. Troy's got his own history and baggage to deal with, too."

She had told Cynthia the reason for Troy's divorce back when she'd first learned about it herself. Madison didn't care for having it tossed in her face. "So we were both cheated on."

"That's the simple version, yes. But who you both are today is a result of that. You both like your independence as much as you want to be close to each other. It's like a little dance."

"As long as you're entertained."

"Oh, I am." Cynthia nodded toward Stacey approaching with a tray holding four shot glasses.

Stacey placed two in front of each of them. Madison lifted a glass and studied its contents. Different liquors were present—three different colors—and they didn't blend. It resembled a nuclear cloud. It didn't exactly look tasty.

"What is this?" Madison held the drink in front of Stacey. Part of her debated whether to send the drinks back.

"It's called a brain hemorrhage." Stacey smiled.

Madison made a funny face. "Sounds pleasant."

"That explains its appearance. Cool." Cynthia sniffed hers.

"I know, eh? Very cool. And they are very yummy. Enjoy," Stacey said.

Before Madison could ask what was in it, Stacey was off to another table.

Cynthia lifted her glass toward Madison.

"Here goes." Madison toasted and flung back the shot.

She expected the concoction would go down with the texture of a raw egg, but it was smooth. And—she licked her lips—it was tasty. Both her and Cynthia's eyes lit as they reached for the second one.

"To a waitress with good taste," Cynthia said. They didn't bother clinking their glasses this time.

The second one went down smoother than the first.

Madison looked over the empty shot glasses. "I wonder what's in these."

Cynthia held up a finger. "To Google." She giggled as she pulled out her phone. "Where's another round?"

Stacey must have overheard her as she held up a finger to signify she'd be back with more.

With the motion, Madison realized that for the span of a few hours, she had turned work off. The distraction of a new life entering the world and a drink—or two—with Cynthia was all she needed. Although that kiss from Troy hadn't hurt. But was it right for her to be having fun while Faye Duncan's family grieved? While Terry and Annabelle worried?

"I can do one more shot, but then I've got to go," Madison said.

Cynthia's dark hair fanned the sides of her face as she leaned over her cell phone. The screen cast a green glow on her features. "It's peach schnapps, Baileys Irish Cream, and grenadine." She slipped her phone back into her purse. "Why only one more? It's Friday night. Oh no. Does this have something to do with the case? You need to learn to have fun, Maddy."

Madison shook her head, determined to focus on work. "I need to find Faye Duncan's killer before the trail runs completely cold."

"Despite the fact she was found in the blaring heat of the day, I think this case was at least cool from the start."

"I can't understand why anyone would do this to her."

"You don't have any suspects?"

Madison shook her head. "Not really. The in-home nurse doesn't seem like a fit. The great-niece never would have done something like this—or at least I'm not seeing any motivation. The girl—it's so wrong when you start referring to a twenty-one-year-old as a *girl*, by the way—her mother volunteers at Peace Liberty Hospital. I haven't spoken to her yet, but she gives her time to others." Madison paused for a second. "That's my next move. I need to talk to her."

"But not right this second?"

Madison shrugged. "I guess not. But go ahead and say it: The old Maddy would have spoken to her already. The new one is too soft."

"The new Maddy took all the amazing parts of the old and added more good qualities to her."

Stacey placed two more shots on the table. "I thought I'd just get one more for each of you this time. Then you let me know if you want more."

"Actually, can we just get the bill?" Cynthia asked.

"One or two?"

"One."

"Thank you, Cyn."

"Don't mention it." She raised the fresh shot glass as if she were going to make another toast but didn't. Instead, she just threw it back.

It didn't prevent Madison from making one for herself, though.

To solving this case.

Chapter 22

THERE WERE WORSE WAYS TO wake up, but a ringing phone had to be near the top of the list. It was Saturday morning, and while Madison usually rose early to walk Hershey before dropping him off at the kennel for the day, the weekends were exempt. She'd lie around and get up only when her mind gave her no other choice. At least that's how it went when Troy didn't sleep over. She'd let herself become raptured in the memory of his kiss from last night if it weren't for the ear-piercing trill of her phone.

"Knight," she answered with a grumble.

"There's another body." It was Winston.

She hated to shift the responsibility, but she wasn't the only detective. "What about—"

"Everyone else is tied up, Knight. And Sovereign and Stanford are at a fresh crime scene right now. That leaves you and Grant."

And after how things had turned out at the hospital yesterday, she wasn't sure how pleased Terry would be to get the call. This also meant the visit to Kimberly Bell would have to wait.

"All right. Where to?" She took down the directions. "I'll be there in twenty."

She hung up and Hershey, who had roused from sleep, crawled up the bed. The ten pounds he had been as a puppy was a distant memory to his current weight of fifty-five pounds. At his growth rate, she'd have to upgrade her bed to a king, and soon. She placed her cell on the nightstand and mussed the top of his head. "Hey, buddy."

Hershey panted, flashing her a doggie smile. Every day was a new adventure, and he was always happy to get started—most times hours before she was. But the compromises had been made. He let her sleep in on the weekends in exchange for regular walks. An easy deal to make—if it was possible to make a deal with a dog.

"I know," she said, "I'll walk you tonight." Then she remembered the gala and could have groaned. But with this new case, maybe she could find a way out of going. Her spirits lifted slightly at the thought.

She buried her face in Hershey's fur and rested her head against his. God, she had fallen for this dog. He was hers since Christmas, so seven months, and somewhere along the line, he had crossed from being an unexpected gift to family. She had never understood why Terry had given his beagles human names. She also had never understood why some people referred to themselves as a mommy or daddy to their canine companions. But now that she had Hershey, all of these preconceptions had changed. A dog wasn't simply a pet or a friend. A dog was family.

She swung her legs over the edge of the bed. Hershey walked along the mattress, stretched out, and placed his paws on her thighs, pinning her to the bed. "I'm sorry, buddy, but I've gotta go to work." Saying *Momma's gotta go to work* almost slipped out instead. She was certain she'd said it in the past, but didn't intend to make it a habit.

Thirty minutes later, she was at the crime scene with Terry. Surprisingly, he was rather eager to work the case. Maybe it was rough being around Annabelle right now or he just wanted a diversion. Madison wasn't sure, but she wasn't about to touch the subject.

Cole Richards was working over the body as Cynthia and Mark were taking pictures and collecting anything that could be evidence.

A woman had found the body when she went out to go grocery shopping. Her background had been checked and had come back clean.

The victim had been propped against the base of a streetlamp in a residential area. The victim, who at first appeared to be a sleeping male vagrant, turned out to be a young woman in her early twenties. She wore a man's full-length trench coat with tattered sleeves, a hoodie underneath, and pants. The men's clothing stood out in contrast to the manicured fingernails and expertly applied makeup. She had no ID and no phone on her.

A female street person in male apparel who placed feminine hygiene as a priority? None of it made any sense. This girl didn't belong here. She didn't belong in this clothing.

Not that Madison knew too much about nail care, but the victim's were gels. Madison only knew this because Chelsea had invited her to go to the salon a couple of times. Madison had yet to get anything done at the salon herself, but Chelsea had talked about it on enough occasions. Madison just couldn't imagine slapping cuffs on a perp if she had white tips or some funky-colored nail polish on. Not to mention the flak she'd get from other officers.

"What do you make of it?" Terry asked.

Madison couldn't take her eyes off the victim's nails. There was something familiar about them. She hadn't yet seen the woman's face and moved in closer. She'd recognize those eyes anywhere. The lifeless steel marbles looking back at her were those of Zoe Bell.

CHAPTER 23

MADISON'S HEART WAS RACING. Terry was staring at her, confused. "What's wrong?"

"Yesterday, after you left I visited Della Carpenter." Madison paused a beat, trying to catch her breath. "I was looking for Zoe Bell to talk to her about her great-aunt."

"You mean to see if she killed the woman?"

"Yes." Madison paced a few feet. "What gets both a woman and her great-niece killed?"

"Whoever did this is close to both of them."

"What's the cause of death?" Madison asked Richards, even though she figured he'd give her a half answer.

He looked up from the body, giving her the same look she'd received from him many times before. It communicated exactly what she'd expected. "If one thing, you're persistent."

"I'll take that as a compliment."

"She's got a large gash in the back of her head, and it lends itself to blunt force trauma," Richards said. "She was clearly hit with something, but until I get her back to the morgue, I won't know for sure if it was the cause of death."

It was the examiner's disclaimer phrase. In other words, if she ran with the case using the initial cause of death and things changed…well, he wasn't responsible.

The killer—she was pretty sure they could safely call the perp as much, now—had let Faye die by negligence but had hit Zoe. He or she was escalating.

"What about the time of death?" Terry asked.

"Between midnight and two. You said this was Zoe Bell, Faye Duncan's great-niece?" Richards asked.

"Yes," Madison confirmed, her heart breaking just thinking about going back to Della Carpenter. While she had planned on talking to Zoe's mother at some point, she wished it were under different circumstances.

"What a shame." Richards stood to his full height and motioned for Milo to load up the body. He directed his assistant to be careful of the hands and feet, even though they were already bagged. He continued. "It's going to be a busy day. There's another call a few blocks over."

Winston had mentioned that Sovereign and Lou had a case of their own. Part of her was curious to see the scene, but she had enough on her own plate. Two bodies. Two murders to solve. And related, at that.

Cynthia was still searching the area surrounding the body for evidence, as was Mark.

"Have you found her clothes?" Madison asked.

Cynthia shook her head. "No. They weren't under the vagrant's clothing, either."

Madison let her gaze travel over the ground. If the girl's clothing were here, it would be clearly visible. There was no place to conceal it. This led to the next question: where did the vagrant's clothing come from? It was men's apparel, so they were possibly looking at another body still to surface.

Sovereign.

Madison pulled out her phone and dialed. Hearing Sovereign's voice had no effect on her, at least not in comparison to the mix of anger and unresolved emotions she had experienced in the past. Now, there was a hint of anger and unresolved emotion in *his* tone. About three months back, he had come to her wanting to rekindle what they once had, but Madison had only been able to offer him friendship. And even that was a stretch at times.

"I understand you're at a crime scene," Madison said.

"Yeah. Why?"

"Describe your victim."

"Male. Midfifties or thereabouts. No ID. It's looking like a vagrant. He was found in an alley next to a Dumpster."

Madison thought back to the way the trench coat hung on Zoe's small frame. "How big is he?"

"Say six feet. Two hundred pounds, give or take."

"Well, I think we found his clothing." Madison mouthed, *Sovereign*, to Terry, and he nodded. She moved toward the department car with Terry in tow. "Where are you?" she asked Sovereign.

He rattled off the location as Madison turned the key in the ignition.

Less than fifteen minutes later, Madison and Terry were walking up to Sovereign. They'd beaten Richards to the scene, which wasn't too much of a shock seeing as he would have had to drop Zoe's body off at the morgue before coming here.

Sovereign and Lou were huddled together, likely comparing their thoughts on the case. Given the way they watched Madison and Terry approach, they didn't much care for the company.

"Don't have enough to keep you busy, Knight? You need my case, too?" Sovereign asked. With those two questions, it was clear why it had been so easy to refuse his invitation to get back together. She had outgrown him.

Madison eyed Samantha and Jennifer—not Jenn, Jenny, or any other abbreviation of the name—as they were collecting evidence. The two of them were only dragged out of the lab when there wasn't any choice. Samantha's specialty was ballistics. Jennifer's was serology or bodily fluids.

Madison brushed past Sovereign to the Dumpster. The stench nearly knocked her off her feet and made her step back. She gagged behind a hand. Her eyes watered.

"What? You can't take a little smell?" Lou was laughing.

"Just because you've acclimated to the scene…" It was a scientific fact that after two minutes of exposure to a strong smell, the sinuses no longer registered the odor.

Madison jacked a finger toward Samantha, who was rummaging through litter, likely in search of a potential murder weapon. The flick of Madison's hand caught her eye, and she stopped moving. "I'm sure Samantha might have something to say about how you reacted when you first showed up."

"We got here at about the same time, but yeah"—Samantha glanced at Lou—"I thought you were going to puke."

Lou waved Samantha off. But there was a spark in his eyes as he looked at the investigator. Nothing tangible and it was very brief, but it was unmistakably present. Maybe Madison was just being paranoid. Lou loved Cynthia and would never hurt her or cheat on her. He had pursued her, not the other way around.

Jennifer eased herself over the edge of the Dumpster and lowered herself inside. Despite the fact that she wore protective coveralls, Madison didn't envy the girl's position. Who knew what was living in that bin.

The initial bombardment of Madison's sinuses soon calmed down and the urge to vomit abated. She took in the scene more carefully.

The man was lying on the ground wearing only boxers. His hair was long and he was unshaven. Death had relaxed his jaw, and then rigor had fixed it slightly open. The teeth that showed through were in a state of rot. His fingernails were caked with dirt, the creases in his fingers and knuckles black.

"When we got here, a blue tarp was covering his body. Sort of like he'd curled up to go to sleep and never woke up," Sovereign said.

"Guess on the cause of death?"

"My guess? Blunt force trauma. Richards will need to confirm, of course."

"Huh." Madison glanced at Terry and got the sun in her eyes. She went to pull her sunglasses down, but they weren't on her head. If they weren't in the car, that was another pair that was lost.

"What do you mean, *huh*?" Lou asked, his gaze going to Madison, then Terry, settling on Madison.

Terry responded. "Our victim was a young woman. The cause of death for her appears to be the same."

"You think our victims are connected?" Lou squinted.

"Well, it appears our victim was wearing your victim's clothing," Terry said. "So, probably."

The way her gut was fluttering and her heart was beating so fast, she had zero doubt about the correlation. How or why they tied together eluded her. Besides the seeming connection between Faye and Zoe, nothing spoke to a serial killer behind all this, yet technically with three bodies, the person they were after was just that.

Still, the evidence in Faye's case leaned toward a person without a record, someone who was close to her. With Zoe, it was way too early to make any conclusions, but the fact that great-aunt and niece were killed within a matter of days was suspicious. Had the aunt died trying to protect Zoe? Although, that didn't necessarily fit with them dying on different days. No, they were separate occurrences, but they had to be related—didn't they?

"Earth to Madison." Sovereign was staring right at her.

"What?"

"I asked if you thought our victims were connected."

She had said as much on the phone before rushing over here. How quickly he forgot.

"Do I normally leave my own crime scene to rush to yours?" She stared back at him until his eyes glazed over. Her message was received. "Was there evidence to indicate this is where he was killed?"

"Besides the seeming obvious?" Sovereign pointed at the body.

She tempered her patience. "If you consider that *obvious*." Again, not very thorough.

"You think he was dumped here and posed as a mostly naked homeless person? Come on."

Nothing could be taken at face value in cases like this. "You'll have to talk to other vagrants in the area. See if they recognize him and whether they saw anything."

Sovereign put both hands on his hips. "Are you going to take over this case, too? I guess Lou and I might as well just leave."

"You never were good at taking direction from a woman." She

stood her ground against him, standing there, shoulders drawn back, posture straight.

"That's where you're wrong. I just never liked taking direction from *you*." With that, Sovereign turned his back on her, and Jennifer popped up from inside the Dumpster, holding a cell phone pinched between two gloved fingers.

Madison and Terry moved closer. The nauseating stench lapped over Madison again. So much for the sense of smell completely acclimating to the environment...

"Can you tell whose phone it is?" Madison asked Jennifer.

"Let me check. One minute." Jennifer punched a fingertip to the screen of the phone. "Good news is it's got juice." A few seconds later, she said, "The *Me* contact is Zoe Bell. Is that who—"

"Pack it up. Get it back to the lab. That's our victim. Let me know the second anything comes back from the phone, including who she had been in contact with recently." Madison stopped within a few inches of Sovereign. "Any doubt our cases are connected now?"

She didn't wait for a response but took off toward the department car. She and Terry had essentially three murders to solve, and step one, they were going to visit Zoe's mother to give her the news about her daughter. After that, they'd go to Della Carpenter and let her know about her granddaughter. They were only required to notify one family member, but the thought of not handling the matter directly with Della wasn't acceptable. She owed it to that poor woman, even if it meant being uncomfortable herself.

Chapter 24

KIMBERLY BELL LIVED IN A white two-story house complete with a picket fence surrounding the property. The grass was short, the gardens weeded, and the flowers stood proudly despite the withering heat. The concrete path from the sidewalk to the front door appeared clean enough to eat off. The paved driveway had a smooth surface with no cracks that Madison could see. No dandelions poked up their heads in the lawn. Everything was pristine. Even the mailbox didn't have a trace of dust, and the front windows were a threat to birds. They made Madison think of those commercials where unsuspecting crows slammed right into streak-free, clean glass.

Madison lifted her sunglasses—which had been in the car—and pushed the doorbell. Seconds later, footsteps were moving inside the house.

The door opened to a woman of startling resemblance to Zoe except for the difference in eye color. She appeared young enough to be the girl's sister, but her eyes disclosed life experience. Kimberly was forty-two and had had Zoe when she was twenty-one.

"Hello?" The woman looked first at Madison and then at Terry. Her chocolate eyes were sparking with fire.

Madison held up her badge. Terry followed suit.

"We're—" They both started talking at once.

"Hey, don't I know you?" She pointed a finger at Terry. "Yeah, I think I do. I saw you at the hospital. When was it? Yesterday? Yes. Your wife was having a baby." She paused to flash a smile.

"How is she? The baby?"

Terry's mouth fell into a tight thin line. "Are you Kimberly Bell?"

Her smile faded, and she crossed her arms. "I am. What's this about?"

"Can we come in? Do you have somewhere we can sit?"

"Yes." For a single word, it was awfully laden with sarcasm, as if to imply who *doesn't* have a place to sit. "Please take your shoes off. The floor was just washed this morning."

The fragrance was a blend of air freshener, carpet powder, and cleaner. This woman was immaculate. Madison observed her wardrobe—a white pantsuit with a short-sleeved top paired with heels. Her makeup was applied with an expert touch, her eyelids painted a rich mocha outlined with black liner. Her hair was smooth and coiffed as if she had just stepped out of a high-end salon. She might dwell in a middle-class neighborhood, but she lived as if she were the upper crust.

"This way." She clicked away from them. Her heels must have been exempt from the no-shoes rule. Madison suspected the shoes had never been worn out of the house.

Kimberly led them to a stiff-looking sitting room, all hard lines and neutrals. She sat in a low chair and crossed her legs. The soles of her shoes confirmed Madison's suspicion—no scuffs. They were definitely only worn indoors.

Madison and Terry each dropped into a chair.

Terry met Madison's gaze quickly, communicating that he had this under control. "Mrs. Bell."

"Please, it's Miss Bell. I haven't been a missus for a few years. It's more fun this way." She smiled at Terry as she ran her hand—slim fingers, thin wrist—down the arm of her chair.

Madison's stomach tossed in revolt. The motions, the eye contact—she was hitting on Terry. Seemingly the fact his wife was having a baby meant nothing to her.

Terry's pulse visibly tapped in his cheek. "We're here because something has happened to your daughter, Zoe Bell. Her body was found this morning—"

"Her what? No, this can't be." Kimberly's fake lashes fluttered, tears wetting them, the odd one sliding down her cheeks. She rubbed her arms. "What happened?"

"It's still too early to tell, but we do believe she was murdered," Terry said.

Kimberly let out such a deep rush of air that it sucked the life from the room. She rose to her feet and rounded the chair she had been sitting in. She held the back of it. "Where did you find her?"

"She was found a few blocks from here, posed in vagrant's clothing."

Another gasp. "Someone dressed her in a homeless person's—" Kimberly's face went stark white with the exception of the blotches of red in her cheeks. "Why?"

"We don't know that yet. There are a lot of things we don't know. It does look like she died of blunt force trauma," Terry said.

"Which still needs to be verified," Madison added.

Kimberly's eyes went from Terry to Madison. "You have to find who did this."

"We have every intention of doing so, but there's something else you might be able to help us with," Madison said.

"Anything."

"First of all, what was your relationship like with your daughter?"

"With Zoe? I love—*loved*—her. She was beautiful and had a big heart. If only it had been a little smaller. I can't believe this is happening."

Her daughter was murdered, but she couldn't believe this was happening, what, to her?

Madison swallowed her anger. "What do you mean by wishing Zoe had a smaller heart?"

Kimberly stared blankly. "She liked men and they liked her back. You did see what she looked like. But I think she played things safe…before now anyway."

"Why do you assume a man killed her?" Terry asked.

"I just thought it was likely the case." Kimberly looked in the direction of a fireplace. On the mantle were several framed photographs of mother and daughter.

"She was your only child?" Madison asked.

Kimberly nodded.

"So you valued your family?"

"Of course. What kind of a thing is that to ask?" Kimberly's hands clasped and unclasped before she slipped them into her pants pockets.

Kimberly *valued* her family but left them in a time of loss to volunteer. That was hard to accept.

"Where were you this past Wednesday evening?" That was the night Faye Duncan was killed.

"Excuse me?"

"You heard the question. Between six o'clock and midnight. Where were you?"

"Well, I…I'm not sure. Probably on a run."

"Probably or you were?"

Silence.

"Last time. Where were you?"

With the resulting silence, the hum of the overhead fan droned. Madison hadn't noticed it before.

Kimberly ran her long fingers down the length of her neck. "I was with a man."

"Your aunt was killed within that timeframe. I'm going to ask again—"

Kimberly held up her hand. "His name is Donnie, but that's all I'm giving you. He is a married man. If this got out—"

"Your aunt and your daughter were both murdered within the span of a few days, and you're worried about breaking up some guy's marriage? It seems to me you should have worried more about that before you slept with the guy." Rage was rushing through Madison, and it took all her willpower not to replace *slept* with the raw F-word.

Tears streamed down Kimberly's cheeks. "There's no way I could have known that."

"Known what? That sleeping with married men breaks up marriages or that during one of your romps your aunt would be murdered?"

Kimberly's face froze, the contortions taking an otherwise striking beauty and turning her into the beast. "Do you think that I killed my aunt *and* my daughter?"

"It's possible," Madison said with a shrug, trying to draw the woman out, get her to contradict herself. "And let's not forget the homeless man who happened to be in the wrong place at the wrong time." It was still early in the investigation, but it seemed a logical conclusion. He could have tried to protect Zoe and paid the ultimate price.

"This is crazy." Kimberly appealed to Terry.

Terry turned to Madison, a question in his eyes: why was she making an accusation without anything to back up her suspicions? She had to admit a woman Kimberly's size could have a rough time overpowering the man. And Zoe had been killed, dressed, and moved to where her body was dumped. Even to get her into a vehicle, that would all be dead weight. Add to that getting Faye Duncan into that wheelchair. But adrenaline could work wonders.

"We're also going to need your whereabouts for last night, as well as a list of all the places you volunteer," Madison said.

Kimberly rubbed her palms down her soaked cheeks and nodded. "Anything. I was with Donnie again last night. Was that when Zoe was killed?"

Madison nodded. "And the places you volunteer?" She gestured for Terry to take out his phone, ready to note the companies.

"I volunteer at the abortion clinic in Peace Liberty Hospital."

"You know, your aunt was an active anti-abortion protestor," Madison said casually.

Kimberly nodded. "That, I knew."

"Did you get into an argument maybe? Things got out of control—"

"No!"

Madison locked eyes with Kimberly.

"And where else?" Terry asked, his jaw rigid.

Kimberly took a deep, heaving breath and pulled her eyes away from Madison. "Only one other place. The soup kitchen down on Fifth."

"The soup kitchen?" Madison reiterated. This was a little too convenient.

"Uh-huh."

Kimberly seemed clueless as to the fact that a body was found thirty feet away from the place. Of course, she might not have been as oblivious as she let on.

Madison narrowed her eyes at the woman. "We'll need Donnie's last name and a way to reach him. Now."

Chapter 25

It killed Madison to walk away. She wanted to slap cuffs on Kimberly Bell right then and take her downtown. But there was the matter of evidence, and at this point, they had nothing to hold the woman. On the surface, she was the least likely suspect— beautiful, put-together, and organized, *and* a community volunteer. The kind of person most should emulate. *Except for being a mistress.* That was a huge exception.

"Just promise me you'll keep your mind open to other possibilities," Terry said as he got into the passenger seat.

He knew her too well. "We have to call Donnie Holland, see what he says about Kimberly's alibis."

Terry continued. "I agree, but Kimberly also mentioned that Zoe had men in her life and, from the sound of it, more than one. Maybe someone got jealous."

"Enough so that they killed her aunt? And first?" Madison pulled her seat belt across herself and faced Terry. "What makes you so sure Kimberly isn't the murderer? Her aunt dies and she leaves her grieving mother and daughter to fulfill a charity obligation."

"Let me ask you this: what was Zoe's attitude about that when you talked to her?"

She thought back and sighed. "I don't think she understood why her mother left them to volunteer."

"It didn't seem like she was upset by the fact she left, in any way?"

"I don't know if I'd say upset per se. It was hard to tell. She was grieving over the loss of her great-aunt."

"All right, then. Let's say she was fine with it."

"Ter—"

He held up a hand. "Listen to me. Please."

"Fine." Adrenaline knotted her gut without mercy.

"We'll head back downtown and find out what's come in so far," he said.

She shook her head.

"What do you mean, no?"

"Just that. First, they won't have much in the way of results yet. Second, when they do, I expect that I'll get a call," she said.

"And since when are you patient?"

"I'm…" Her gaze locked on the front step. Kimberly Bell had come out and was hugging herself in the sunlight.

"Leave it alone, Maddy."

"We have to go see Della Carpenter and let the poor woman know about her granddaughter."

"You know that's not our responsibility. We've notified next of kin."

"I know. It's just something I need to—" Her cell phone rang, cutting off her sentence. "Knight."

"What's this about three murders being connected? You don't think to pick up your damned phone? Of course, why should I expect any communication from you?"

Oh, she really wasn't in the mood for him.

She held the phone away from her ear, trying to collect herself. "Sarge, nothing indicates that we have a serial killer."

"Three bodies are leaning to the opposite of that statement, Knight. First, the old lady, then the girl and a bum."

His ignorance certainly hadn't decreased with the lack of McAlexandar's presence. And here, she thought McAlexandar fueled it in Winston.

"I'm not fully certain how the man fits in, but there's something that connects these women," she said.

"Yes, the murderer."

She paced her breathing. "There's nothing to indicate the work of a violent serial killer."

"Three bodies in the morgue would say otherwise."

"One collapsed of a heart attack and the other two were struck in the head." She wanted to throw the phone, and with Kimberly watching them from her front stoop, Madison knew she needed to get out of the woman's driveway. "I've gotta go."

"Don't you hang up on—"

She ended the call and tossed her cell into the console.

"You hung up on him, didn't you?"

She didn't answer Terry and put the car into reverse. "Call this Donnie Holland on our way to Della Carpenter's."

Her anger turned her vision red. Curse Sovereign for opening his big mouth before she had a chance to fill in the sergeant. Sovereign was always worried about appearance while she concerned herself with getting the job done. And sadly, right now, she wasn't sure how to go about that exactly. Hopefully by the time they finished with Della, they'd have someone to talk to from the contact list in Zoe's phone. There was also Angels Incorporated where Zoe worked, but one thing at a time.

Chapter 26

Officers hadn't found any signs of a struggle at Zoe's house— inside or outside. Zoe wasn't killed there. Just another indicator pointing to the alley.

Madison and Terry were back at the station at their desks. Terry had gotten ahold of Donnie Holland, and he had confirmed Kimberly's alibi.

Telling Della Carpenter about her granddaughter was one of the hardest things Madison had done in her years as a cop. While every notification of kin was unpleasant, painful, and even heartbreaking, going back to the same person within twenty-four hours was enough to rend the heart in two.

Della had known before they'd arrived, though. Her cheeks had already been wet, her eyes red. She had been shivering in her warm house. Kimberly Bell had called her, delivering the news by telephone. What kind of a daughter did that when she lived in the same city as her mother?

None of it went far toward improving Madison's opinion of the woman. She might volunteer her time, but she had a selfish streak. According to Della, her daughter had been too distraught to drive.

So take a cab? That had been Madison's thought, but she'd kept her mouth shut.

Della had turned out to be as much at a loss regarding Zoe's murder as she was Faye's. According to her, neither death made sense, and it was almost as if a random person spotted them and fixated on them.

It was the motivation that didn't make sense. Faye was in her sixties, Zoe in her twenties. Then there was the homeless man who was aged somewhere between the two women. So far, there wasn't a common denominator that would attract the same killer.

Zoe's murder struck Madison as a passion kill—in the heat of the moment. With Faye, the person had watched her die, put her in a wheelchair, and positioned her outside the hospital property. The only similarity was that neither body was left with ID.

The vagrant may just have been in the wrong place at the wrong time. He also provided the killer a means to conceal Zoe's identity. Yet, as far as they knew, Zoe's clothing wasn't found in the alley. Did the killer take them?

The man's body and Zoe's had also been found a twenty-minute drive apart. Whoever killed them had a vehicle—just as Faye's killer would have needed to in order to steal the wheelchair. They likely had wheeled Faye to the final spot to be less conspicuous.

A question applied to both Faye's and Zoe's murders: why take ID but leave their bodies somewhere to be easily found? The sign strapped to Faye's chair and the fact that she was left where she used to protest abortion seemed indicative that the killer was making a statement, but what exactly?

Surely, they'd get an update on Zoe's phone contacts soon. They needed to figure out who she was close to, who her friends were, if she had a boyfriend. When they had asked Della, she hadn't known any names and had broken down over not having had as close a relationship with Zoe as Faye had had.

"Terry?"

"Yeah." He didn't take his eyes from his computer monitor. Madison wondered what he was doing but didn't care enough to ask.

"We have to go back to the alley and see what else we can find. I say that's ground zero." What she didn't add was that she hoped Sovereign was gone by then.

CHAPTER 27

"WHERE ARE YOU GOING NOW?" Terry jogged to keep up with Madison.

Hadn't I made myself clear enough?

"We're going back to the alley," Madison said.

"You do have a problem letting go, don't you? Two murders aren't enough. Now you want to take over Sovereign's investigation?"

She stopped walking and spun to face him. "His case is really ours. Zoe was wearing that man's clothing. She was in that alley."

"At least her phone was."

She rolled her eyes. "We need to figure out why, and the only way we're going to do that is to go back to where his body was found." She resumed walking, her strides eating up feet of the hallway at a rapid rate until she reached the station's lot. "There wasn't much by way of evidence where we found Zoe. She was hit with something, and it has to be in that alley." She unlocked the car and slipped behind the wheel.

Terry got into the passenger seat. "They'll still be working on the scene."

"I'm counting on it." At this point, she even suspected that Cynthia and Mark would have joined Samantha and Jennifer. That alley would be littered with potential evidence. She needed to know if they'd found anything else and if the information from Zoe's phone was ready. She couldn't wait much longer.

Ten minutes later, she had parked on the street near the alley. Officer Tendum—a rookie—was guarding the perimeter. She barely looked at him before sliding under the tape. They had their history, and it wasn't a good one. First of all, she found his attitude deplorable. And second, Tendum was why her friend and training officer, Higgins, had been shot during a recent investigation. Tendum wasn't the one who pulled the trigger, but as far as she was concerned, he might as well have been. Higgins was recovering and had been assigned to modified duties when his "backup" should have protected him. Tendum should be stationed behind a desk, not entrusted with protecting a crime scene.

"Detective Knight," Tendum called out.

She was already a few feet away. She ignored him.

"This isn't your case!" he yelled.

Terry reached out and touched her forearm. It was hardly effective at stilling the rage that pulsed through her system. Tendum had the nerve to tell her what was and what wasn't her job? He's the one who had failed to use his authority to kill the man who'd shot Higgins.

When an officer is shot in the line of duty—even off-duty—it's traumatic. When that shooting could have been prevented and the appropriate action wasn't taken, it was inexcusable. That was the case here. Yes, the perp had put his weapon on Tendum after shooting Higgins, but Tendum shouldn't have hesitated. Instead, he'd frozen and let fear render him paralyzed. Meanwhile, Higgins had been bleeding out on the ground.

She'd never forgive Tendum. Higgins could have died, and Tendum would have let the man walk away. Not to mention another civilian had paid with her life because he had failed to handle the situation properly.

Cynthia was hunched over and picking up a piece of blood-soaked newspaper. It dangled from her hand, ready to be inserted into an evidence bag. "What are you doing here, Maddy?"

Richards must have come and gone. The body was no longer lying beside the Dumpster.

"I guess you haven't heard. This case ties into ours," Madison said.

"I still don't think it's a good idea for you to be here." She put the paper in the bag and sealed it closed. Next, she scribbled the location on it and other pertinent information.

"What you think doesn't matter."

"Oh really?" Cynthia walked toward Madison.

"You know what I mean, Cyn."

Cynthia raised her brows and dragged a pointed finger from Madison to Terry. "Can you believe this girl? She pulls out *Cyn* when she's put on the spot."

"It's not that," Madison said. "Listen, we need to speak to Jennifer."

"It's about Zoe's phone, isn't it?"

"Yes."

"Well, we were just about to call you."

Madison pointed toward the pile of garbage and debris from where Cynthia had emerged. "Yeah, it sure looked like it."

Cynthia smirked and shook her head. "You have no patience." Her gaze went to Terry and Madison followed suit. He was smiling, too.

"Would you guys cut it out and focus? The phone, what did you find?" Her cell chimed, notifying her of an e-mail.

"You might want to get that," Cynthia said.

"It can wait."

"If you want to know what was on Zoe's phone, then no, it can't."

Madison rolled her eyes. "Jennifer sent the list to my phone?"

"Yes."

She opened up the message's attachment to see Zoe's contact list. There were fifty names and numbers. Nothing was ever easy. She went back to the note Jennifer had included. Zoe's recent history showed several calls and messages to various people including Faye Duncan. But correspondence with an Elias Bowers was of a personal nature.

Madison lowered her phone. Cynthia had already gone back to evidence collection, and Terry was staring at Madison. She shared the information with him but remained standing there, thinking everything through.

So Zoe had actually had a boyfriend. How did he factor into her death, or did he even? And if he did, why kill Faye Duncan?

Assuming the vagrant was collateral damage—God, she hated to think of anyone that way—the murders were prompted by either Faye's or Zoe's actions.

Their deaths were personal.

Personal. There was something there, but she wasn't quite grasping what.

Faye Duncan had been passionate about two things: her great-niece and protesting abortion.

Zoe Bell was somewhat of an unknown at this point. Her mother had said she got on well with men, and she'd had a male contact, Elias, who seemed like a possible lover.

The vagrant, who she was tiring of labeling such, deserved a name. She'd think of him as *Charlie* until she knew otherwise. Assigning him a label or considering him a John Doe was too impersonal.

She didn't know anything about Charlie at this point. Nothing.

Her eyes scanned the area, settling on the back door of the soup kitchen. The same soup kitchen where Kimberly Bell volunteered.

How did this all fit together?

"What are you thinking, Maddy?" Terry asked.

She wrested her gaze from the door to look at Terry. "I'm just trying to figure out how the murders and series of events are connected. First, Faye dies and her body is left outside the hospital. Then, Zoe is found in vagrant's clothing. The reason for this I have yet to understand."

"Maybe the killer didn't think we'd identify her that way."

His theory had merit. The killer wasn't counting on them to recognize Zoe Bell. That could rule out the mother, Kimberly, right there. Say, she had let Faye die and Zoe confronted her. She could have lashed out, resulting in Zoe's murder, and Charlie's because he'd witnessed the event. But what purpose would Kimberly have to conceal her daughter's identity? Regret,

maybe? As if by doing so, it would minimize what she had done?
   Another circle.
   And standing around wasn't going to do them any good.
"We've got to meet this Elias Bowers, figure out exactly who
he was to Zoe Bell and whether or not he's the one behind the
murders."

Chapter 28

Elias Bowers was a prenatal doctor at Peace Liberty Hospital. If Faye had died defending her stance on abortion, it wouldn't be Elias pushing the buttons. He would have been on her side—at least one would think. It was possible the doctor still believed in the right to choose.

Madison and Terry caught up with him at home. According to the hospital, he had just come off a twenty-hour shift.

His Lexus was in the driveway of his bungalow. The property was well maintained and in a nice part of town, but not in one of the fancy neighborhoods where many doctors settled down.

The curtains in the front were all closed. Terry pressed the doorbell and the chime echoed through the otherwise silent home as if it were a yell in a canyon. It told Madison the doctor was sparse on furnishings. He must have put most of his money into his car.

They waited, and still there was no movement from inside.

Madison pressed the bell this time.

"He must be knocked out not to hear this thing," Terry said.

It was a possibility Madison didn't like. She imagined Elias in bed, door shut, maybe an air cleaner on, a fan overhead. It's possible he had even invested in soundproofing his room seeing as he worked long shifts at the hospital.

"Wait…did you hear that?" Terry asked.

She strained to listen. "Ah—"

"There."

It was the clunk of a gate closing.

"Hello?" A man's voice called out from the side of the house. He rounded the front and Madison recognized him from his DMV photo. Elias Bowers. Just like Zoe, his eyes were piercing, but instead of being the color of steel, they were as blue as a clear sky. Facial growth shadowed his angular jaw and his build was firm.

"We're detectives with Stiles PD." Madison held up her badge. "We have some questions for you about Zoe Bell."

He raked his fingers through his already-tousled hair. "What about her?"

"Do you have someplace we could sit?" she asked.

His eyes glazed over—maybe from exhaustion?—but they registered confusion. "Ah, yeah, sure. This way."

He led them to a back deck, where a man was nursing a beer and sitting with his feet up on another chair. There were four empty bottles on the table next to him.

He stood up quickly.

"This is Ben," Elias said.

Ben acknowledged them with a small wave from hip level. His eyes darted between Madison and Terry.

"They want to talk about Zoe," Elias explained to his friend.

"Okay?" Ben said, clearly confused. He went back to his chair but didn't put his feet up again.

"Why do you want to talk about her?" Elias asked Madison. Then his eyes darted to Terry and he dropped onto a chair next to his friend. "Is she all right?"

Coming straight out with it was the best way, she decided. "Her body was found this morning," Madison said.

Elias rubbed the stubble on his face and his eyes misted. "What happened?"

"We believe that she was murdered. The cause of death is looking to be blunt force trauma."

"Someone beat her?" His brow furrowed, crease lines etching into his skin with the depth of the question.

"Yes, it appears that way," Madison said. "When did you last see her?"

"Over a week ago. My shifts at the hospital kept getting in the way."

Madison nodded. She'd get to alibis soon enough. "What was your relationship like with Zoe Bell?"

He sniffled and looked at Ben, who was shaking his head.

"I'm so sorry, man," Ben said.

A few seconds had passed before Elias responded to her question. "We were lovers." He blew out a rush of air. "Heck, we were more than that." His body was shaking, and his eyes had glazed over.

Ben stepped in for his friend. "He was going to propose to her."

"So it was serious?" Madison queried the obvious.

Elias met her eyes. "You could say that." He waited a few beats. "She was a special girl."

With his comment, their age difference became more apparent. Zoe had been twenty-one, and according to his record, Elias was in his early thirties.

"Where did you meet?"

"At the hospital. She came in to visit her aunt—great-aunt. Anyway, she had hip surgery or something like that..." He paused for a few seconds and then continued. "Well, Zoe was all turned around and I helped her find her aunt's room. The hallways down at Peace Liberty can get pretty confusing when you're not familiar with them."

Madison could attest to that. "Did you know her aunt?"

"Yes and no. I know more *of* her. We weren't introduced."

"So, you never met?" she asked yet again.

Elias shook his head. "No, like I said. By the way, how is she doing? I know the two of them were really close."

He either didn't know about Faye's murder or was playing dumb. "She was also murdered."

"She— What?" Elias's lips twisted. "What is going on?"

"That's what we're trying to figure out," Terry said.

"And you thought I could help with that?" Elias looked from Terry to Madison.

She wasn't about to say he was a suspect…just yet. "You were going to propose to Zoe but never met her aunt? Like you said, they were close."

"I had brought it up to Zoe, but it never seemed like a good time. I know it sounds crazy, wanting to marry a girl when she didn't even want to introduce me to her favorite relative, but Zoe wasn't like other girls. She had a spark in her. Her best friend was her aunt. Maybe in some ways—" He waved a hand. "I'm not finishing that thought. It's going to sound wrong."

If he were going to say that Zoe was better dead than having to grieve the loss of her aunt, yes, it would sound wrong. And very bad.

Madison turned her attention to Ben. "Did you know Zoe?"

His gaze was looking over the back lawn. He faced Madison and nodded. Then he turned to Elias. "I'm so sorry, man."

"I just can't believe it," Elias said.

It seemed apparent that Zoe had been killed in that back alley, and if so, they needed to figure out why she'd been there in the first place. Did Zoe volunteer at the soup kitchen like her mother? And what would either of them be doing there at the time of night that Zoe was killed, anyway?

"Did Zoe do any volunteer work?" Madison asked.

"Not that I know of. Her job kept her pretty busy."

"She worked at Angels Incorporated?" Usually, Madison would have let him say where, but she wanted to see if the name elicited any reaction. The motive for the two women's deaths had to be buried underneath outside appearances.

Elias's light-blue irises had turned stormy. "Yeah. She worked in the office there."

"What do they do there?" Madison asked.

"I can't say we talked much about business," Elias said.

Yet, he was going to propose to her? Had Zoe been hiding something? It seemed more likely that a young girl would have enemies over that of an older woman, but what would result in *both* of them being killed?

"Like I said," Elias continued, "our relationship was relatively new. She did mention she liked her boss."

New? But he was ready to make a lifetime commitment. No wonder so many marriages ended in divorce when people gambled like this.

"Where were you this morning between midnight and two?" Madison asked.

"I'm a suspect now?" Elias looked at his friend. "I should have just gone to bed. First a long shift, then a couple beers, and now this? I'm going to have a breakdown." His eyes went heavenward, and then he ran his hands down his face. He took a moment to compose himself. "I was doing a cesarean section at that time."

"And around six o'clock three nights ago?" That was the estimate for Faye's time of death.

"Again, I was at the hospital. I'm usually there. Check with them."

"We will," Madison said.

Chapter 29

"So what are you thinking?" Terry asked as they walked back to the car.

"Too early to say, but I have a feeling he's not behind the murders."

"You're taking his word for this? That's something new in the history of Madison."

She narrowed her eyes. "Oh, shut up." If he were closer, she'd punch him in the shoulder.

She pulled out of Elias's drive. "A twenty-one-year-old woman like Zoe had one man she was in regular communication with, according to her phone, but her mother said she got along well with men. She had other contacts in her phone." She remembered the tally—over fifty.

"We'll speak with them," Terry said.

To think of speaking with each one of them was an overwhelming thought. "Fifty-plus people? There has to be another way to narrow things down. Maybe Zoe had a secret life if she didn't want to tell her boyfriend about what she did for work. There could have been a good reason for that." They needed to firm up what Angels Incorporated was all about. "It might not be what's on her phone, but what isn't."

"What do you mean?"

"Isn't there a way to extract a phone's message history even in the cases where messages have been deleted? If so, maybe our answer may lie in there somewhere. We'll have to speak to Cynthia and see what she has to say." She considered calling now, but Cynthia was probably still investigating the alley. "Fire off a text message to Cynthia. Tell her what we're looking for." She watched Terry until he pulled his phone out. With her eyes back on the road, she swerved around an SUV, and then pulled back into their lane.

"If you could take it a little easy, I'm trying to text here."

"Don't you mean peck?" Madison laughed. He might have been getting faster, but he still tapped each key. She wasn't the queen of technology, but she believed there were apps out there that made texting an easier process.

"Where are we off to anyway? Shouldn't you be getting ready for that event tonight?" Terry asked.

Oh shit! She had forgotten all about it.

"I can't go. I'm in the middle of a case," she said, satisfied with the plausible excuse.

"And you always will be. It's time you got a life."

"Excuse me?" She turned to him, ready to fight, but his smile washed away her rage. With his expression, she remembered the promises she had made to herself, which included opening up to people and doing more for herself than working all the time. "He wants me to wear a dress." She heard the moan to her voice.

"Imagine that." He had tucked his head down, his attention back on messaging Cynthia.

"I don't wear dresses."

"But you *can*."

Leave it to Terry to bring up Christmas Eve and the small dinner party he'd held at his house. She had worn a dress that night.

"Let me rephrase this: I prefer not to wear dresses."

He shrugged. "Sometimes you have to do things you don't want to because it makes someone else happy."

He was exasperating, but he had a point. And she didn't want to let down Troy. He might never kiss her again. She laughed at the thought. "Fine, I'll go."

He pointed at the dash: 5:00 PM.

How did it get to be that late? But it wasn't the first time she'd gotten so absorbed in a case that time had passed without her noticing. This job was never going to be the standard nine-to-five, Monday to Friday.

She thought of Hershey. He might have to forego the walk she'd promised him today. Because Terry was right: whether she liked it or not she had to go tonight.

"First stop tomorrow, Angels Incorporated," she said.

"You got it."

"So I'll see you there tonight?"

"Nope."

She slammed the brakes at a yellow light.

"Please don't break my neck." He stretched his neck left, then right.

"Terry, if I'm going, you're—"

"Nope. Not with Annabelle's situation right now."

"You could go alone." Was she desperate enough to pull him from his nearly bursting pregnant wife?

He shook his head. "It's not happening."

"But I have to get all dressed up," she sulked.

"Yep." He tucked his phone into a pocket. "The message is off to Cynthia."

Oh, Cynthia should be there, she realized. Madison might not end up facing Troy and this thing on her own, after all.

CHAPTER 30

THE FOUNDATION FOR FALLEN HEROES in the Line of Duty had gone all out for the affair. They had rented a banquet hall in a ritzy hotel, hiring everyone from decorators to caterers. Round tables, each one with seating for eight, were covered with white linens. Place settings consisted of crystal wineglasses, fine china, and silverware. Floral centerpieces with flameless candles were positioned in the middle of each table along with two bottles of wine—one red, one white. The latter was in an ice bucket.

Tables framed three sides of a dance floor, and on the fourth side, there was a podium with a microphone. Behind it was a banner displaying the Stiles PD logo alongside the one for the foundation.

Next to the makeshift stage was a live band playing some jazz standards, and the singer wasn't doing a half-bad job of "If I Ruled the World."

As Madison took in the grand room, she wondered how much money would actually make it to the cause. But with a thousand plates at two hundred dollars each—and with the silent auction still to be held—funds would add up quickly. The person who headed up the committee to arrange the event was definitely in a white-collar position. It wasn't that cops didn't appreciate the finer things in life, but most were happy with the basics—a BBQ steak and a beer. But as Troy had told her when he had extended her a ticket, "Sometimes you just have to get dressed up."

She focused on that thought as she slipped into a dress. It was a simple piece—black, fitted, and came to just above her knees.

She wore makeup, including eye shadow and mascara, and she even put on a pair of dangling diamond earrings. The fact that they had come from a previous boyfriend mattered little to her. They'd suit the event tonight. And if she was forced to doll herself up—sticking with the crooning-era terminology—that meant Troy would be wearing a suit, and with his body...

"I see you made it," he whispered in her ear, having come up behind her.

She stayed there, letting his warm breath cascade along her neck. "Isn't the first thing you're supposed to say is how nice I look?" She turned to face him.

He pressed his lips together and bobbed his head side to side. "Actually, I had no intention of saying you look nice."

Her jaw stiffened, as did her entire body.

He slipped a hand behind her neck, teasing her as if he were going to kiss her, but instead he brushed his fingers against an earring. "I was going to say you look absolutely beautiful."

"Thank you." It took a lot to pry the two words from her throat. Her heart was beating so fast, she feared it might jump out of her chest. It didn't help that his green eyes were peering into hers.

She really needed to get a grip. She had made so many exceptions for this man. He told her things; he didn't make suggestions. He slid into a booth and kissed her in public. To top his presumptions off was the nickname he had for her—Bulldog. She detested the term of endearment. It had nothing to do with the breed's looks; they were cute in an acquired-taste sort of way. But it made her sound like a dog with a bone. That he'd based the name on her tendency to obsess over a case to the point of it becoming all-consuming didn't matter.

She stepped back from him, and he didn't move with her. A waitress approached with a silver tray full of champagne-filled flutes. The woman smiled at them as they each took one.

"To tonight." Troy clinked his glass to Madison's.

Hers was to her lips when he added, "To you in a dress."

Somehow, she succeeded in swallowing the amount she had sipped. "You just had to say that, didn't you?"

The smile flashed in his eyes but didn't show on his lips. "Guilty."

"Detective Knight." She looked toward the voice to find it was Leland King, the journalist from the *Stiles Times*, who had addressed her. He was in his early fifties with numerous awards to his credit, but he never let his success affect his modesty. And it had no bearing on his wardrobe. He was an average dresser, and by most counts, a man of average looks.

She looked around his general vicinity. "No date?"

"You should know me well enough by now, Detective. I fly solo." His eyes drifted to Troy.

Madison made the introductions, and Troy held out his hand. King held the shake as if he were assessing Troy. Madison wasn't sure why King would be analyzing him. It's not as if the man should care who she dated. But when everything had happened between her and the Russians, King had taken her side and they had bonded.

The crowd clapped at the end of the song. After an instrumental introduction, the singer began to sing "I Can't Believe That You're in Love With Me."

"If you'll excuse us." Troy took her glass and passed it off to King, who managed to hold their two flutes in one hand. He had his own in the other. Troy then took Madison's arm and led her to the dance floor.

"What are you doing?" Madison asked.

"What does it look like? We're going to dance."

"You think so?"

"I know so."

Madison caught King's eye and mouthed, *Sorry*. He just nodded at her.

She and Troy were swaying to the classic song before she had a chance to dispute the matter. First, she was in a dress and "gussied up," as her grandmother would have said, and second, she was dancing with Troy for everyone to see.

As he led her around the floor, her eyes took in the room. She swore people were watching them but was happy that most weren't paying them any attention. Then her eyes found Cynthia's. There was no hiding the thousand-watt smile on her friend's face. Madison shook her head.

Heat was blooming in Madison's cheeks. She hated being put on the spot in any capacity other than an actual investigation. As they rotated, King lifted a glass to her and then pointed to a table next to him where he had set their glasses. She smiled her thanks, then dropped her head to Troy's shoulder. He held her tighter.

Before Troy, it had been so long since she had felt secure in a man's arms. Since Sovereign had broken her heart all those years ago, she had always been one foot out the door with the men she'd dated. She had taken the comfort of their embraces—at the time—but had never expected or anticipated any more. She had convinced herself she didn't want—or need—any more than that. The truth was that she had been hurting inside.

But she had been able to release herself from the burden she carried over their failed relationship. It was liberating, though a part of her still refused to buy into the fairy tale of happily-ever-after. It was probably only a matter of time until Troy would see that he was too good for her. Then this, too, would end. It was inevitable, wasn't it? She was a seven, and he was a ten. That meant one thing: when the relationship did end, he'd have initiated it.

She straightened up and let out a deep breath.

He lowered his face close to hers. "You smell nice, Bulldog."

She gently slapped his chest, becoming even more aware of the firm muscles beneath his shirt. "Would you stop calling me that?"

"I thought I'd test it out again just to see if you'd changed your mind about the nickname."

"I don't know. Do you like Hotshot now?" She had assigned the nickname months ago on reflex. It alluded to his ability to acquire his target when under pressure. To Madison, it was more complimentary than Bulldog.

His response was swift as he shook his head. There was the

hint of a smile playing on his lips. "Not at all."

"Well, then." It was in the following lull of silence that she realized what he had done. He had pulled out *Bulldog* to put her at ease. God, the man was good.

She put her elbow on his shoulder, moving in tighter against him. She inhaled his cologne, a heady blend of birch and sandalwood. The fragrance was crisp.

Speaking of smelling good…

She closed her eyes to savor the scent, and when she opened them, McAlexandar was right in front of her.

Chapter 31

Madison hoped her eyes were playing tricks on her. What was McAlexandar doing here? Of course, she already knew the answer. If there was an opportunity to make headlines, he always found his way into the spotlight. She should have known that he'd be here. As former police chief, his presence would seem appropriate to others, but she knew him better than most. He hadn't dedicated his life to the brotherhood of blue. He stood in opposition to all that they represented. And there wasn't much worse than a dirty cop, and of those, McAlexandar was king of the shit pile.

Troy must have sensed her stiffen. He slowed down, the two of them almost static on the dance floor. A few of their colleagues swirled around them.

"Are you okay?" he whispered in her ear.

Before she could respond, McAlexandar guided his wife closer to her and Troy. "Madison Knight."

She clenched her teeth and forced a tight smile. Even now, he couldn't address her by formal title. Not that it should surprise her. He despised that she worked as a detective and had sought to take her badge on many occasions.

"Patrick McAlexandar, I didn't expect to see you here," she said.

The two couples moved across the floor until they were standing at the edge.

McAlexandar touched his wife's hand. "Darling, why don't you get us a glass of champagne?" She nodded and excused herself.

With his wife's back to him, his niceties ended. The Viper was back in his eyes, in the set of his jaw. He was ready to strike. He held his gaze on her for a few seconds before his demeanor softened, and he extended his hand to Troy. "Nice to see you again, Matthews."

Troy shook the man's hand, but the encounter was brief, a mere touch and release.

To Madison, McAlexandar said, "In answer to your question"—he tugged down on his suit jacket—"why wouldn't I be here?" He put on his media smile and extended his arms to take in the room.

"I'm surprised that you'd want to draw attention to yourself. After you withdrew from your position as police chief, I thought you crawled back into your hole."

He wagged his finger at her, a mannerism with which she was all too familiar. Nothing this man could say or do would stop her from trying to nail him to the wall. He had to pay for his involvement with the Russians. Who knew many lives he had a hand in executing?

"Now, that's not playing nice, Knight."

"And you, of all people, should recognize that," she hissed. Troy's hand fell to her lower back. She sensed it was his way of asking her to keep things polite. But she wasn't feeling inclined. "How many deaths are you responsible for, hmm? Two, four, or more? Come on, tell us."

Troy removed his hand from her altogether now and clasped both in front of himself. He stretched his neck side to side, and it told Madison that not only was he uncomfortable with this confrontation, but he was also angry.

McAlexandar shoved his hands into his pockets. "You always have had quite the imagination."

"Some people might think you're worth respecting, but I see you for who you really are. I'm sure I'm not alone in that, either." She refrained from completely speaking her mind. She could have been even more candid.

McAlexandar turned his gaze to Troy. "She's always had an

issue with male authority. Do you know what you're getting involved with?"

She felt the surge of energy around him. Troy didn't want to be roped into this conversation on any level.

"I love a woman who stands her ground and speaks her mind," Troy simply replied.

Madison glanced at Troy, impressed by his candor.

"Well, then, you have that in spades with this one. Don't say I didn't warn you," McAlexandar said.

His wife returned with the champagne and spoke something in a hushed tone to him. "Ah, yes," he said, and then turned to Madison and Troy. "I guess I won't be winning your vote."

Vote? Her heart raced. He had to be joking. She knew his past aspiration had been to run for mayor, but when he'd stepped down as police chief, she had hoped he no longer desired the electoral seat. Surely, he was just trying to get a rise out of her. Did he really have the nerve to go through with this?

"That's right. I'm running for office in the fall. This city needs a major overhaul." He lifted his champagne flute to them before slithering into the crowd with his wife.

"I can't believe it," Madison said, even though she did believe it.

"Neither can I." Troy's tone was sharp, and it was clear he wasn't impressed.

Was it her doing or McAlexandar's? If it were hers, she'd cut and run from this relationship. She wouldn't change who she was for anyone, not even for six-pack abs and a handsome face. McAlexandar was a snake, and she would stand by that no matter the repercussions. If Troy wasn't going to support her, or at least allow her space in this area, well, then, they weren't meant to be together.

Despite her galloping heartbeat, she turned to him. She didn't reach out for him and let the space between them do the communicating. "What can't *you* believe?" she asked. The trust she had extended this man may come hurtling back in her face, but she stood strong.

Troy snatched a glass of champagne from the tray of a passing server. "I can't believe that he talks to you like that. What a piece of shit." He flung back the bubbly.

She was certain the expression on her face must have been convoluted—part smile, part confusion. Surely, a dazed look filled her eyes.

He jutted his empty glass in the direction that McAlexandar and his wife had gone. "You didn't think I was going to take his side, did you?"

There was something there, in the tone of his voice, in the hardened edge his green eyes took on. If she admitted to considering just that, he would cross from agitation to rage. If she tried to cover up what she had been thinking, he'd tell and be angry anyhow. Where was that proverbial bell to save her?

"Honestly, I didn't know—"

"You thought I'd take his side." He wasn't looking at her now. Instead, his eyes carried over the growing crowd, seemingly fixed on nothing.

She touched his forearm, and his gaze went to where her hand touched him, then up to her eyes. His eyes already haunted her soul, and now they tormented her. In them was a storm, and she had no idea whether to seek shelter or face it head-on.

Troy laid his hand over hers. "You never have to doubt whose side I'm on. Do you understand that?"

She nodded, albeit barely. Her breathing was so light it was almost nonexistent. She was one beat away from her heart stalling altogether.

"All right. Now what is the deal with you two?" he asked.

"The deal is that man is in cahoots with the Russian Mafia."

"And you know this for a fact?"

She tempered her impulse to direct her anger at him. None of this was Troy's doing. McAlexandar was to blame. "I have a witness who says he was in contact with Dimitre Petrov when he was at his last prison," she said.

"And you're the reason Petrov was transferred."

Her jaw dropped slightly.

"Don't look at me like that," he said. "Of course I know."

She raised an eyebrow. "You keep tabs on Dimitre?"

"I keep tabs on you and I know you watch Dimitre."

Madison saw Leland King across the room. When everything had come to a climax with the Russians a few months ago, King had written an article and exposed the history between her family and the Russians. The short version was they were responsible for her grandfather's death and her motivation for becoming a cop. She bobbed her head in King's direction with her eyes on Troy.

Troy nodded. "Yes, I read his piece on your family."

"I should have known."

"You should've. What concerns you concerns me."

That direct statement had her taking notice, and not in a good way. "I don't need you to watch over me or take care of me."

"That's not what I'm—"

"That's exactly what you're implying."

"I just meant— Never mind. You're only going to hear what you want to, anyway," he said.

"And what do I *want* to hear?"

"You don't think I know you're looking for a way out of this relationship, Maddy? I know your history."

"More prying?"

His jaw hinged tighter, and he glanced up at the ceiling. Then he met her eyes again. "You told me about your past. Maybe you're forgetting that part."

The adrenaline cooled in her system. "Fine, but—"

"No buts. I've got you now, Madison, and unless you really do something to piss me off, we're a couple."

"Unless *I* do something?" She was heating up again.

"Detective Knight." The new police chief, Andrea Fletcher, was suddenly right next to Madison.

Madison peeled her eyes from Troy. There was such a determination in his aura, a raw maleness that was determined to dominate and conquer. He was the exact type of man she should avoid.

Madison tried to smile at the chief, wondering if the effort was pointless. She always had a hard time conveying emotions she wasn't feeling.

Fletcher was breathtaking, though. Madison had only seen the new chief in pantsuits, sometimes skirt suits. But the red gown with a sweetheart neckline hugged her slender frame. Her chestnut hair was swirled back into a soft chignon with curly strands left out to frame her face. Her delicate facial features were lightly touched with eye shadow in muted tones and a soft-pink lipstick.

"Good evening, Chief. How are you enjoying the gala?" Madison asked. "That is a beautiful dress."

"Thank you. It's going wonderfully so far. I love seeing people come together for a good cause." As if to emphasize her point, Fletcher scanned the crowd, and then looked back at Madison. "You clean up well yourself, Detective. Doesn't she, Troy?"

"Yes, and I told her as much," he said, a slight scowl on his face.

Madison's eyes widened. She knew Troy had been upset, but he normally put on such a good face when it came to his emotions.

Fletcher smiled and shook her head. "I've always had to watch out for him."

Watch out for him? That was an odd thing to say. How well did they know each other? Troy *had* said on numerous occasions that tonight would be a good opportunity to get to know the chief…

Then it struck her: those eyes. They were the same green. And the way she spoke to Troy… Those weren't the words of a police chief to a subordinate. It was the prompting of a… Madison's heart thumped rapidly. They had different last names, but that meant nothing. Fletcher was married.

"You're brother and sister?" Madison asked tentatively.

Now Troy smiled. "Yes. I wanted to tell you tonight."

Fletcher was still grinning, too.

Madison was the only one who wasn't impressed. He was related to the chief and he hadn't told her? And now he sprung the news like it was no big deal? If Fletcher hadn't come over, would he have followed through? When exactly had he planned to tell her? The large room was closing in and her vision blurred.

"Maddy, are you all right?" Fletcher asked.

She felt the chief touch her arm, of Troy's supportive hand on her shoulder. She glanced from the chief to Troy. "I have to go."

"But you haven't eaten," Troy said.

The master of ceremonies took position behind the microphone. No doubt he was going to tell people to sit as dinner was about to be served.

"I'm not feeling well." She brushed between brother and sister and headed for the exit. *Brother and sister?* That changed things. How, she didn't know yet, but it did.

She passed Cynthia on her way out of the ballroom.

"Maddy, what's wrong?" she asked.

Madison kept moving. She wasn't in the mood to discuss this right now. She didn't even know why this revelation bothered her so much. Maybe because she had trusted the man to be forthcoming, and once again, her faith had been misplaced.

Chapter 32

"Are you all right, Troy?" The doting gleam in his older sister's eyes showed quite often, and now it had turned to one of worry. Andrea had always been protective of him—often to a fault.

"I'm fine."

"She'll be back." She put her hand on his shoulder and squeezed. Her effort to soothe him only fanned the flame of his irritation.

"I'm fine." His repeated statement was a dismissal, and his sister was astute enough to nod and leave him be. She walked away, and he remained standing there. Alone.

How dare Madison just walk out on him? Maybe he had put too much faith in this relationship. He knew she was ready to run given an iota of motivation. She had literally one foot out the door at all times. It was Lauren, his ex-wife, all over again. Only now he had the gift of hindsight, and he wasn't going to let a woman strong-arm him again.

But there was something about Madison. Despite her rough exterior and defiant attitude, she needed someone in her life. And he wanted to be that someone. There was no denying that his feelings toward her went a long way back, but the timing had never been right. When he was a married man, it wouldn't have mattered if Madison had come to him naked. He would have turned her away. He was nothing if not faithful.

Damn it.

And now that he had Madison in his life, he wasn't willing to let her go. But at what point should he accept that he might be more into this relationship than she was?

He was pathetic, needing a committed relationship the way he did. Hadn't his failed marriage taught him anything? Happily-ever-after was an illusion, an outcome that existed only in fiction.

And, God, she could be so stubborn. Like tonight. Why did she run off on him like that?

A member of his team waved to him from across the room, and Troy saluted the man nonchalantly as he took a seat at his assigned table. The empty chair beside him was enough to stir his pride. And his anger. He must've been crazy to think he even had a chance to make this—whatever *this* was—work with Madison.

But maybe he should have been more forthright. Of course, maybe this had to do with that dick, McAlexandar, and not with Troy at all. Madison didn't seem to realize how much he had been keeping tabs on her, but he knew enough. She had suspicions about McAlexandar, and the two of them had battled it out more than once. Troy was also aware that the departmental strain had extended to the sergeant and probably still remained. Both men were old-school, preferring a world where women either stayed at home or answered phones and brought them coffee. Troy had observed Madison fighting the dynamic duo at every turn.

It was why, when his sister had told him she was taking over for McAlexandar, he'd encouraged Andrea. She had always had a mind for business and was a do-gooder. Her new position would allow her to utilize these two natural gifts.

Troy spread his cloth napkin across his lap. His eyes darted around the room. It felt like everyone was watching him, probably wondering where Madison had gone. Maybe some of them thought she had excused herself to use the washroom, but that summation would evaporate when she never returned. And Troy knew she wasn't coming back. It had been in the set of her jaw and the fire in her eyes.

But there was no way in hell that he was chasing after her.

Was this what he really wanted? A strong-willed woman who could catch flame without a spark? Or had he provided the flicker that had ignited her anger?

No. He refused to accept that. He was always too eager to make exceptions for the women he fell for. It had been the same with Lauren. He'd loved her from the time he had first heard her laugh and had been faithful to her for the fifteen years of their marriage. He had been oblivious to her infidelities. They did say love was blind.

She was always "going out with the girls." It wasn't until she had forgotten their anniversary and gave him the same line that he noticed something was up. Still, he was the mongrel who had believed she loved him. Foolish.

He'd planned to surprise her with flowers and a fancy dinner out, but he was the one who had ended up being surprised. Or shocked was more like it.

The signs had been there all along, but he had refused to see them. How often did a woman need to go out with her friends? It was getting to the point that Lauren was out most nights of the week. Sometimes she'd even go out on Saturday afternoons. But he had accepted her word. He had been busy building his career, and he had actually liked the fact that she was independent and had a life of her own. She'd deserved to be out living while he worked. He just hadn't been thinking about the kind of *living* she was doing.

He had shown up at her best friend's apartment that day and had been told that she hadn't seen Lauren in months. That should have been his first serious clue, but it didn't have his gut churning. His training as a cop had gone out the window wherever she was concerned. They were in love...right? Why would Lauren lie to him? Their life together was perfect, was it not? Those were the things he would say to himself to ease the doubt niggling in his belly.

He'd even felt guilty, as if he'd betrayed her, when he'd opted to find Lauren through the GPS on her phone. He hadn't believed it when he saw it. According to the tracker, she—or at least her phone—had been at his best friend's house. The rose-colored glasses were taken off then.

A bouquet of red roses had wilted on the passenger seat

that night as he drove to confront the two people who had been the closest to him. Sadly, his newfound suspicions had been confirmed. It had marked the end of a marriage and the destruction of a friendship, both beyond reconciliation. To this day, the smell of roses was nauseating to him.

"How's it going, Troy?" Officer Beck sat down across from him and held up a champagne flute.

"Good." It was a knee-jerk response. There was no meaning behind it. In fact, everything wasn't good, certainly not him.

With the recollections of Lauren, that seed of betrayal grew, weighing him down. But it didn't bring in a wave of nerves or an upset stomach. Instead, his system vibrated with rage, a defense mechanism he must have developed since Lauren.

Madison Knight was a beautiful woman. She was tenacious. His Bulldog. But was she worth chasing after and risking his heart?

Troy lifted his champagne flute, following the lead of the others in the room who were toasting something the master of ceremonies had said. He went through the motions as he dwelled on Madison and the conflict she brewed within him. And he hated that the answers to his questions came so readily. He'd give her space for a few days, but Madison was definitely one in million, clichéd as he knew it sounded.

CHAPTER 33

MADISON WENT HOME FROM THE gala to change, but she had no intention of staying there. She walked Hershey for a few blocks, both to give him the attention he deserved and in an effort to cool her temper. But even moving at a brisk pace wasn't enough to still the feelings of betrayal churning in her gut. Maybe laying it all bare and exposing oneself wasn't worth it. No matter what perspective one had on vulnerability, that's what it was: a weakness.

Troy hadn't called her, and she hadn't expected him to. His temper ran as deep as hers did, if not deeper. She had seen it directed elsewhere and didn't relish the thought of it coming her way. But what did he think would happen? Announcing that the police chief was his sister wasn't a small thing. Potentially, it was loaded. Any future accreditations would be rumored as being the result of her sleeping with Fletcher's brother. And the last thing Madison wanted was to stand on anyone's shoulders. Really, how could Troy figure this news hadn't been worth sharing from the start of their relationship? He could have told her the night Fletcher's position was announced. They'd gone out for dinner afterward, and there had been plenty of time.

She dropped Hershey back at home with plans to go into the station. If she wasn't at the gala, she might as well do some good elsewhere.

IT HAD BEEN HARD TO leave with Hershey giving her those puppy eyes, but it was for the greater good. He was the dog of a cop.

He had to know there were going to be sacrifices involved. Then again, maybe she was giving the canine too much credit.

The hallways of the station were almost barren with most of the brotherhood at the gala. There was only a minimal staff on tonight, making it the perfect night to rob a bank.

She typed *Angels Incorporated* into her system. Seeing as it was an incorporated company, her database should list the president's and directors' information. It should also have a brief description as to what sort of business they conducted.

Scrolling down, she noted there were only two names. The president was Mario Cohen and the director was Ken Shelton. She pulled their backgrounds and noticed that Mario Cohen's address matched that of the company. She grabbed a pen and then searched for a piece of paper.

Her desk was cluttered, overflowing with case files and things she intended to tidy up—not that Terry would believe it. She glanced over at his desk. It was pristine. Not one thing out of place.

She found a sheet and pulled it from her tray. She wrote their names on the back.

Next, she looked at the business information: ENTERTAINMENT INDUSTRY. To describe that as vague would be generous. It could mean any number of things, from movies to novels and anything between.

What would Zoe Bell offer the entertainment industry?

Her stomach sank with the answer. Zoe was young and beautiful. She never told Elias what her employer did for work. She had disclosed that she was a manager and that corresponded with her credit report. But there were at least two reasons for not telling Elias. One, Zoe may have been ashamed of her position, or two, she was hiding it for some reason. It was even possible the motives blended.

Looking closer at the report on the corporation, Angels Incorporated was the parent company of a local strip club. And it wasn't just any club. It was one located in a dangerous part of the city. A quick look into the establishment showed its mailing address matched that of Angels Incorporated despite a different physical location. The reason for that wasn't clear.

But what all this equated to was that Zoe Bell may not have been the sweet girl her family thought she was. Sure, Zoe could have been the club's manager, but most likely, Zoe was a stripper.

CHAPTER 34

MADISON RANG THE DOORBELL AND waited, the smell of barbecuing meat wafting through the neighborhood. She wasn't sure if it was coming from Terry's backyard or someone else's, but someone somewhere was having a late dinner.

Terry answered the door. "What are you doing here? Shouldn't you be at the gala?"

"I was and now I'm not. Listen, we have to check out Angels Incorporated."

"Maddy—" Terry glanced over his shoulder back into his house "—it's nine o'clock at night. We were going there first thing tomorrow."

"Change of plans."

"Why would they be open now? And didn't you say they worked out of a house?"

"I said the address was residential." She wasn't going to tell him she'd already went by there and no one was home. She continued. "But there's a lot more to this. Angels Incorporated is the parent company of Club 69. That's the strip club on Industrial Plaza Road."

"I know what 69 is."

"*Club* 69." She shook her head. "Never mind, I'm not even touching that."

He narrowed his eyes at her. "Get your head out of the gutter, Maddy."

"Me? You're the one who abbreviated the name."

"If I were referring to *that*, I would have said *sixty-niner*. I also know what that—"

She snapped her fingers. "Terry, listen."

He sighed. "What, Maddy? What do you want?"

"After what happened with the Russians, you made me promise never to jeopardize my life again. You also told me to get you to come along if I was going to do something I considered even a little risky. And if you know of the club, then you know it's a rough crowd."

Terry took a deep breath and glanced back into his house again, then to Madison. "What about the big Troy Matthews?"

She was starting to feel silly for having come here. What was she thinking? Annabelle was due at any moment. Terry and his wife had enough stress in their lives. "Never mind, Terry. I can go alone."

"You have a fight?"

"What?"

"You and Troy?"

She had interrupted his evening so she'd give him an answer, but she wasn't going to get into any detail. She certainly wasn't going to mention his relation to the police chief. "He's still at the gala."

"What happened?"

"I don't want to talk about it."

"Don't mess this up, Maddy."

"Excuse me?" She crossed her arms over her chest. She should have known he'd take Troy's side.

"I'll come with you. Just give me a minute." Terry left the door open and went inside.

She noticed how he'd ignored her counter and she was happy he was respecting her wish. Still, his words stung like a pinprick—a little pain at first, but then it began to fester. Why did he think *she* would mess things up? Troy was the one who hadn't bothered to communicate. He was the one who had withheld information.

Seconds turned to minutes as Madison listened to Terry explaining the situation to Annabelle, who obviously didn't like him leaving the house so late. Madison shouldn't have come.

And if the double life of a young woman wasn't possibly behind the three murders, maybe she could have walked away. But Zoe Bell had been involved with a dangerous crowd. One of them could have gotten even for something.

Still, Faye Duncan had been boiling water for tea. Madison found it hard to imagine anyone from Club 69 tipping a teacup to his or her lips.

Madison was about to tell Terry she'd go it alone, but then he hurried past her to the department car she had checked out from the station.

"We've got to be quick. She's not happy about this. At all," he said.

Inside, Annabelle was standing down the hall. Madison waved, but Annabelle kept her hands on her stomach.

"I'm sorry, Terry. It was a bad idea coming here."

"You think?" He got into the passenger seat of the sedan and Madison got behind the wheel before Terry continued. "But you did the right thing. It might be bad timing, but I'm glad you came to get me. Club 69 isn't anywhere you want to go alone. Just promise me one thing."

Her chest became heavy and she took a deep breath.

"What is that?" she asked.

"If I come with you tonight, I don't work tomorrow. Besides, it will be Sunday."

"I didn't realize you observed the Sabbath."

"If I did, today would have been the correct day to observe it."

She let out a moan.

"What? I'm trying to educate you. Sharing this useful information."

"That wasn't exactly what I was thinking." She smirked at him before glancing in the rearview mirror and backing out of his driveway. Her mind was no longer on his *useful information*; it was on the investigation. Was it someone from Club 69 who landed both Zoe and her great-aunt in the morgue?

THE SIGN OUTSIDE CLUB 69 advertised that they had the sexiest dancing girls in the city—a brave claim. But it was worse for Madison to note the push for patrons to book a private room. Goons guarded the entrance. Their eyes followed Madison and Terry, but they didn't try to stop them.

The music in the club pumped loudly—the bass vibrated in Madison's chest. Through a fog-machine haze, colored strobe lights danced across the stage, spotlighting the current act—a trim blonde flinging around a pole and bending in ways bordering on contortionism.

"Welcome to Club 69. My name is Kitty."

Kitty was another blonde—sort of. The color was too pale next to her tanned skin to be natural. She wore a black bustier paired with a lingerie skirt. Garter belts were fastened to its base, holding up thigh-high netted stockings. Her heeled boots came to midcalf. Kitty was more scantily clad than a woman working the streets.

Madison held up her badge and so did Terry.

"Whoa." Kitty gestured for them to move to the side. She shuffled them down the bar until Madison was next to a bald-headed black man with a chest like a tank. He wore a leather vest and a bronze crucifix hung from a black cord around his neck. He passed Madison a sly smile, but it faded when Madison showed him her badge. A second later, he walked away.

Kitty put a hand over Madison's badge. "Please. Mario don't like cops in his place."

Well, isn't that too bad.

Madison could request that she fetch him but figured it was best to start with Kitty. "Do you know Zoe Bell? I understand she works here." For now, she also thought it best to go with present tense.

"Zoe?" Her pixie nose wrinkled up. "I only know one Zoe, but she was a friend back in college. She got messed up with drugs and ended up dying last year from AIDS."

Madison should have known better. Zoe would have worked under a stripper name. She extended her phone to Kitty with Zoe's DMV photo on the screen. "Do you recognize her?"

"Oh, you mean—"

"Hey, Sweet Cheeks, get me a table." A man with a substantive gut brushed his way in the door. He leered at Madison. She glowered back. If he made one move, she'd take him down. He only had to lick his lips and Madison needed a shower.

"I'll be right back." Kitty handed Madison's phone back to her and sauntered off, her hips swaying left to right, right to left— no doubt putting in extra effort for showmanship. Even from behind Leer Boy, it was apparent he followed the movement, his head angling in direct correlation.

Pervert.

Before the interruption, Kitty had clearly recognized Zoe. God, Madison hated to think of her as *Kitty*. It was demeaning to the female sex. A woman should own her sexuality, not exchange it for a dollar. By doing so, she was giving her power away, gambling on her femininity, and setting women's advocacy back decades. Women like Zoe and Kitty may have viewed it from the opposite perspective, feeling that it gave them influence.

It was still hard to fathom that Zoe was a stripper. The image Madison witnessed at Della's house was very different from this world, this lifestyle. Even judging Zoe's house from the outside, it seemed kempt and proper.

Kitty's hips swung at a gentler pendulum on her return saunter back to them.

"You recognized this woman?" Madison asked, flashing Zoe's photograph again.

"I knew her as Eden."

"Eden?"

"Yeah, as in the Garden of Eden."

Madison knew exactly what the Garden of Eden was from church as a child. What happened in Zoe's life to take her from religion to a place like this?

Madison's back was to the bar, but it was apparent that Kitty caught eyes with someone behind Madison. Madison turned to see the bartender pouring a stream of golden liquor into a shot glass. It seemed like he was avoiding making eye contact, but she kept her gaze on him long enough that he raised his eyes to meet Madison's.

"Is there something you'd like to add to our conversation?" she asked.

He shook his head and headed down the bar with the drink he had poured. He set it in front of a man in a suit.

Madison watched after the bartender, but he never returned. Interesting. She'd talk to him before they left the club.

She turned to Kitty. "Did you know Eden well?"

"I don't pay you to talk." A man sidled up next to Kitty. He was Ioan Gruffudd's doppelganger from the mussed brown hair to soft facial features and subtle cleft chin.

"I'm sorry," Kitty said.

He slapped her on the ass, and she let out a yelp, one Madison figured was more for show than from pain.

"Are you here for the entertainment?" His dark eyes scanned over them with an air of indifference. "Because something tells me you're cops."

"I'm Detective Knight, and this is—"

"I'm Detective Grant." Terry took a step toward the man. "Now that you know who we are, who are you?"

"That doesn't really matter."

Madison regarded Terry's protective stance. "We believe it does," she said.

"Name's Ken." His jaw loosened, and his eyes wandered around the bar before returning to them.

There were some similarities to his DMV photo, but he looked quite different in person. "Ken Shelton?" She had Terry pull a detailed background on him along with Mario Cohen as they drove over. They had both served time.

Ken remained silent and peacocked his stance—widened legs, rigid shoulders, straight back, hands clasped in front at his waist.

"We understand that Eden worked here," Madison said.

He guffawed. "There's probably an Eden at every strip club in the city."

She brought up a crime scene photo of Zoe and held it for him to see. "We're concerned with this one."

He glanced at it. "That's a girl?"

Madison pulled her phone back and loaded Zoe's license photo. "What about this one? Easier to make out?"

He visibly swallowed. "I recognize her. Someone killed her?"

No one said the man was a genius. Madison wasn't in the mood to placate by responding to such a stupid question after the man had just seen Zoe dead. Men's clothing or not—the implication should be clear.

"Do you know anyone who could have done this to her?"

"Everyone here loved her."

Madison found it odd how the director of an establishment like this could have affection for his girls, especially ones he just *recognizes*. It was more a legalized brothel. "'Loved her'? Are you sure that's what you mean?"

"I wouldn't expect you to understand."

"Who was she closest to around here?"

"You mean customers?"

Madison shrugged. "Sure."

"She had regulars. I can't see any of them doing this to her, though." He pointed toward Madison's phone.

"What was your relationship like with her?" Terry asked.

He broke eye contact with Madison to look at Terry. "We got along fine."

"Everyone around here loved her, but you got along *fine*," Madison said.

Ken shoved his hands into his pockets. He licked his lips. "She never gave me a shot."

"She wouldn't have sex with you?"

"Exactly. But she'd spread her legs for everyone else. Not customers, of course. Outside of the club and on personal time."

"Of course not," Madison said dryly. "We'll need a list of her regulars."

"You're kidding, right? She was one of our most popular features."

To hear her referred to as a "feature" nauseated Madison. Zoe had been flesh and blood, a human being, not a sideshow, not an attraction at Disney World. Madison wasn't naive to how the world worked; being a cop opened her eyes to the depravity of the human race. It didn't mean she had to like it when it smacked her in the face, though.

She steadied her breath. "We'll still need the list."

"I'll have to talk to Mario."

"By all means, get him now."

"Fine. The truth is, I don't know where he is tonight. He just called to say he wasn't coming in."

Seeing as Mario lived at the address listed for Angels Incorporated, he was somewhere other than home. "When was the last shift *Eden* worked?" Madison asked.

"Last night."

What if Elias found out about what Zoe really did for a living? Would that have proved to be enough to push him over the edge? The fact that he brought lives into the world didn't mean he couldn't be responsible for taking three out.

CHAPTER 35

"IT'S NOT LIKE I HAVE a list of names I can just give you." Ken crossed his arms. "It's not like we take them here."

"But you take plastic?" Madison asked.

"Yes, we do, but—"

"Your accounting records will do." Cynthia might hurt her for making such a laborious request, but depending on the direction of the case, it may be of benefit to have the information.

"No, no way. You're not seeing those without a warrant." Ken unlaced his arms. "I think I've been more than hospitable to you—"

"We'd like to see in Eden's locker, speak to some of the girls before we leave," Madison said.

"You do realize it's Saturday night—the busiest night of the week? I can't be holding up my girls to talk to you."

"Let us go backstage, then. We'll talk to them as they come off and before they go on," Terry suggested.

The music amped up. Another thumping, bass concoction that hardly deserved to be termed *music*.

Ken hesitated, seeming to give thought to Terry's proposal. She couldn't imagine Mario being too happy about it if Ken agreed to the request, but that wasn't her problem. She had only one thing to worry about and that was catching a killer. If it inconvenienced people along the way, it was of little consequence. Murder investigations demanded prying into recessed corners that people would rather keep in the dark.

"I guess you could. You should probably get a warrant for that, too," Ken said.

"You served ten years for stealing a car back in '98. You've only had freedom again for less than a decade. Are you sure you want to go behind bars for interfering with a police investigation?" Madison asked.

"Now you're threatening me? And this is to get me to cooperate?"

She'd try going about this another way. "You said Eden—" She almost said Zoe this time "—wouldn't sleep with you, but she slept with everyone else?"

"I think I said she'd 'open her legs' for everyone else."

Madison curled her lips downward. The fact that she wasn't impressed with his direct nature would have been clear.

"Yes and no," he said.

"This probably made you angry. She wouldn't put out for you. Did she have sex with Mario?"

Ken's face contorted. He started breathing from his mouth.

Madison continued to prod him. "She put out for everyone but Ken Shelton. Maybe you took what you felt was yours?"

"Now I raped her?" He flailed his arms in the air. "This is ridiculous."

"Is it? I'm not so sure."

Terry nudged his foot against hers, but she kept going.

"What's to say you didn't kill her to keep her quiet about what you'd done? Or maybe you really didn't have the balls and never did have her. But other men did, and you couldn't stand it. You killed her because of it."

Ken scoffed. "You're a good storyteller."

"Am I? Who do you think the DA would believe? An ex-con or a respected Stiles PD detective?"

"Cops invent things to convict people. I didn't steal that car."

"The report says you were found behind the wheel. The car wasn't registered to you."

He waved his hand. "Small point."

"Small point? That is the definition of car theft."

"I borrowed the car. I was going to take it back."

"Uh-huh. Listen, I don't care. I'll be honest. What I do care about is why Zoe Bell—Eden—is in the city morgue. Cooperate with us and it will look good when you come up before a judge again." It was a fact that 40 percent of those who had served time were convicted at least once more. As for her promise, it was a load of hogwash. She hoped he was stupid enough to buy the line.

"Fine. I'll take you backstage," Ken said.

Jackpot.

THE DRESSING ROOMS WERE AN extension of the backstage area. There were no privacy curtains. Of course, when these women bared all in front of strange men, what was a show of flesh among one another?

The blonde who had been on stage when they first entered the club was sitting in front of a mirror applying rouge to her cheeks. She wore a silk wraparound robe that reached her upper thighs. She paused application of the powder, stalling the brush midway between the compact and her face. Her blue eyes reflected back at them in the mirror. "I don't know who you two are, but you're casting shadows." She touched the brush to her cheeks.

Neither Madison nor Terry said anything and she set the applicator down next to the blush.

The woman shot to her feet. "Ramone!" she shouted.

Madison stuck her badge in the girl's face. Her lips fell in a straight line and twitched as if she were going to say something but hesitated doing so.

"We're detectives with Stiles PD," Madison said.

Her eyes traced up and down Terry. "Are you here to arrest me because I've been a naughty girl? I've been meaning to pay that ticket, I swear."

They didn't have time for this nonsense. "How well did you know Eden?" Madison asked.

Her blue eyes ping-ponged between Madison and Terry. "Did something happen to her?"

"She was murdered," Terry said.

"Oh my...God." The girl backed up until she reached the makeup table and rested her hips against it.

"Do you know anyone who might have done this to her?" Madison asked.

She turned over her left wrist. There was a daffodil tattoo with a ribbon tied on its stem. The word *SHINE* was inked below it. She rubbed her fingertip over the tat, seemingly lost in her thoughts.

Madison gave her a few seconds, but time was moving along and concern about Annabelle became a factor. "Do you know—"

"My mother was my beacon in this world." She continued pawing at her wrist. "This was her favorite flower." She sniffled. "She said that they are the color of sunshine to make us happy." There was a scoffing tone in her voice, but it seemed she was desperately trying to cling to her mother's belief. "When I'm down, I look at this." Her fingers stopped moving, but she kept them pressed to her skin.

"Were you and Eden close?" Madison asked.

The girl just stared blankly at Madison.

"What's your name?"

"I wanted Daffodil, but the doofuses who own the place thought it was a dumb name for a stripper. Said it sounded like Donald Duck or something. Jackasses."

"What is your *real* name?" Terry asked with evident impatience.

A partial smile had only one side of her mouth rising. "I rarely use it, but it's Vicky Hart."

"Were you close to Eden?" Madison repeated.

"You mean Zoe? Yes." Her eyelids lowered. From grief, from exhaustion? It was hard to tell.

The hoots and hollers of the lechers in the bar area echoed backstage. To be in this line of work took a unique individual, that was for sure. Madison hated it when men simply leered at her. To think about them groping her, sticking dollars in her G-string—not that a G-string was a comfortable choice to start with—and yelling for her made her blood curdle. She'd likely end up behind bars for beating their asses.

"You were close to Zoe..." Madison prompted, realizing Vicky had only provided her name, not the answer.

"We are—were... It's odd to think that she's dead. She and I were both popular so we talked about business a lot. We worked out together."

"Did you meet her boyfriend?" Terry asked.

"Zoe had a boyfriend? Oh, do you mean that guy who came in here the one night yelling at her?"

"When did this happen?"

"Hmm." Vicky pressed a finger to her lips and then pointed it in the air. "A month ago...give or take."

"This guy. Describe him for us," Madison said.

"Ah, blond hair, blue eyes, unshaven. He was handsome. A little old for my liking, though. I like 'em before they're thirty." She winked at Terry. Ironic, as Terry was in his early thirties.

"He was also a little on the short side," she continued.

The description didn't match Elias, who had dark hair and was over six feet tall.

"What did they fight about?" Terry asked.

"I couldn't hear all of it. They holed up in the bathroom. Everyone was gathered around the door."

"Everyone?" Madison asked.

"Us girls. Raven, Barbie, and me."

And that was *everyone*?

Terry tapped on the screen of his phone.

"Whatcha doing there?" Vicky brushed her hand toward him. "Neither of those girls would have hurt Zoe."

Terry disregarded Vicky's claim and punched something into his phone. They'd need to talk to the other girls and see what they overheard, regardless.

"You said you couldn't hear all of it, so you did hear something? What was that?" Madison asked.

"I heard the words *money* and *pay up*. Raven thought she owed him money, Barbie thought maybe he was her pimp. Some of the girls do that outside the club, in their own time. If Mario found out, he'd flip. He'd want first stab."

Confirmation yet again that this place was a tar pit.

"What did you think it was about?" Madison asked.

"I think he was her boyfriend and he found out that she danced and didn't like it one bit."

"And how does *money* and *pay up* fit into that?" Terry asked.

Vicky itched the bridge of her nose. "Hell if I know. I just don't think he wanted her working here anymore. It was more or less the feeling I got. Hey, you're cops, you should know about hunches."

Madison disregarded her latter comment. "Do you know if she had issues with any customers?"

"Nah, the guys loved her. They got a little touchy at times, but it didn't bother Zoe. She enjoyed the attention."

Running with Vicky's rendition, Zoe's boyfriend found out about her stripping, didn't like it, and possibly killed her because of it. What didn't jibe was the man's description when compared to Elias. How many lives had Zoe lived, and which one of them had caught up with her?

CHAPTER 36

BEFORE THEY HAD LEFT THE club, Madison had made a point of talking to the suspicious bartender. It turned out that he just had a bad relationship with cops. His parents had been taken from him when he was young, and he'd been placed in foster care. He had been working at the time of all three murders, and Ken Shelton had confirmed his alibis.

Madison had dropped Terry home at about eleven thirty. When they'd arrived, the outside porch light was on, and he'd told Madison that it was a promising sign that Annabelle wasn't too upset with him.

That had been seven and a half hours ago. Plenty of time to get some shut-eye if one slept solidly for that duration. Instead, Madison tossed and turned, thinking about what Zoe may have done to get herself, her great-aunt, and a seemingly innocent bystander killed. Maybe the vagrant—*Charlie*, Madison remembered naming him—had tried to protect Zoe and had taken the first blow instead. Still, she was left with the question of why there was so much death and who had the motive to kill all three in the first place.

Madison was on the couch in her living room, a notepad on her lap, a pen in her hand, a coffee on the side table, and Hershey snoring beside her.

Without knowing more about Charlie, Madison considered three potential suspects: Kimberly Bell, Elias Bowers, and Jody Marsh.

What did each stand to gain? What did they stand to lose?

What were their means, motive, and opportunity?

Kimberly Bell had the most to lose. Zoe was her only daughter. Faye was her only aunt. As for gain, a search of Zoe's house didn't reveal any life insurance policy, and Faye had left all her money to a children's foundation.

The dynamic between Kimberly and Faye would likely have become heated on occasion since the women had diverse opinions on the matter of abortion. When it came to putting Faye's dead weight into a wheelchair, adrenaline could have given Kimberly the necessary strength.

As for the relationship between mother and daughter, Madison sensed that they weren't very close. Kimberly didn't even know the name of the man Zoe was seeing. Of course, Zoe could have kept her love life private, as she had her work. Kimberly had vaguely summarized that men liked her daughter, but that was an easy assumption to make just by looking at Zoe.

Kimberly was a volunteer at the soup kitchen, but Zoe's time of death was placed between midnight and two in the morning. It was unlikely that Kimberly would have been in the area at that time. Not to mention, what would be her true motive to kill her only child?

Still, Madison would speak with the people at the soup kitchen, whether Sovereign felt as though they were stepping on his toes or not.

Next.

Elias Bowers. With Zoe gone, he lost a lover and possible wife. Did he, in fact, know about Zoe's secret life? Then again, he didn't match Vicky's description of the man who had confronted Zoe at the club.

Madison added the unknown man to the list of suspects.

Back to Elias. When it came to Faye, he said he had never met the woman, but that may have been a lie. Did Faye stand in the way of Zoe and Elias? If so, why? He was single—so not an adulterer—handsome, and a doctor. Faye would also have respected his career as someone who delivered babies into the world. They would have shared that bond. The motive for him to kill Faye wasn't a clear one. In fact, the means, motive, and opportunity were all missing. His alibis had cleared him. She drew a line through his name.

Next on the list was Jody Marsh. She'd seemed genuinely upset that Faye had been murdered. Still, Madison had seen her fair share of killers put on a show for the cops. She had admitted that Faye hadn't treated her with much respect. Was that enough for her to let Faye die and put her body on display? She *had* refused to provide her DNA without a warrant. Madison made a note to follow up with Cynthia on the results.

Zoe had also mentioned Faye's behavior around Jody, so the two of them must have met, but without more to go on, it was impossible to establish a strong motive for the other two deaths. She hated to admit it, but Terry might be right when it came to her. So far, she was kissing that forty dollars good-bye.

Hershey yawned and stretched out on the couch beside her. He placed his legs over hers and then rested his head on her lap. She set her notepad on the side table next to her mug and rubbed his head.

"Who is the killer, buddy?"

Her eyes traced to the clock. Noon.

She considered calling Terry, but he had made it clear that he wasn't interested in working today. There had been no room for misinterpretation.

Troy still hadn't called her, and maybe it was best this way. He could go his way and she hers. It was less complicated than having "the talk" and then parting ways, wasn't it? She tried to convince herself of this, but there was something about obtaining closure. With it came a sense of peace. Without it, things were in turmoil. She questioned her choices, possibly even her sanity. He was a good man. And he seemed committed to her. Hadn't he said that unless she did something truly awful, they would remain a couple?

In the light of day, the sentiment made her angry. Who was he to make such a statement? It was as if he had assumed all the power in the relationship, leaving her to follow along blindly.

Well, she wasn't blind anymore. In fact, her eyes were wide open. He was the police chief's brother. How could she just overlook that?

She had let herself buy into the prospect of having a happy relationship when maybe it just wasn't meant for her. She had done fine on her own, and she had Hershey for reliability. She didn't need a man to complete the picture. There was only one solid thing in her life that had trumped everything else—her career. And she wasn't about to forfeit all she had worked so hard for in exchange for a man.

That's it. She couldn't just sit around all day. She had murders to solve.

She'd start with finding out more about the man who'd argued with Zoe at Club 69. She'd leave the soup kitchen for tomorrow and visit there with Terry. Today, she'd visit the strippers, Raven and Barbie. Vicky had told her right where to find them, and conveniently for Madison, they lived together.

"Momma's gotta go to work, buddy."

Momma? Whether she wanted to or not, she was falling into the role of a furbaby momma. What was her world coming to?

Chapter 37

THE SHINGLES WERE CURLED BACK as if they were yawning. The wood siding was in desperate need of a fresh coat of paint, and the roof on the front porch sagged in the middle. The building didn't appear sound enough to enter, let alone live in.

Given the amount of money these women likely made, they must have had other priorities. Madison surmised that Raven and Barbie—whose real names were Peggy and Lynda, respectively—must have some expensive habits. Clothes? Alcohol? Drugs?

Madison knocked on the front door, and a brunette with a bob cut answered within a few seconds. She was wearing short shorts and a fitted tee with the name of the retailer stamped across the front.

Her eyes were alert and curious. "Can I help you?"

Madison held up her badge and made the introduction. "I'm looking for Peggy and Lynda."

"I'm Peggy, but I'm not sure why you'd want to speak to me."

No hesitation. No show of emotion. Vicky hadn't told her about Zoe.

"I understand that you were friends with Zoe Bell, known as Eden down at the club. Her body was found yesterday morning," Madison said.

Peggy gasped, tears filling her eyes. She stepped back into the townhouse, and Madison followed her inside.

The home smelled of cat litter and stale beer, and tumbleweeds of cat hair whirled in the front entrance. Madison's stomach clenched and had her wishing for fresh air again. But returning outside wasn't an option.

Peggy leaned against a half wall, her chin to her chest, her gaze on the floor. "What happened exactly?" Peggy asked. "You said you 'found' her yesterday. Did someone kill her?"

Madison ignored the question. "Vicky said that you overheard an altercation take place between Zoe and a man. I'd like to hear the story from your perspective. What took place that night? What did he look like?"

"An *altercation* might be exaggerating things a little. They argued. They were yelling in the bathroom."

"Had you seen the man before that night?"

Peggy shook her head. Her gaze had lifted from the floor, but it was distant and unfocused.

"Can you describe him?"

"Blond hair. Blue eyes. Handsome."

Madison nodded. That description coincided with Vicky's observations. "Did you notice his height? Was there anything that stood out about his voice? An accent or anything?"

"Short and not that I noticed."

"And how old would you say he—"

"Peg? Who are you talking to?" A woman with red hair came out from a side hall, wiping her eyes. Her bangs covered half her face.

"It's a detective," Peggy answered. To Madison, she said, "This is Lynda."

Lynda ran a flattened hand along the length of her hair and then tucked a bunch of strands behind an ear, clearing her face. Her eyes were at half-mast, and Madison pegged it on exhaustion, not drug use or a hangover.

"What do you want?" Lynda asked.

"Zoe is dead, Lynda. I think she was murdered," Peggy said.

"What?" Lynda dropped onto the arm of the sofa closest to her.

"The detective wants to know about that man. You remember *him*. He came in, and then he and Zoe were yelling at each other in the bathroom."

"I think he was her pimp." Lynda's words came out nonchalantly, as if every woman had a pimp.

Madison directed her next comment to Peggy. "Vicky mentioned that you thought she owed him money."

Peggy nodded. "Well, it was definitely about money. I'm not sure I buy Zoe prostituting herself, though."

"Then you live in a make-believe world, Peg. Zoe was unscrupulous, just like her mother." Madison's ears perked at that, and the fog seemed to be lifting from Lynda's eyes. She scooped her hair in her hand, spun it around, and grabbed a pen from a nearby table. She then stuck the pen into her hair, creating a makeshift chignon.

"What about Zoe's mother?" Madison asked.

"She was a whore. She'd sleep with anyone," Lynda said.

"What do you mean by that?"

"Oh, married, single, whatever, she does 'em. Even women."

Madison hadn't expected that last bit. She still wasn't sure if, or how, Kimberly's lifestyle factored into the investigation, but she did want to know more about the man at the club. "Is there anything you can tell me about his looks or something that stood out about him? Peggy mentioned he was blond with blue eyes."

"He looked to be in his thirties maybe. I don't think he had shaved for a few days. He was trim. Short."

Still nothing new. "Any lisps or stutters when he spoke? Accents?"

"No." Lynda chewed on her lip. "He was really possessive of Zoe, though. She was finished her act and getting ready to leave for the night. She went to head out our door—it's located backstage—and when she swung it open, the next thing we knew this guy had her by the arm and seemed to be either forcing or coercing her into the bathroom."

"Yet none of you thought to get security?" Sweat beaded on Madison's skin, and along with it a chill zipped through her body. The man could have pushed Zoe into the bathroom to rape her. The memory of Constantine's hands on her, groping at her...

"It will only hurt a little bit." He laughs, and she feels him

growing against her. He puts his hands on her lower abdomen.

She places herself out of body and closes her eyes briefly.

He sits back and lifts his shirt over his head.

She had a second, or less, at most. She maneuvers and grabs the gun.

She swallowed hard and blinked. She opened her eyes to look at Peggy again. Skepticism laced her irises, but if she suspected Madison had left them for a moment, she didn't say anything about it.

"I don't know this for a fact or anything," Peggy began, "but I think Zoe made a deal with the wrong people and this guy came to collect. I can't see Zoe selling herself." She projected a glower toward Lynda.

Lynda rolled her eyes.

"So no one from the club guards the back door?" Madison asked. Her heartbeat was coming down. Slowly.

"Nope. Kind of stupid, I know. We have them covering the entrance to backstage from the club side, but really, any creep could help himself by coming in the back."

"Ramone?" Madison remembered that Vicky had called for him when she and Terry were backstage.

"Yeah," Lynda said.

"Did you overhear anything else?" Madison asked both girls.

Lynda shook her head. "You think the music's loud when you're in the crowd, try backstage."

Madison recalled the pounding in her chest of the bass. She conceded with a nod.

"I heard just enough to know it involved money," Peggy said.

"And you?" Madison looked at Lynda.

"Same."

Nothing new, but it was confirmation. It also didn't net a motive. There could be many explanations for arguments involving money besides prostitution. A bet made with the wrong person. A drug dealer collecting on a debt. And the list went on.

Zoe's autopsy was scheduled for tomorrow, and Madison was

ready for some answers. Richards should be able to tell from a quick examination whether Zoe was a drug addict, so that could narrow down the list, perhaps.

Madison came back to Lynda's take on the argument. "You think it's possible she was prostituting herself?"

Lynda glanced at Peggy and then answered. "I do."

"And why is that?"

"She had nice clothes, jewelry. She was always showing us new shoes. The girl was obsessed with them. We can make good money stripping at Club 69 but not enough to live that kind of lifestyle. I mean, look at where we live"—Lynda opened her arms to take in the home—"and that's the two of us pooling money to rent this crap hole."

Madison thought back to Zoe's house, how tidy the yard was, how sound the structure. Zoe was getting money from somewhere else. It could have been the man who had confronted her at the club, and that same man could have been her killer.

Chapter 38

Answers. That was all she needed, and it seemed like it was too much to ask for. Her sleep was fitful. She saw almost every hour on the clock, but more than the case weighed on her thoughts. Troy did, too. He still hadn't contacted her since she'd stormed from the gala Saturday night. Maybe she should have expected that. Eventually everyone let you down, given enough time. She recognized the cynicism, but it was there for good reason. Life had taught her this lesson repeatedly.

She grabbed a Starbucks on her way to the station and, once there, headed for the lab. She sent a quick text off to Terry to let him know where she'd be.

Madison found Cynthia perched behind her computer. Her black frames rested on the end of her nose. Cynthia pushed them up when she turned to Madison. "Good morning."

It didn't much feel like one to Madison. The liquid stimulant would need to wield the power of the gods to wake her up. If it hadn't been for the driving force to find Zoe and Faye's killer, she'd still be in bed.

"So why did you leave Saturday night? Troy didn't look too happy," Cynthia said.

Rage pulsed through her. "He didn't seem too happy? Well, that's too bad."

"Oh no. What happened?"

"Why do guys keep secrets? Is it a genetic thing? You work in a lab. Do men have a clandestine gene?"

Cynthia laughed, but it faded under Madison's stare. "I guess you weren't joking. Ahem."

"No, I wasn't."

Cynthia rose to her feet, tilted her hips to the right and placed a hand there. "Spill it."

"You promise you won't tell a soul." Madison realized the stupidity of requesting such a thing. Troy's relationship to the new chief wouldn't remain a secret forever. Anyone could find out if he or she cared to. Of all the times for her to forego a background check on a man she was dating...

Cynthia extended her little finger toward Madison.

A pinkie swear?

Madison slapped her hand away playfully. She loved how her friend had a way of trying to lighten the mood.

"Did he kill someone? Oh, I know! He likes to cross-dress on the weekends?" Cynthia grinned.

Madison couldn't help the small smile that pulled at one side of her mouth. "Would you be serious please?"

"Sorry. I'm listening," Cynthia said. Her mouth twitched from trying to suppress a smile.

"Chief Fletcher is Troy's sister."

Cynthia's eyes lit up. "How awesome."

"Awesome? That's not exactly how I'd describe it."

"And this is why you left on Saturday?"

This conversation wasn't going the way Madison had imagined it would. She had expected some empathy, some understanding. "Yes, it's why I left. He sprung it on me."

"He probably thought you'd like the surprise."

"He should know I don't like surprises," Madison mumbled.

"So you left because of who his sister is and you haven't talked since?"

"If he wanted to talk, he has my number."

Cynthia winced.

"What?"

"You think he's the one who should be calling *you*? You left him there. You—"

"You think I overreacted?" Madison pressed her hands to her

own chest.

"Uh, yeah. There's no question."

"You weren't there. Fletcher was there and Troy didn't even come out and say it. I put it together. He swears he had every intention of telling me that night, but who the hell knows." She realized she had started gesturing wildly and crossed her arms.

Cynthia put a gentle hand on Madison's arm. "Remember when the Russians had you?"

"Now, that's a stupid question." Cold sweat coated her skin—the precursor for most "events."

Anatolli cocks the hammer, and Madison closes her eyes, anticipating the bullet.

"*Three.*"

Then the delay.

She opens her eyes, staring blankly at Sergey, and hears the click of the hammer.

"*Bang! You're dead!*" *Anatolli exclaims, and both men start laughing.*

"*Looks like fate has other plans," Sergey says.*

"Maddy, are you all right?" Cynthia was shaking her slightly as she spoke.

Madison pulled back. "Yeah." Would the flashbacks ever stop? Dr. Connor had told her they would, but some days it was hard to believe.

Cynthia studied her eyes. "You told me that you promised yourself some things. Do you remember those promises?"

Madison took a steadied, deep breath as she ticked them off in her head.

She would open up to people and try to trust them.

She'd let herself forgive, forget, and heal.

She'd love with all her heart.

She'd accept herself as she was. The few extra pounds she carried didn't measure her worth.

She'd give more of herself to those around her, including her parents.

Madison swallowed. She wished she'd had never confided

those vows in Cynthia. Had she done so for the purpose of accountability? What had she been thinking?

"Do you remember, Maddy?"

"Yes, of course, but this is—"

"This isn't an exception," Cynthia interrupted, shaking her head. "You promised to love with your full heart and to be forgiving."

She could argue that she'd made those specific promises in direct regard to Toby Sovereign, but she knew the excuse wouldn't fly with her friend, even if they had been made with him in mind.

"Are you still with me?" Cynthia asked.

Madison nodded.

"Troy is a good thing for you. Plus, the guy is hot." A mischievous grin curled her lips.

"Cyn—"

Cynthia held up a hand. "This is one case where you're going to have to swallow your pride. He's related to the chief. So what? You do remember how many times I listened to you bitch about the last one. The chief, not your ex-boyfriend. Although, we could go there, as well."

"Okay. Enough." Just Cynthia's reference to McAlexandar had Madison's core temperature heating. What an arrogant man. And what nerve he had to show himself at the gala! He put on the face of standing up for the brotherhood of blue when he was a dirty cop. A *bloodstained* cop.

Cynthia snapped her fingers. "Are you listening to me?"

"Yes."

"Good. Then I suggest you talk to Troy and work this out."

"And if I don't?"

"Then you're a stupid, stupid girl." Cynthia held eye contact until Madison received the message.

Maybe she *was* overreacting to the situation. Troy had said he'd planned to tell her. But what had taken him so long? What if he had just said that to cover himself? The questions kept slamming into the forefront of her mind.

Deep breaths. Still thoughts. Focus.

What real difference did his relation to the chief really make in their relationship?

"Maybe I'll text him," Madison conceded.

"Maybe? You should *at least* text him."

Madison nodded but wasn't feeling as committed to following Cynthia's advice as she might have thought. "Now, can we focus on business?"

"I don't know. Can you get your mind off lover boy?"

"Hey, you brought him up."

Cynthia laughed. "It's always someone else's fault."

"Just tell me what you've got on Zoe, Faye, or even the vagrant."

The door to the lab swung open then, and Terry came in. "What did I miss?"

Madison and Cynthia glanced at each other, an unspoken agreement not to say a word about Troy to Terry passing between them.

Chapter 39

"Did you find the murder weapon?" Madison asked Cynthia.

"Well, let's just get right to it, shall we?" Cynthia smirked and headed to the table.

There was an assortment of photographs spread on the surface. They captured everything that was collected at the various crime scenes. The items would be secured in evidence lockup and checked out for testing to ensure chain of custody.

Cynthia continued. "In direct answer to your question, no, the murder weapon hasn't yet been found. As you know, Richards will be conducting the autopsy within the hour. Of course, I'm sure you're going to be there."

Madison strove to be present for all autopsies related to her investigations. There was always the potential for something to stand out to her and spark a lead.

Cynthia continued. "We know from looking at both the vagrant and—"

"Charlie."

"What?"

"Let's just call him Charlie." She was tired of discussing the homeless man in generic terms.

"Usually it's John Doe, but oooookay." Cynthia pulled her eyes from Madison and sorted through the pictures.

Terry raised his eyebrows. "Charlie?"

"Just accept it," Madison said.

"You'll be seeing this in person soon enough, but here you go." Cynthia handed her a photograph of the back of Zoe's head.

Blood had soaked and matted her hair. It was pushed aside and there was a wound at the base of the skull.

Madison passed the picture to Terry. "It looks rather small."

Cynthia nodded. "The killer hit her in exactly the right place. The trauma broke her neck."

"So you're saying that her death was likely not an accidental homicide?" Madison said.

"I don't think so, no. There was a lot of force behind the blow."

Cynthia went to another pile on the table. "This isn't your case, but—" Cynthia handed a picture of Charlie to Madison "—the blow to his head looks similar. We collected bloody evidence from the alley. Newspapers. Tattered blankets. There was even some blood on the Dumpster. And before you ask, I will clarify. He had another gash—this one on his forehead and nonfatal."

"So he was struck from behind, fell, and hit his head on the Dumpster on the way down?"

"Precisely."

Then the killer had stripped him of his clothes, laid him on his back, and covered him with a tarp. She wondered how Sovereign was making out interviewing those from the street or whether he had uniforms do the job. The latter wouldn't surprise her. Not that Sovereign wasn't a good cop, but he delegated anything he could. She'd rather handle everything herself.

"From the evidence, it appears that whoever killed Zoe also killed Charlie," Cynthia summarized.

"No doubt. I think Charlie was just in the wrong place at the wrong time," Madison said.

"Do we really have to call him Charlie?" Terry asked.

Both women looked at him, and he held up his hands. "Fine—" Terry created a circle in the air with a pointed finger beside his ear "—Charlie, it is."

"Continue, Cyn," Madison said.

"There were three blood profiles on a newspaper we collected. I came in to analyze them early this morning, and one came from Zoe and another from Charlie. There was no hit in the system for the third."

Madison looked at her friend, surprised. "You analyzed it already?"

Cynthia jacked a thumb at Terry. "She's usually all 'Hurry things up,' and now I have something and she's like, 'Already?' There's no pleasing this one."

"You guys do realize when you get going like this that I'm right here, in the room?" Madison angled her head and widened her eyes.

Cynthia raised her brows, and Terry smirked.

Madison sighed and then got back to business. "It's possible the third profile belonged to the killer. Maybe they hurt themselves in the struggle?" Madison theorized. "Is there any indication she was in a struggle before her death?"

"Unlike Faye Duncan, Zoe didn't show signs of bruising, but one of her fingernails was broken."

"And it takes a lot to break gels," Madison added.

Cynthia and Terry stared at her.

"You knew that she had gel nails? That is a rather girlie thing to know." Cynthia crossed her arms. "You never cease to surprise me. Just when I think I know you…"

"Cut it out. My sister gets hers done and is always trying to get me to try them."

"You should."

She narrowed her eyes at Cynthia. "Not really my thing. What about the cigarette butts? The one found next to Faye's body and the one from her backyard?"

Cynthia scrunched up her nose. "Nice subject change."

"Uh-huh."

"Well, testing showed the cigarettes came from two different people."

"Did you compare the DNA from them to the third blood profile?"

"Do you think I just started in the lab yesterday?"

"I never said—"

Cynthia waved it off. "Not yet, but it's on my list of things to do."

"I'm appalled. You said you came in early." Madison did her best to mask her tone in seriousness, and she had almost pulled it off. But Cynthia crossed her eyes and had Madison's lips curling upward.

Cynthia flailed her hands in the air. "See, you're never happy."

A full-fledged smile now. "I wouldn't go so far as to say that. But I do know what I want. What about Faye Duncan? Is there anything pulled from her house that could prove helpful?"

"Jumping all over today, aren't we?"

Madison shrugged.

"Okay," Cynthia continued. "First off, the only person touching those teacups was Faye. No other prints. Prints from the front door—not even going there. But before you set into me, we were able to lift prints from the handles on the wheelchair."

"And?"

"And there wasn't a match in AFIS."

Automated Fingerprint Identification System was a database used to store, obtain, and analyze fingerprint data found in relation to committed crimes.

Jody Marsh, although she would have been printed as an in-home nurse, would have had her records stored in another database. To gain access to that would require another warrant, in addition to the one already served for her DNA.

"What about Jody Marsh's DNA?" Madison asked, assuming it had been obtained by this point.

"Doesn't match either cigarette."

Unless evidence became known and implicated Jody Marsh, Madison was going to have to focus the investigation elsewhere.

Cynthia carried on. "Now, the direction of the blow indicates the assailant was around five and a half feet tall, give or take a few inches," Cynthia clarified.

The mystery man from Club 69 was described as short. For a guy, that height would definitely qualify. Maybe if Madison went back to the club, the girls would know where he measured to against the doorframe… It was a reach, but it was a possibility.

Then it hit her.

"What about street cameras? Are any pointed at the back entrance to Club 69? Or behind the soup kitchen?" Madison asked.

Cynthia shared a look with Terry. "That's a good question," she said. "I can call the city and see if any are pointed in the direction of the club, but we won't hear back right away. Regarding the soup kitchen, there was a camera, but it's live feed only."

"You looked into it for Sovereign already?" Madison asked.

Cynthia nodded. "Sometimes I have to do work for his cases, too."

"Hardy har."

"Hey, that's my line," Terry said.

Madison shot him a glare. He shrugged.

"You got anything else for us?" she asked.

Cynthia fanned her hand over the table and all the images. "As you can see, there's a lot here. And with the three cases tying together, it's all a rush and due yesterday. I've got the team in for a twelve-hour shift today."

By "the team," she meant Mark, Jennifer, and Samantha.

"There's no doubt in my mind that both Zoe and the vagrant—Charlie—were killed by the same instrument," Cynthia added. "An X-ray will show the wound better, but it's oval shaped. If you find that, you'll be closer to finding who did this."

Madison recognized the throwaway phrase, the implication obvious. What she hated was that the longer it took them to sort through the facts, the longer the killer lived a full life.

"And what are your thoughts on Faye?" Madison asked.

"I doubt a sixty-eight-year-old woman was the prime target. I think she was rather like Charlie. An innocent bystander in all this."

"I agree. And, Cyn, about your calling the city—don't worry about it. Terry and I will go to the club and see if we can spot a street cam."

Cynthia gave her a thumbs-up. "Okay. Keep me posted."

"Likewise." Madison gave her friend a tight smile as she and Terry left.

It was time to find out what the autopsy could tell them.

Chapter 40

"I GUESS YOU OWE ME FORTY." Terry held out his hand, palm up, and flexed his fingers. "The nurse didn't kill Faye Duncan. I seem to recall a bet where you said she did it."

Madison brushed past him down the hall, now recalling the actual particulars of their bet. "I actually said someone from Heaven's Care was involved, not Jody Marsh specifically."

Terry came up on her side, and his smile had become a frown.

"We could amend our existing bet," she began, "I say this case will be solved by dinner tomorrow." She was grasping but doing her best to stay positive. Maybe the wager would help.

"Tomorrow?"

She stopped walking and held her hand out. "Let's shake on it."

"For forty dollars or double or nothing again?" he asked.

"Eighty dollars? That's getting a little rich."

"What? You can't afford to—"

They shook on the bet.

"I hate taking money out of your baby's mouth," she said. "But you've brought this on yourself." She winked, turned, and resumed walking toward the morgue.

They found Richards suited up in a smock and a face shield. He lifted the shield and eyeballed the clock on the wall. Madison followed the direction of his gaze.

10:10 AM.

"I was just about to start the internal autopsy," Richards began, "and in another couple minutes, it would have been without you present."

Zoe Bell was on the slab, her once-vibrant silver eyes now vacant and clouded over and her flesh ashen white. Her hair was fanned out around her head in dank tendrils.

Her gaze remained on Zoe. Unforgiving stainless steel was the last stop on everyone's journey. To be a witness to the process made reality sink in further each time. It never got easier. Only the faces changed—those of the murdered and those of the loved ones left behind.

A heavy cloak of mortality draped over her, compressing her chest and making breathing slightly difficult. But she was practiced at putting on a front. Those around her would think she had things under control. And maybe she was naive to think that she was alone in this experience. Death was a shared reality, an outcome beyond human intervention.

"An overview of the body indicates that time of death was, in fact, between midnight and two o'clock Saturday morning," Richards said. "The cause of death was blunt force trauma to the cervical vertebrae. The instrument used was oval shaped, approximately four inches wide."

"A golf putter?" Terry suggested.

"Maybe, but I can't say definitively," Richards said.

"What about signs of drug use?" Madison asked. "Witnesses saw a man arguing with Zoe about a month ago. It could have been a drug dealer."

"No visual signs on her body to indicate drug use. Her weight was a little under for her height and bone structure, but otherwise she seemed in perfect health. That was until someone hit her, of course." He paused. "Now there is something that you may find interesting. The victim had unprotected sex before she died."

A flashback to Constantine threatened a repeat performance, but she successfully suppressed it. She'd have to tell Dr. Connor about this on her next visit.

"Was she raped?" Madison asked.

"No signs to indicate that."

She let out a deep breath.

"Now, the sperm were dead, so all I can say for sure is she

had sex within three days before her death. Sperm only lives for twenty-four to thirty-six hours in the body but can still be tested for up to five days. Today's the fifth day, and I've rushed the testing to obtain the DNA profile or profiles," Richards continued.

Elias had told them he'd last seen Zoe over a week ago. So either he was lying or Zoe was sleeping around.

"You think she had sex with more than one person?" Madison asked.

"Testing will confirm for sure."

Flecks on Zoe's skin picked up light, winking when Madison moved her head. "She's wearing body glitter."

"You'd be correct," Richards said.

"She was a stripper," Terry added.

She narrowed her eyes at him. "I understand that, Terry. I was commenting on the fact. We know that she worked the night she was killed..." Madison's external brainstorming stopped there but continued in her mind.

The strippers witnessed the argument between Zoe and the mystery man a month ago. She had latched onto him being the killer, but the murders might not have anything to do with him. If it had been him, why hadn't he acted sooner? Why wait thirty days? To throw suspicion off himself?

"I will be requesting a full toxicology panel be run on her," Richards said. "It will tell us the state she was in the night she died and whether she was under the influence of any drugs or alcohol. The internal autopsy will also tell me if she had any serious drug problems."

Madison nodded. Again, her eyes drifted to Zoe. How tragic to have a life cut so short—and for what purpose? A possessive lover, a debt, or was it for some other motivation they had yet to uncover?

"I'm going to start now." Richards grabbed a scalpel from a nearby table and put his face shield down. He then hit a button on his recorder. "This is the autopsy for Zoe Bell, age twenty-one, case number..."

Madison looked away, knowing that he was making the Y-shaped incision across Zoe's chest. She had been present for the procedure on several occasions, but she had never actually watched the full process. The sight of blood combined with the nauseating stench of death was almost too much for her constitution to handle *without* watching the blade actually slice through...

She caught movement from the corner of her eye as Richards lifted the flaps of skin back. He was a veteran and conducting autopsies had become routine and fluid for him. He balanced a delicate hand with that of a skilled medical examiner, and he was thorough and methodical. He exchanged the scalpel for a saw and cut through her rib cage, then proceeded to weigh each organ and add commentary.

To signify he was finished, Richards nudged the face shield up with his forearm. Red stained his gloves and the front of his smock. "Her organs are the right color and size. As I had suspected, she was neither a smoker nor a drug abuser."

On the positive side, that eliminated the likelihood of the man being at the club to collect a debt related to drugs. On the negative side, it opened up the field for possible motivations.

CHAPTER 41

IT WAS AROUND NOON BY the time they made it back to Club 69. The parking lot was empty except for one Range Rover. According to the sign by the main door, the place didn't open for another hour. Madison and Terry headed toward the back of the building.

Six men loitered on a nearby street corner smoking weed or whatever concoction was this week's special. Two guys had dispersed when they saw Madison and Terry, while the remaining four watched the detectives with rapt attention. Either they were smoking regular cigarettes or they didn't fear the cops.

She let her gaze leave them to search for a street cam but remained cognizant of the men. She pointed up the poles as they walked along the rear of the building. "It looks like we're out of luck when it comes to the cameras."

"I had a feeling we would be." He sighed.

Since when did Terry keep his pessimistic thoughts to himself?

"Are you doing all right?" she asked.

"Yes."

"That was a quick answer."

"It's the truth."

She wasn't the only one in this partnership who didn't care for discussing feelings, and he clearly wasn't in the mood to talk. But it was also apparent that something was bothering him.

"How's Annabelle?"

He locked eyes with her. "Can we just focus on the investigation?"

"Sure," she said, assessing his words. His mood probably had to do with the fact Daniel wasn't here yet.

The back of Club 69 stank heavily of garbage, cigarettes, beer, and marijuana. Black garbage bags were piled against the wall of the building next to an overflowing Dumpster. With the amount of cash that surely moved through the place, money to get the bin emptied wouldn't have been the issue. Sex was a lucrative business.

Speaking of sex… It had been five days since she had sex with Troy. Her breath stilted as she recalled the touch of his fingers on her skin, his breath on her neck… It was ridiculous that she was letting him get to her like this, especially right now.

She had told Cynthia she'd text him, but she hadn't been able to bring herself to follow through yet. She was still mad. His sister was appointed police chief back in March. It was July.

Terry pulled the handle on the back door and it opened with a screech. "It's unlocked."

She smirked at him. Always one for the obvious. She brushed by him and entered the club first.

"Hello?" a man's voice called out. "Who's there?"

"Stiles PD," Madison answered.

"Hold up a minute." The man's breath was labored and definitely coming closer. He stepped out from around a corner, carrying a case of empty liquor bottles. He maneuvered the box under an arm. His raven hair had an iridescent quality and looked purplish from some angles. Unlike the mop on his head, his eyes were flat.

Madison recognized him but not from having met him in person. "Mario Cohen." Not a question.

"That's me." He licked his lips and rubbed his jaw. "What do you want? I'm busy here."

She lowered the badge she had held up for him. "I'm sure you heard about your employee Zoe Bell."

"Yeah." The implication in his tone was *so what?*

How could he be so blasé about the death of an employee? Then again, Madison remembered the type of business he ran.

"She was murdered, you know." She stated it bluntly, hoping

DEADLY IMPULSE

for a shred of humanity to make itself evident in the man. Nothing surfaced except for seemingly ratcheting irritation over having his day interrupted.

"In less than an hour, this place will be open, so if there's—"

"Do you know who would have had reason to kill her?" Madison crossed her arms. She wasn't going to back down because of some prick with an attitude.

"I really don't have time to discuss this."

"Yet you had time to take off two nights ago," she said.

Mario put the box on the floor.

"That's right, we were here, and you weren't."

"I'm allowed a night off."

"Where were you and what were you doing?"

"*Who* I was doing would be the correct question. And the last time I checked, it's not against the law to get some." He tossed a smirk, one he must've thought was full of machismo, Terry's way.

Terry remained stone-faced, though, and Mario's expression faded.

"Some of your girls mentioned Zoe had a fight with a man on your premises last month," Terry said.

"My girls talked to you?" Mario looked to the ceiling and let air hiss out between clenched teeth. "I don't know what they think they saw—"

"Who are you trying to protect?" Madison asked.

"I'm not trying to protect anyone. I don't know who they are talking about. I only saw customers around Zoe. And she was popular. She'll be a tough act to replace."

Madison narrowed her eyes on him. "My heart goes out to you." Sarcasm. Every word.

"I'm sure it does." Mario glowered back at her and then continued. "I don't mean this with disrespect—not that I care if you take offense—but no one here would have done this to Zoe."

"And you know all your customers? They are all regulars you can vouch for?"

Mario held up a hand. "Now, I never said that."

"By all means, clarify it for us, then," Madison said.

"I'm just saying the guys who come in here may look like shit, they may smell like shit, but they're not killers."

She wasn't going to argue with two out of the three. The latter claim she contested. "Are you sure?"

His eyes glazed over like a reptile. "All right, some have done time, but they don't want to go back."

"So no one *that you know of* would have killed Zoe," Terry said.

"Not that I'm aware of."

"Which is it, Mario? You vouch for them or you're not so sure?"

His facial features hardened. "I guess I'm not sure," he ground out.

"Does anyone, in particular, stand out to you as being suspicious?" Madison asked.

"No. Now, I need to get back to business."

"Do you have any cameras backstage?" She figured it a reach but had to ask.

"No."

"What about out back to cover the girls' door?" She hadn't seen one, but surveillance devices could be tiny these days.

"No! I don't want to get involved in anybody's business just like I don't want them involved in mine. If that will be all?" Mario picked up the case of bottles.

"No, that's not all," Terry said. "So you never saw a man with blond hair in an argument with Zoe?"

"Blond hair? That's descriptive. Later." Mario turned his back on them, but Madison grabbed his arm and spun him around. He kept the bottles balanced but glared at her.

She stared him down. "I think you're lying. You told us that you know who is going in and out of your place, but this blond guy connected to Zoe, you have no idea who he is."

He hoisted the box under one arm as he had earlier. "Lots of blond guys hung around Zoe. I even had a few escorted from the premises, but none of them would have killed her."

"Again, you seem pretty certain," Terry said.

"I'm sorry she's dead. Please pass along my condolences, but I've got a business to run."

When he walked away this time, Madison let him go. He didn't care that one of his girls was murdered. He claimed to know everyone who stepped foot in his establishment, but he didn't know the particular blond male, who was clearly associated with Zoe in some way, that they were after. Something wasn't settling for Madison. He knew more than he was sharing.

CHAPTER 42

MADISON WASN'T READY TO LEAVE the club's property just yet. She wanted to speak to the girls again and see if they could give her a better idea of the mystery man's height. She and Terry waited in the department car for Club 69 to officially open. If Mario didn't like talking to them when they entered from the rear of the building, he definitely wouldn't appreciate their presence among his paying customers.

But she didn't care. Right now she just wanted to get in that club and out of the humidity. It was stifling out here. Even with the vehicle's air-conditioning cranked up, it did little to relieve the mugginess that clung to her like a second skin. They were essentially baking in a convection oven on four wheels, and she hated the feeling of sweat dripping down her torso.

The dash read 12:57 PM.

A few vehicles pulled into the lot, and the men who had occupied them ambled toward the club's door. There was no self-consciousness or shame about their entertainment choice, no furtive glances over their shoulders.

The door opened, and the men started filtering in.

"Thank God." Madison got out of the car.

She came up behind a man she pegged in his late fifties. He wore a biker jacket, and his silver mane was pulled into a sad-looking ponytail. His hair was thin and greasy. His cheeks were concaved, and his red-rimmed eyes testified to drug abuse. He held the door for her and flashed her a toothy grin.

Mark off dental hygiene as one of the man's priorities.

"Wait…are you cops?" the man asked.

She glanced at the badge she wore around her neck.

"Ah, son of a bitch." He pushed Terry aside and set off at a run.

Son of a bitch was right. She hated running!

She helped Terry gain his balance, but he shrugged free of her. She breezed right past Terry, caught up with the man, and slammed him against a vehicle. His hand had just touched the handle of a jalopy—a beige number dating back a couple of decades.

"Why'd you run?" She yanked on his clothing until he was spun around and facing her.

He leaned back against the car door, heaving for breath.

She was…not winded in the slightest. And Terry? She had beat him in a running pursuit? The smile started to grow when she met her partner's eyes but died when she faced the gray-haired man again.

"I didn't do it! You cops never want to believe me!" He turned and then wrenched on the door handle. With the amount of rust caked around it, Madison was surprised it didn't just rip off.

Terry put his hand on the man's shoulders and he stopped moving. "What's your name?" Terry asked.

"Ah, man." He straightened and jammed his hands into the pockets of his jeans. "I didn't do it. And I served my time. I ain't never seen no cent in compensation for the wrong done me, either. My guess is you're not here for that reason."

Madison almost laughed. Out loud. She shook her head. "We're here about Eden." She almost said Zoe.

"What about her?"

"She was murdered. Do you know anything about that?"

"Ah, no! Please don't send me back."

"Name." She made the request this time, in the way of a demand.

"Nick Stanley, and before you comment on the fact that I have two first names, forget it, I'm sick of hearing it." He started to pull his hands out of his pockets.

"Stop right there," Terry barked.

"I don't have a weapon or anything, I swear."

Madison nodded to Terry. "Bring them out nice and slow," she said.

Nick's hands emerged…empty.

"See, I told you." Nick shot heated glares at Madison and then Terry.

"What did you do time for?" Madison asked.

"For robbery. A robbery I *didn't commit*." He leaned against his car again, crossed his arms and his ankles.

"You keep saying you're innocent," Madison said.

"That's because I am!"

It was a detour, but the man was talking. "Was anyone hurt during this robbery?"

"Someone was stabbed."

"And you weren't involved?" Terry asked.

"No, man. I found out about it when the police came down on me. They only saw the way I looked and went from there. Thank God they found the guy who did the murder or I'd be rotting behind bars. He's still there."

"If they got the guy, why were you still doing time?" Madison asked.

"For the robbery. They figured it must have been the two of us working together."

"So you knew the guy who did the stabbing?"

A big sigh. "Yes. We were childhood friends."

Madison didn't want to go any further down memory lane. "Tell us what you know about Eden."

"I know I didn't kill her."

"And?"

"She was flexible on the pole." A creepy grin spread across his face and his eyes glazed over. The boy in his pants was conjuring the image of a scantily clad Zoe Bell.

Madison swallowed her disgust. "Did you ever see her arguing with anyone? Think hard," Madison said, realizing her horrid choice in words.

Silence passed. The hamsters were just a-spinnin' in that head of his.

Nick wagged a pointed finger, directed at neither of them.

More silence.

Madison glanced at Terry, who was fighting back laughter. She, on the other hand, was no longer amused. They didn't have time to be wasting with this guy. "You either have or you haven't."

"Yep"—he was nodding—"I have."

"All right, and?" Madison prompted him to continue. He seemed to need constant encouragement. Or he was just plain slow. Or both. He was a prime example of why drugs weren't good for you.

"It was, say three weeks ago now. I didn't see him with her, but I heard him cursing her name. I said, 'Hey, pal, what's your problem?' He told me to shut the fuck up."

Terry cringed.

Three weeks and a month were close enough to be the same guy as the one that had been arguing with Zoe backstage.

"Around what time was that?"

"Say around nine?"

"So continue to paint the picture for us. He just came out of the club saying her name…" More leading.

Nick shook his head. "He was already in the parking lot talking on the phone to someone when I saw him."

"He was in this parking lot?" Madison asked.

"Ah, yeah."

How could she have missed that? They had been so fixated on coverage of the back, they hadn't thought about the lot. She spotted the camera right away.

Club 69 was located on a corner, and it was mounted on the stoplight. The watchful eye probably captured some of the lot. She bobbed her head in the camera's direction for Terry's benefit. Nick didn't seem to even notice.

"He was saying something about Zoe not being who they thought she was," Nick continued. "I just thought it was a jealous boyfriend, ya know."

"Zoe? You knew her real name?" Madison asked.

"Yeah, but it's… Never mind."

"It's what, Nick?" Terry pressed.

"I hired her for a lap dance."

The bile came up into her mouth. She swallowed. Sour. Vile.

"And she just happened to tell you her real name?" Madison raised her brows.

"Not exactly. I just overheard someone call her that."

"And that's all?" She asked the question but had a feeling it just might have been that simple.

"Yeah, I swear."

"This guy, then, what did he look like?" Terry asked.

"Blond hair, about thirty or so, average looks, and he was small. I don't even think he was six foot. Probably half a foot shy of that."

It was the same description they had received about the mystery man who had argued with Zoe. Now they had the man's general height—if they could trust their source—and it lined up with Cynthia's findings on the angle of the blows to Zoe and Charlie.

Nick said that he had never seen him in the club, only in the lot. But he could have already been inside and had the argument with Zoe. He obviously had something to reveal about the girl. He could have parked in the lot and walked around back.

"Did you catch the make of the car?" Madison asked.

Nick indicated his piece of crap. "I don't really care about stuff like that. Four wheels are a mode of transportation, nothing more."

"A color?"

"Blue."

"Light blue, dark, bright?" Madison kept the questions rolling.

"Bright."

"Two-door or—"

"Four."

"Older model or newer?"

"There was some rust around the wheel wells. It was maybe six years old? I might not know cars, but rust… Rust, I know."

Madison pulled out a card and handed it to Nick. "You think of anything else, you call me. You got it?"

"Sure. What about the time I served? I didn't do the crime."

"You'll have to take that up with the prosecutor's office." She already had her back to him when Nick cursed. She wasn't sure if the expletive was directed at her or the system in general.

They had come to check on surveillance cameras and to see Peggy and Lynda. And while they might not have spoken with the girls, they possibly had the mystery man on tape.

She slid behind the wheel of the department car, and Terry got into the passenger seat.

"'Paint the picture for us'?" He laughed. "And you say I talk funny."

"Oh, you do, Terry, you do." He could tease her about her choice of words all he wanted. She was in too good of a mood—for a couple of reasons—for anyone to spoil it. She grinned. "By the way, I beat your ass back there."

"How do you figure that? I was pushed."

Madison laughed.

"What? I was."

"Any excuse you can pull out. Just admit it. You were beaten by a girl." She put the car into reverse.

Terry rambled, but she was basking in the headway they had made with the case.

CHAPTER 43

MADISON HAD CALLED CYNTHIA, AND she was going to obtain the camera footage from the city. Madison and Terry would be visiting Elias Bowers again. Someone had sex with Zoe Bell within the three days before her death, and he had claimed to have last seen her more than a week prior. And while his alibis may have checked out, Madison was curious if he had lied about the last time they had sex, and if so, why.

They tracked Elias down at the hospital, where he was only a quarter way into his twelve-hour shift.

He entered the waiting room where Madison and Terry were seated. "Come with me."

He led them through a maze of corridors to his office. Etched on the glass window next to the door was ELIAS BOWERS.

The space was compact and organized. The base of a large-screen computer monitor took up a good chunk of his desk space.

Elias took a seat behind his desk and pointed to the two chairs across from him.

Terry sat, but Madison remained standing and perused the room.

A three-door, vertical filing cabinet was up against one wall. A potted plant with long branches shooting out from it fanned out atop the cabinet. Besides the flora and a framed motivational poster, the place was void of personal touches. Elias had zero personality, if one was to judge him based on this room.

"Did you find Zoe's killer?" Elias's voice cracked with his

question. Was it from guilt or grief?

His eyes followed her gaze around the room, but she acted as if she weren't aware of his attention on her.

"You said the last time you saw Zoe was over a week ago. Is that right?" she asked. Given what Zoe did for a living, it wasn't a stretch to believe Zoe was having sex with more than one man, but she wanted to see if his answer would change.

"Yes."

"And you are sure you don't want to change that answer?"

Elias sat back in his chair and crossed his arms. "I swear. Am I a suspect again? My alibis should have cleared me."

"There's evidence that Zoe was sexually active within three days before her death," Madison said. Maybe she should feel like shit for exposing Zoe's lifestyle. Maybe he was better off carrying a false image of Zoe.

Elias's face contorted, first leaning toward heartache, then rage. His chest heaved.

But it wasn't time to play nice. There were three murders to solve. "So either you were lying about when you saw her last, or she was screwing around on you," Madison continued.

The way Elias's lips quivered twisted her gut. "You checked with the hospital. Confirmed my work schedule?"

"We did."

"Then you know I was here the night she was killed."

"You could have taken a dinner break." She was pushing it. It would have taken a bit of time to orchestrate Zoe's and Charlie's murders. She held eye contact with him.

He was the first to look away. "No, I didn't. It was too crazy."

The door to his office burst open, and his friend Ben, the one who had been with him the day they'd first met Elias, rushed into the room.

"I just heard, Eli, that the detectives"—Ben's eyes went over to Madison and Terry then back to his friend—"are here. Did they find out who killed Zoe?"

"We're still working on that," Madison answered even though he had asked Elias.

Elias wheeled closer to his desk and rested his forehead in his hands.

Ben went over to his friend. "What's wrong?"

"You were right about her," Elias said, his voice muffled.

"I was—"

Elias raised his head and met his friend's eyes. "She was a slut."

Ben glanced at Madison and Terry, and then went behind Elias and put his hands on Elias's shoulders. The top of Elias's head came to Ben's collarbone.

Our mystery man is short…

"You have to let her go," Ben said while lightly massaging Elias.

Elias shrugged him off. "I have to let her go?" He bound to his feet and turned toward his friend. "I was going to marry her."

"You know she wasn't any good. I told you that." Ben's face reddened from anger or maybe embarrassment. It was hard to tell.

Elias raked a hand through his mop of brown hair. "I didn't believe you… I didn't *want* to believe you."

The man Nick saw in the parking lot had said that Zoe wasn't who they thought she was. Could it have been Ben and the person he spoke to, Elias?

Ben's structure came in around the estimated height for the killer. He was in his midthirties. But his hair was brown.

He could have colored it…

The two men were staring at each other, their torsos only inches apart. Both their chests were expanding with deep breathing.

"Ben, why don't you sit?" Madison gestured toward the chair that had been offered to her.

Ben kept his eyes on Elias as he rounded the desk and took a seat.

Madison walked around in front of Ben. "Where were you two days ago from midnight to two?"

"Me?" Ben's eyes pleaded with her and then petitioned Elias. "You think I did this?"

Elias dropped back into his chair and pulled out a desk drawer.

Madison braced a hand over her holster, ready to draw. Terry rose to his feet. This situation could go bad quickly. Two men, both visually emotionally charged over Zoe.

"I'm just getting—"

"Don't move." Madison walked behind the desk and spotted the aspirin bottle. She handed it to Elias.

"Gee, thanks." He snatched the pills from her and took one out. He popped it into his mouth and swigged back a couple of gulps of water from the bottle on his desk. He wiped his mouth with the back of his hand.

Madison shifted her attention back to Ben. "Answer the question."

"Where was I—"

"—two days ago. Midnight to two in the morning," she reiterated.

"How the heck am I supposed to know?"

"It wasn't that long ago. Do you have a memory problem?"

Ben's eyes flickered, confirming the reason for the hue to his cheeks. Rage. "If you think I killed her, think again. She wouldn't be worth going to prison for."

"Hey, you watch how you talk about her," Elias barked.

"Or what, Eli?"

Elias's jaw jutted out and then stiffened. In the very least, Zoe's murder had cast a wedge between the friends.

"Ten seconds before I haul your ass downtown," Madison threatened. And she had every intention of following through if she needed to.

"I was at home. Sleeping," Ben said.

"Can anyone testify to that?"

"My cat. If she could talk."

Madison nudged Ben in the shoulder. "That's it. Stand up. You're coming down—" Madison's cell phone rang, and with her aggravation already notched high, she could have thrown it across the room. She held up one hand, directing Ben to stay still, and with the other accepted the call.

"Knight," she said, waiting a beat for the response. "You're sure?" She let her eyes drift between Ben and Elias. "Tomorrow?" She listened for a moment more. "Okay." She hung up and turned to Terry. She'd fill him in later, but it had been Cynthia. The feed from the camera would be to the lab by the morning. But that wasn't everything. In fact, things were finally coming together.

"Where were we? Oh yeah." She grabbed Ben's arm and tucked her phone away with her other hand. "We were going downtown."

"Eli, aren't you going to say anything?" Ben begged.

"What do you want me to say? Maybe you did do this. You never liked her." Elias swiveled his chair to face the window, turning his back on Ben.

CHAPTER 44

BEN HAD WHINED THE ENTIRE ride from the hospital. Or at least until she'd threatened to shoot him. It wasn't something most cops would be proud of—and she'd be disciplined if it reached the sarge's ears—but Ben's silence made it easier to think. Before that, he'd kept repeating that he never would have killed Zoe because "she wasn't worth going to prison for." They'd at least gotten his last name out of him before he'd shut up: Dixon.

Ben wasn't under arrest, but it was clear that he didn't have a choice about whether or not he was coming along for the ride. Once they got Ben secured in the backseat of the department sedan, Madison filled Terry in on Cynthia's messages outside of the car.

When they got to the station, she and Terry each gripped one of Ben's arms and led him toward the interrogation rooms.

Sergeant Winston was outside his office, curling an index finger at her to imply that she was to stop what she was doing and speak with him.

"I'll be there in a sec." To Terry, she said, "Don't start without me."

She watched after Terry and Ben for a few seconds before going into the sarge's office. "It's really not a good time."

"Shut the door."

Lord, now what?

"He's a suspect in our two murder investigations," she said.

Winston stared past her to the door. "Close the door."

She latched it. "This guy could have done it, Sarge. He has a good motive. He had something at stake when it came to Zoe Bell." She might have been stretching the facts a bit.

"Which is all conjecture at this point."

Was she that easy to see through?

"It will be proved. You'll see." She spun to leave, her frustration getting the best of her.

"Knight, not so fast. Sit."

It was apparent that she didn't have a choice. Now she knew how Ben felt. She dropped into a chair across from Winston.

"Sovereign tells me you've been putting your nose into his case."

"And what is this, kindergarten? Besides, you and I have already had this conversation. His murder case is connected with my two cases. There's no denying that."

Winston tapped a flat hand on a piece of paper. "This report confirms that blood from your young victim—"

"Zoe Bell."

"—was in that alley where the vagrant was found."

She wasn't going to ask him to say Charlie. He wouldn't understand, and she didn't have time for this discussion. Their first solid suspect was sitting in an interrogation room, and she was stuck here with Winston.

"Yet, you don't think we're dealing with a serial killer? See, Sovereign, he isn't too sure about that," Winston said.

"Well, Sovereign has always had a flair for the dramatic."

Winston's eyes summoned her to watch herself, but she wasn't going to follow the silent directive.

"Sovereign hasn't had a large profile case in a while," she continued. "He wants to make a name for himself."

"Where is this coming from?"

"Reality? I think I nailed it, actually. It's about the media. But I'm not on board with this being a serial killer. That doesn't sit well with you, though, I guess. You'd rather the headlines."

"I'm warning you, Knight."

"McAlexandar's gone and you don't like it." Whoa, her words were coming out without a filter, but she couldn't stop the torrent.

"Now, Sovereign's trying to butter up to you."

Suddenly, all her fury about Troy being related to the police chief fired to the front of her mind. And her words fell flat. Sovereign must be trying to create a name for himself with Fletcher early. Maybe he knew about Troy's relation to her.

"Are you still seeing that shrink?" Winston asked coolly.

Madison shot to her feet. "That has nothing to do with this. I've always taken shit because I'm the only female detective, and there are only a few female officers at that."

"Oh, here we go again. Women's lib, Knight?"

She was seething, and her pulse was racing. Shit really did float to the top.

"Well, things have changed if you haven't noticed. Your boss is a woman," Madison began, "and I have a suspect to question."

"Knight."

Her hand was on the doorknob. She didn't face him when she spoke. "Winston."

"I know you have your own opinions about me, but I'm doing my best here."

She turned. "Doing your best? McAlexandar used to pull your strings. Now who is?"

By the way his mouth set in a flat line, she knew she had gone too far. "Unless you have concrete proof this suspect of yours killed those people, let him walk."

"Concrete—"

"Yes, concrete. As in no room for doubt. And one more thing, Knight." He paused for effect. "Get out of my office."

And don't let the door hit you on the way out. Winston hadn't said it, but Madison received the implication.

She stormed out, mumbling, "With pleasure," and headed to interrogation room one. Enough with the delays and hiccups of this investigation. She'd deal with Troy and Sovereign later. Right now, she had a suspect to question.

CHAPTER 45

WHEN MADISON ENTERED THE INTERROGATION ROOM, Terry stopped jingling the change in his pocket and Ben's gaze went straight to her.

"Why did you bring me here?" Fear wormed its way into his tone. "I didn't kill Zoe."

Madison opened the case folder that Terry would have brought in and set on the table. She glanced inside at Ben's background. He had marked an asterisk beside the fact that Ben owned a blue, four-door Buick Regal. That aligned with Nick Stanley's testimony. Ben's home address was within walking distance of Elias's, too, and that probably explained why they hadn't seen his vehicle in Elias's driveway.

She was going to play this questioning slow. Usually, she went in with cannons firing. Ben hadn't requested a lawyer, though, and she didn't want to provoke him to request one. She needed her "concrete proof."

"Tell us how you knew Zoe," Madison said. Terry glanced at her, likely because of her relaxed approach. She was being a tiger cub when she was normally a tigress pouncing on her prey. Winston had forced her hand, or in keeping with the analogy, her paw. She'd have to stalk her target *patiently* from a distance.

"My best friend was dating her." Sarcastic. Blunt.

"So Elias introduced the two of you?"

"Yes."

"You mentioned at the hospital that you had told Elias that Zoe wasn't who she said she was."

"She wasn't."

"And what did you mean by that?" Madison asked.

Terry jingled the change in his pocket.

Ben glanced over his shoulder and then clasped his hands on the table. "Just that. Elias is a doctor, and she was money hungry."

"How did you know that?"

"I know the type."

"See, I think there's more to it." There was no avoiding it. She had to sink her teeth into the meat—just a little, get a taste. It was time for the reveal. For the other part of Cynthia's message, another finding that would have connected Zoe and Faye. "Zoe was pregnant when she died."

Silence.

"So? Doesn't that prove she was trying to trap him? She's with a kid, and then he has no choice. Even if he left her, he'd owe child support."

"Except I'm not so sure it was Elias's baby," she said nonchalantly. She sank back into the chair as if relaxing.

Ben flailed an arm. "With good reason."

She put on a shocked face. "She slept around?"

Silence.

Acting never was her strong suit. "Did you have sex with her?"

Ben shifted, straightening out. He clasped his hands together and cupped them as if easing arthritic pain.

"I mean, who could blame you? She was a pretty girl." Madison caught another glance from Terry. This time he was smirking. Was he impressed by her restraint?

"She was my best friend's girl."

She maintained eye contact with Ben. "Oh, come on, that doesn't matter these days."

"Fine, we did. Once."

"Only the once?"

"Okay, three times, but that's all."

Madison nodded and gave it a few seconds before speaking again. "Have you ever been to Club 69?"

"That's a strip club?" He sounded unsure.

"You know it?"

"Yeah."

"Have you been?" she repeated.

"No."

"So you never saw Zoe perform?"

"What?" He lunged forward, his hands now grabbing the edge of the table.

"Zoe. Did you see her perform? She stripped there."

"I didn't. I'd have no way of knowing that." Ben's shoulders sagged, and he sat back in his chair.

"But you said that Zoe wasn't the woman Elias thought she was."

"Because she had sex with me. And she went down on me. And, God, she was hot!"

She didn't even have to pretend to be disinterested. "And that's the only reason?"

"Yeah." An exasperated sigh.

"You seduced your friend's girl—"

"She"—he splayed his hands on his chest—"seduced me. Thank you very much."

She pulled a photograph of Faye Duncan from the case file and slid it across to Ben. It was one of Faye with Zoe. "What about this woman? Do you recognize her?"

"No. Is she a relative of Zoe's or something? It's not like Zoe and I talked much."

He was there the day she and Terry delivered the news of Zoe's murder to Elias, and she knew they'd brought up Faye Duncan. While he wasn't shown her picture when they'd first met him, one would figure something would connect. Unless he wasn't paying any attention to their conversation, he should know it was Zoe's great-aunt and that she was also murdered.

"You were at Elias's house when we told him about Zoe…" God, she wanted to call him out.

"Yeah?" He shoved the photo back to Madison's side of the table.

His fingernails had a yellowish tinge. He could be a smoker.

Madison made a point of brushing her hand against his when she retrieved the photo. His eyes rose to meet hers.

"Oh…that woman was Zoe's relative? The one that was also murdered?"

Ding. Ding. Ding. Tell him what he's won.

"Uh-huh." Being nice and cooperative was killing her. She'd rather tear into his flesh.

"What was she? Her aunt? Grandma?"

"Great-aunt." This guy either sucked at listening or excelled at acting.

"For the record, where were you this past Saturday in the wee hours from just around midnight to two in the morning?" Madison asked while putting the photograph back in the folder.

"I would have been at home sleeping. I told you this."

"And what do you do at the hospital? You're not a doctor." She knew his file said he was on the nursing staff, but she wanted to hear him say it.

"I'm a nurse." Based on the way heat scorched his phrase, he must've defended his position on a regular basis.

"So you're telling me that Zoe cheated on your friend, who is a doctor, for a male nurse?" She poured a little salt in the opened wound. A girl had to have a little fun.

"I'm telling you, Zoe was easy, but Eli was going to make a wife out of her. It wouldn't have lasted. I couldn't let it happen. Even if it meant telling him about Zoe and me."

Madison bought his words. "Elias means a lot to you."

"He does."

"That woman"—Madison pressed a finger to the folder indicating Faye Duncan—"was left in a wheelchair outside Peace Liberty Hospital. That's where you work."

"Now you think I killed her, *too*? This day keeps getting better. Can I leave?" Ben stood, but Terry backed him up until his options were to bump into Terry's chest or sit down again. Ben sat.

Madison continued. "The wheelchair was stolen from the hospital. You wouldn't have stood out."

"So I killed two people—"

"I'm thinking three, but all in due time." She leaned back and crossed her legs.

"Three?" Ben's face paled, and he took a few deep breaths. "And you think I took the chair, too."

Madison angled her head to the right. "Did you?"

Terry jingled the change in his pocket again.

"I didn't kill anybody. This is police harassment. I want to go home."

"You still haven't provided an alibi for five nights ago. Let's say from around six o'clock until midnight." That was the estimated time of death window for Faye.

"Are you asking now?"

She remained silent.

"Last Wednesday? Well, unless you have more against me, you won't be getting an answer. I know my rights."

The urge to pounce on him was almost unbearable—the tigress wanted to act—but Winston's words drilled into her skull. *Concrete proof.* She didn't have it. The fact that Ben was withholding an alibi for the time of Faye's murder wasn't enough. His flimsy alibi for the time of Zoe's murder wasn't even enough. The system demanded more.

She stood, fingertips pressed to the table. "Zoe's baby is being tested for DNA."

"I already told you I slept with her, but we used protection."

Madison smirked. "You never mentioned that latter part before. It still doesn't mean the child wasn't yours. Wouldn't you want to know?"

Ben glanced back at Terry before standing. "What good would it do?"

"You want to know what good it would do?" Madison walked over to Ben and leaned close to him. "It would be a sign of good faith. We're letting you go—"

"Only because I didn't do it and you can't prove that I did," he interrupted.

Madison shrugged. "Then what's a little fingerprinting and a

DNA swab?" If he volunteered his prints, she wouldn't have to secure a warrant to obtain them from the hospital.

"You need fingerprints to prove I'm the father?" Ben rolled his eyes. "Fine."

CHAPTER 46

"We confirm that little shit's the father of Zoe's baby and we're halfway there," Madison said to Terry on the way back to their desks. He cringed a little at the four-letter word but didn't comment on it. He must have appreciated how much effort it took to hold herself together with Ben.

Ben had provided his prints and DNA, and it was just a matter of time before they had their *concrete proof*. He'd be a paternal match to the baby's fetus. He'd fit with the forensic evidence left at the crimes—the bloody items from the alley and tie back to one of the cigarettes. It would all make sense. She hadn't noticed any cuts on him, but they could have been hidden under his shirt.

He matched the physical description provided by eyewitnesses at Club 69 as arguing with Zoe backstage, too, minus the hair color. He also lined up with the man Nick Stanley saw in the parking lot. His blue Buick Regal would soon be shown in the city's camera footage, and he'd be trapped in his lies.

Ben also had a motive. If he'd known Zoe was carrying his child, he could have wanted her to abort it and she could have refused. Then Faye could have admonished Zoe to keep the baby, and Ben found out. He could have gone to speak to her. Faye made him tea, but he wasn't there to make friends; he was there to confront an older woman who had overstepped her bounds. And they'd know soon enough if his prints were on the wheelchair.

Madison was confident that by tomorrow morning, when

they had all their results and footage in evidence, they'd have everything they needed to lock up the guy for life. If he lied about knowing that Zoe danced at Club 69, it would go a long way in getting them the time they needed to gather all the necessary evidence to hold him accountable for her murder. From there it would be easy to connect him with Charlie.

"I'm surprised you let him go," Terry said.

"It wasn't my choice."

"Winston?"

"Yep. He gave me a lecture about butting into Sovereign's case, but is it my fault he can't take care of his own?"

Terry's eyes flicked to something behind her.

She spun around to come face-to-face with Sovereign. "I take it you heard?" she asked.

"I did." He was expressionless. Nothing to indicate hurt feelings or anger. Just total indifference.

"Why did you go crying to the sarge?"

"I didn't go *crying* to anyone. I'm doing my job, Mad—Knight. You should do yours." He brushed past her, but she couldn't let this go. She grabbed his arm and torqued him around.

"We have three bodies among us. This isn't about our past. This is about finding justice."

"Save the speech." He shrugged her off him and resumed walking.

Terry put his hand on her forearm. "Let it go."

"Argh. He makes me so angry." She held out her hands. "I'm shaking."

"Just let it go," Terry repeated.

Madison watched Sovereign walk away, wondering what she ever saw in the man. And to think she had recently agreed to resume a friendship with him. Ridiculous.

"We've gotta go." She took a few steps before noticing Terry wasn't falling in line with her. "Are you coming?"

"Actually, I'm calling it a day. It's already seven."

She halted. "Annabelle?"

"You got it. Until that baby comes…"

Madison waved him off. "You don't have to explain it to me. Just promise me something: first thing tomorrow morning we go to that soup kitchen. We've got to do what we can to tie Ben Dixon to that back alley."

Terry consented with a nod and left through the doors before she did.

They'd have time to use up in the morning anyhow. Cynthia would be working through the footage from the city's video and Samantha would be running the comparisons on the DNA and fingerprints.

"Madison?"

She closed her eyes. It was Troy.

"It's not a good time," she said. With Sovereign just storming off and being forced to release Ben, discussing Troy's relation to the police chief—right now—wasn't going to go well.

"I think it's the perfect time." He came around in front of her, his piercing green eyes wielding less power than they had in the past.

"Then you're not hearing me." She moved to sidestep him, and he slid his hand along her side, catching her arm at the crook of her elbow.

She stopped. The place where his hand touched her flesh burned. The smell of his cologne was oaky. Familiar.

"I'm not going to chase after you. Nor will I make you do anything you don't want to do."

She mustered the strength to free her arm from his hold. "Then let me go."

And he did.

As she walked toward the front doors, he held true to his word. He didn't chase after her. She swallowed the lump in her throat and her tears until she reached the privacy of her car.

How could she be so selfish? It was all too easy for her to turn her back on their relationship. Maybe he was better off without her. She was the most challenging, hardheaded woman… And God, he didn't want it any other way.

He wasn't generally one to brood over issues of the heart. He was cool and calm—in every situation. It's why he excelled at being a SWAT leader. The position required logic and the ability to fend off emotional influences, the skill to read a situation and act. There wasn't time for hesitation or self-doubt. He wished these attributes crossed over to his dealings with Madison.

She probably thought him cold, but inside, he seethed with furnace-like intensity. He had to make her see that they belonged together.

Stupid? Illogical? Possessive?

Maybe all three. But the heart wants what the heart wants. He just wished it wasn't Madison his heart wanted. God, she made him so angry. She threw him off-balance.

But it was for this very reason he didn't want to let her go. She had a way of stoking his flame—and that made him feel alive.

Damn it all to hell.

He'd witnessed her prior relationships disintegrate. He should have known better than to ever pursue her. But now it was too late. He was in too deep.

CHAPTER 47

THE SOUP KITCHEN WAS OPEN and serving an assortment of carbs, bacon, and scrambled eggs. Stepping through the door, the stench of body odor overpowered the food. It was nauseating and had Madison longing to retreat outdoors. But that wasn't an option. Regardless of whether Sovereign was doing his job or not, she had her own things to check out. And if he felt she was stepping on his toes before, just wait until he found out about their visit here.

But this wasn't about him. It was about finding closure for three murders.

For eight in the morning, the place sure was busy with people lined up out the door for a meal. It was a heartrending sight to see this many in need.

The place was painted a bright yellow and Madison questioned the choice. Yellow could soothe and uplift, but it could also stir up tempers. Either way, she never gravitated toward that part of the color wheel.

Three women and two men distributed food from behind a counter and onto the trays in front of them. Ladles went in. Ladles came out. Home fries, bacon, scrambled eggs, French toast. Tables were filled to capacity with people scarfing down their breakfasts as if they were late for a job. Of course, that was a possibility for some of them. The majority, based on the way they were dressed—tattered clothing, sneakers with flapping soles—had no job to be late for. The street was their home and living there a full-time occupation.

Madison caught the eye of one woman who was seated at a table talking to herself. Then wildfire sparked in her gaze, and she pointed a finger at Madison.

"You! You!" She rose to her feet. The entire time she was wagging her finger. Her shirt was three times her size and hung off her thick frame, and she wore a red visor. Eggs were stuck to her mouth and face, and she had a hairy upper lip.

Terry stepped between the woman and Madison and held up his hand. "Please take your seat."

She watched over Terry's shoulder. The woman's finger remained raised.

"She! She!"

People were staring now.

Terry's stance remained grounded, protective of Madison. "Take a seat," he repeated.

The woman's beady eyes remained fixed on Madison. Enough was enough. Madison maneuvered in front of Terry.

"Take your seat or we'll take you downtown." She steeled herself, ready to take physical action as her insides quaked from the rush of adrenaline. Who knew what this woman was on—or rather, what she should have been on?

"I see you." She hunched her head down, snickering.

Madison went to take hold of the woman's arm and didn't even make contact when the woman lashed out. Her fingernails cut into Madison's flesh.

"Son of a bitch!" Madison cupped her cheek and pulled her hand back to see that the woman had drawn blood. Now she needed a tetanus shot. Great. She should have left these people to Sovereign.

"That's it. You're coming with us." Terry cuffed the woman.

"I see you," the woman hissed on her way past Madison. Terry glowered at Madison.

Yes, maybe she should have stayed positioned all nice and safe behind him. Maybe she should just have stayed at home—today and every other day. Period. Like women back in the day when all they did was cater to the men.

Madison noticed that the one woman behind the counter had stopped midway between the serving tray and a man's plate. It was there in her eyes. This woman managed the place.

"We'll be back to talk to you," Madison called out to her.

The woman resumed movement and emptied the loaded ladle onto the plate. She pasted a smile to her face and then said, "Enjoy."

The entire time she never took her eyes off Madison.

Chapter 48

THE WOMAN WOULD BE CHARGED with assaulting an officer, but until that happened, Madison and Terry were stuck waiting for a uniformed officer to show up and escort her to a holding cell.

Madison was in the driver's seat of the sedan with the visor flipped down and antiseptic spray in one hand. Her cheek was raw and the area surrounding the cut was a bright red. She gingerly dabbed at the wound with a tissue.

As she worked to clean her face, she saw the woman watching her in the mirror. She scrunched up her face when she noticed that she had Madison's attention.

Madison snapped the visor back in place. She was too angry to talk. Too angry to react. She was just going to sit there and pretend she had patience while they waited for an officer to get this woman out of her sight…and so the woman could no longer see *her*.

She leaned her head back and shut her eyes in an effort to detach from the current situation and soothe the uneasiness pulsing through her. It wasn't working.

She shot forward. "Where the hell is—"

Flashing lights appeared in the rearview mirror. The woman's eyes were still on her. They had just jumped mirrors. God, this woman gave her the creeps.

Madison bounded out of the car, slamming the door behind her.

Officer Tendum got out of the patrol car and strode toward her. Of all the uniforms, why did it have to be him? The day had just started, and she was ready to crawl into a hole.

Terry was working to get the woman out of the backseat.

"Ouch." Tendum pointed to her cheek. "It looks like she did a number on you."

"Conversing isn't necessary." Madison glanced back to Terry, who had finally met with success. He handed the woman over to Tendum.

"Book her for assaulting a police officer," Terry said.

"Will do." Tendum assumed control over the woman, guiding her by her cuffed wrists. "This way."

Madison rolled her eyes and shook her head. "This is a joke."

"You've got to let what happened go."

"Let it go? He shouldn't even wear a badge, let alone be entrusted with a car." Hearing her words, she finally understood the exemption. Tendum was a man; therefore, he received a pass. Now if she had been in the same predicament as Tendum had—which she never would be, as she would have pulled the trigger—she'd be out on her ass. And deservedly so.

"How is Higgins these days?" Terry asked her.

"I like how you sail right over this." She swept her hand in front of her. "And it might work as a nice diversion if Tendum wasn't the reason Higgins is on modified duty."

"I'm not trying to *sail over* anything, Maddy, and I'm not going to talk about this again. Cut the kid some slack."

"Cut him some—"

"If Higgins can forgive him, so can you." Terry left her standing there and headed back toward the soup kitchen.

She hurried to catch up with him. "Let me take the lead in there."

"Guess we'll see if you beat me to it." He opened the door, and she snuck under his arm.

She strode toward the woman from earlier, badge held up high. "Detective Knight." She bobbed her head to indicate behind her. "Detective Grant. Do you have someplace we could talk in private?"

She placed the ladle she held into the serving tray and

addressed the burly man beside her. "Barry, I'm taking five."

"Sure. Don't bother me none." Barry's eyes traced over Madison and Terry.

THE WOMAN'S NAME WAS VALERIE Armstrong, and she led them into an office that made Madison's desk look organized. Papers were stacked on four three-drawer horizontal filing cabinets that lined the back wall and atop a table that served as a desk. There was a computer monitor, but Madison couldn't see a keyboard. It must have been buried beneath the sheets that were fanned over the desk's surface, along with an assortment of pens, markers, and paper clips. It was as if an office-supply-laden tornado had passed through.

Valerie gestured around the space. "Sorry there's no place to sit. If there were, I'd offer you a chair." Her eyes met Madison's, diluting the sincerity of her offer. "You know that I spoke to another detective…blond hair, good-looking."

It was easy to see Sovereign as "good-looking" when you didn't know his personality.

"We're just here to ask some follow-up questions," Madison began. "You have a camera that covers the back alley, but it's live-feed only, correct? It doesn't record?"

"No, it doesn't. It's mainly there as a deterrent to make people think twice about trying anything." Valerie crossed her arms and angled her head. "I told all this to that other detective."

"Who is responsible for watching the feed?" Madison asked.

"Barry."

"He was the one serving food next to you a moment ago?"

"Yes. We don't have the funding to hire someone to monitor that thing full time. We're happy to just keep the doors open, give people food for their bellies."

What was the point of having the surveillance equipment if no one watched it?

Madison steadied her patience. Her cheek was welted and throbbing. It wasn't as if her mood had been a good one to start with today. She really needed a solid night's sleep.

"Is anyone here between midnight and two in the morning?" she asked.

"No. And, again, I told that other detective all this. I'd love to help with your murder investigations, but I'm not sure what else I can say."

Investigations. Plural. Madison's blood heated. "So you know about…?"

"The young woman as well? Yes. Although she wasn't killed in the alley."

"Who told you that?" Madison's question came out as a snarl.

"The detective."

Unbelievable. Here Sovereign was all over her, complaining to the sarge about her overstepping boundaries when he was guilty of that very thing. What nerve he had to tell this woman that Zoe was killed somewhere else.

"The investigation is still under way," Madison said coolly, providing a blanket statement.

Valerie glanced at Terry. "I can only tell you what I've been told."

Madison took a few deep breaths. If Sovereign were sitting across from her, there might be bloodshed, even though she hated the sight of blood.

She took another deep inhale and exhale.

With Kimberly volunteering here, Valerie might have met Zoe, and if so, she might know why Zoe had been in the area.

Madison pulled up a photograph of Zoe Bell on her phone and showed it to Valerie. "Do you recognize her?"

Valerie nodded. "He showed me her photograph."

Son of a bitch—Sovereign, and the fact that she hadn't met Zoe.

"We"—she gestured between herself and Terry—"believe that she was killed in the back alley at the same time as the homeless person." So much for presenting a united front as Stiles PD and for keeping case particulars confidential. "Did you know the girl? Did she volunteer here?"

"Before he showed me her picture, I had never seen her

before."

"What about this woman?" Madison showed her a photo of Kimberly Bell.

Valerie leaned over to get a good look. "Her, I know. She volunteers here."

If Madison relayed that Zoe was Kimberly's daughter now, she might lose Valerie to an emotional reaction. She couldn't take that chance. "Would Kimberly have any reason to be here between midnight and two in the morning on a Saturday?"

"Not that I can imagine."

"She has a key to the building," Madison realized aloud. The fact had been contained within Valerie's response.

Valerie's eyes slid from the phone to meet Madison's eyes. "How did you know that?"

"Well, you would have said things differently if she didn't. When asked if she had any reason to be here, you would have said that the kitchen is closed at that time."

The woman nodded. "Reading between the lines."

"Something that is necessary for the job," Madison said.

Valerie dipped her head. "Fine. Yes, she did have a key. Sometimes she'd open up. She is a huge help around here."

Open up... Madison ruminated on that. A place like this, located where it was, would have more than just a camera. "Does the place have a security system?"

"Of course."

Many companies assigned different passcodes to each employee. "Did Kimberly have an individual access code to disarm it?"

"Yes." The word slithered out on a hiss with a tinge of uncertainty.

Madison glanced at Terry. Again, Sovereign's lack of thoroughness was epic. She and Terry would get ahold of the security system records and find out if Kimberly, or anyone else, disarmed the place that night. Why Kimberly would have been here in the first place was another issue. She could have killed her daughter and the vagrant in the alley without it even involving the soup kitchen.

"Did Kimberly use her alarm code Saturday during the wee hours?" Madison asked.

"I can find out." Valerie gathered some papers and moved them aside to uncover her keyboard. A highlighter fell to the floor in the process, but Valerie didn't bother picking it up. She started typing.

With each keystroke, the fact that Sovereign had interfered with her investigation hammered into Madison's skull. If he could ask questions about her case, she could do the same. "You didn't happen to know him, did you? The homeless person?"

Valerie stopped typing and shook her head. "No, sorry. I saw him in the alley several times, but he never came in. I even personally invited him on a few occasions. He said he wasn't into accepting 'no handouts,' phrased just that way."

It was curious why he decided to position himself near their back doors when he had no interest in taking advantage of their services.

Madison nodded at what Valerie had said, and Valerie went back to her computer. "As I suspected, there are no entries in the system at that time."

It could never be that easy, could it?

Chapter 49

MADISON AND TERRY LEFT THE soup kitchen and walked to the back alley. With the camera from the soup kitchen rendered useless, they were at a dead end. There were no other businesses that backed up to the alley and no cameras were mounted anywhere. Even apartment buildings with bars on the windows that would fetch more a month in rent than they were worth didn't offer any surveillance equipment.

Madison sighed and scanned the area one last time, then got back in the car. Her phone rang as she was buckling up. Cynthia called to confirm she had the footage from the city's camera and would have it ready when Madison and Terry arrived back to the station.

And, true to her word, when they walked in, Cynthia had the black-and-white video onscreen.

"What happened to you?" Cynthia asked, angling her head to assess the damage to Madison's cheek. Her hand reached out to touch the wound, but Madison shrunk back before her friend made contact. Shivers laced through her just anticipating Cynthia's fingers brushing against the inflamed skin.

"Please," said Madison, "let's not go there."

"What did you say or do to piss someone off?"

Terry chuckled.

Madison glared at him, then at Cynthia. "Excuse me. How could you even believe that I have the ability to piss people off?" She played innocent and then continued. "Killers probably hate me because I put them behind bars." She carried on with the monologue in her mind. The word *tenacious* came up and then carried over to thoughts of Troy. She had been rough on him yesterday, and their interaction was partially to blame for her shoddy sleep and foul mood.

Madison gestured to the video. "Let's watch it."

Cynthia raised her brows. "What, are you not going to tell me?"

"Nope." She stared at the screen, waiting for the video to start. It didn't.

Cynthia was looking at Terry, arms crossed.

"Some old lady attacked her," Terry said.

"Really?" Cynthia's facial expression was a mix of amusement and fascination.

Madison leveled her eyes on her friend. "It doesn't really matter. Let's watch the video."

Cynthia held up her hands and pulled a remote out of her pocket. The video came to life.

The time stamp was for nine in the evening four weeks ago. Apparently, Nick Stanley had lost track of the days as he'd thought it was three weeks ago. It was dusky from nightfall setting in, but the picture was rather clear. But still not clear enough to make out facial details.

Cynthia paused it. "Just so you know, I worked through to find this incident you said that man had witnessed. I searched the time frame you requested, starting a month back, and got lucky quickly. I only had to work through a couple evenings." Cynthia hit "play" again.

The man came out of the club, close to a run. He sidled up next to his car and opened the driver's door, but he didn't get in. He pulled out his cell, dialed, and then put it to his ear. He rested his left arm on the roof of his car and talked animatedly. His free arm was to the camera, and it was coursing through the air, up, down, left, and right. Flailing.

There was something about his movements that was familiar. "Can you zoom in?" Madison asked.

"I'll see."

The video was paused in a position where the man's arm was down. Cynthia went over to the computer, clicked here and there, and enlarged the picture.

His facial profile was too pixelated to distinguish.

"What about the license plate?" Terry asked.

Madison glanced at him. That was going to be her next question.

Other vehicles blocked part of the plate and what remained was at a sharp angle, but Cynthia could work miracles.

She did her thing with the computer, selecting the plate and dragging it to another monitor and into another program, where she made some adjustments. She grabbed corners of the image and straightened it.

The letters *AAW* stared back at them.

Cynthia keyed those letters into the DMV database and searched in Stiles. In seconds, they had their answer.

"Son of a bitch!" Madison balled her fists and stomped her heel into the floor. She shook her head and looked at Terry. "Winston made me let him go."

"Who is he?" Cynthia asked.

"Ben Dixon."

"The one whose DNA and prints we have to test?"

"That would be him." Madison paused for a second and then continued. "Did you watch much more of this segment? Does the video show him going around the club to the back door?"

"He came out the front door and got on the phone—the part you saw—and then he leaves."

A minor technicality. He could have argued with Zoe on another occasion. She hadn't forgotten the hair color issue, either. The girls and Nick had said the man who'd argued with Zoe was blond.

Madison hurried to the door.

"Just a second," Cynthia called out.

"What is it? He could be anywhere by now."

"Surprised you didn't ask, but just so you know, Samantha's working on the DNA comparisons today. I'll let you know as soon as I get something."

"Thanks, Cyn," Madison said while on the move. She'd turn on the lights to part traffic and get to Ben Dixon faster. It was one thing not knowing who the killer was—that was the cat and mouse game—but it was quite another thing to have had the mouse in her claws and have let him get away.

Chapter 50

They'd given Ben two choices: come with them the easy way or the hard way. The latter she would've had no problem executing. It would've involved slapping cuffs on him and escorting him from the hospital in front of his colleagues. Unfortunately, he'd chosen option number one.

She hated having to retrieve him when he shouldn't have been released in the first place. It was all because Winston had wanted to make some sort of point. What that point was she didn't know. What she saw was an effort to establish control. The sergeant should be more concerned about how this fiasco made the department look to the city's residents.

An hour had passed between picking up Ben and the three of them being back in the interrogation room.

Madison sat at the table, and Terry leaned against the back wall. The change jingling would start any second.

"You told us that you never went to Club 69," Madison said. She'd play it cool. For now. There was a pleasure to derive from providing the rope for him to noose himself.

"That's right." Ben leaned back in his chair, bending one leg over the other. Somewhere along the way, he'd lost all trepidation. He still hadn't called for a lawyer, and he was being cocky.

"How do you explain this, then?" She slid a photograph across the table. It was a still photo of him leaning on his car outside the club. The image didn't capture any signage, just the building's red brick.

"So what? It's me outside my car." He placed his hand over the photo and looked her straight in the eye.

This was how he wanted to play things? It was one of the oldest, most ridiculous routes for any suspect to take, playing dumb and arrogant. They must have all missed the memo about cooperation going a long way in reducing prison sentences. But that's fine. She rather liked it when no deals needed to be extended.

"Can you tell us where you were?" She picked up his hand by one finger to clear the photo.

He glanced down at it. "Not sure. The mall, maybe."

"Try again." Her bullshit meter was screaming.

Ben crossed his arms. "I don't know."

Madison exchanged the photo for another one from the folder and tossed it toward Ben. He stopped it from going over the edge of the table.

The focus of this second image was the same as the first, but it hadn't been cropped. It captured a rectangular sign with flashing lights around it that said DANCING GIRLS.

She tossed another photo to him. This one showed Club 69's sign.

She leaned back in her chair, crossed her legs, crossed her arms, and waited.

"Maybe I should get a lawyer." His confidence was a thin veneer. He now avoided eye contact, and his voice was weak.

"You could, or you could be honest with us." Madison lifted her chin.

"Fine. I went to the club."

"Club 69?" Madison named the establishment to provide clarity for the record. She didn't need this case going sideways.

"Yes."

"And you were on the phone talking to someone about Zoe?"

He stared at her. "How do you know that?"

"Let's just say we have our ways."

Ben rolled his eyes. "Where did you get these pictures?"

"The city was nice enough to share the footage with us." She told him where the video camera was placed.

"Shit," he muttered.

Change jingled. Terry circled him. "Getting it off your chest will make you feel better."

"You've already lied to us about not ever being there. What else aren't you telling us?" Madison demanded.

"Fine. I found out Zoe was a stripper there. I was on the phone with Elias telling him what kind of girl she was." He still wouldn't make eye contact.

"Did you sleep with her before, or after, you found out what she did for work?"

"After."

Terry jingled his change louder.

"So you used her line of work to bribe her into sleeping with you?" Madison asked.

"I might have taken advantage of the situation. She was a stripper. She took it off for a dollar. Girls like that don't have morals."

"But she didn't sleep with you until you had something to hold over her." The insult registered in Ben's eyes, but he was smart enough not to lash out at her.

She stood and paced. "So you showed up at the club, saw Zoe, and called Elias. That's all? You never confronted Zoe, yelled at her?"

"No."

"Interesting. People are saying that Zoe argued with a man matching your description." She couldn't ask if he dyed his hair or she'd show her hand. With each step, she kept her eyes on Ben. "Think before you speak again because we're getting sick of the lies, Ben. It doesn't look good for you. So I'm going to ask again: did you confront Zoe at the club?"

"No." Ben straightened in his seat and pressed a fingertip to the table. "Eli had us both over one night, and when he stepped away to get us fresh drinks, I told her I knew what she was about. She was desperate to keep the news from him, said it would break his heart. But I think what she really meant was there goes her payday." Hatred filled his voice and his eyes.

"So you guaranteed your confidence if she had sex with you?" Madison asked.

He nodded.

"Even though you had already betrayed that trust by calling Elias?"

He shrugged. "He didn't believe me."

Disgust settled in the pit of her gut like a ball of acid. If she verbalized the way it made her feel personally, it could come back to bite her later on. A seasoned lawyer could use it to claim she was prejudiced against Ben. It was one thing to think a certain way and another to broadcast one's opinions. Broadcasting resulted in repercussions.

The change jingling was hitting her last nerve. She shot Terry a look to stop. He did, and then there was a knock on the door.

Madison got up and opened it to Cynthia. She shook her head as she handed her a folder.

Madison peeked her head back into the room. "Terry."

He came out and closed the door behind him.

"Tell us, we got him," Madison said.

"One man had sex with Zoe before her death and Ben Dixon was that man."

"So much for the guy using protection. Just another lie," Madison said.

Cynthia continued. "His DNA wasn't a match to anything else, though. Not to the cigarettes, not to the—"

"What about the baby?"

Cynthia shook her head. "He's not the father. Now, I'm running the DNA profile through the system, but something will only come up if the father has a criminal record. There are no hits so far, but it's still going. In regards to the fingerprints pulled from the wheelchair, Ben is not a match to those, either."

"So all we can prove is he had sex with Zoe," Terry said.

"Forensically, I'm afraid so." Cynthia let her eyes drift from Madison to Terry, then back to Madison.

"It still doesn't mean he didn't kill her."

"He's not the father," Terry began, "and his prints weren't on the chair."

"I'll leave this with you two," Cynthia said. "Remember, though, just because his prints don't match up doesn't mean he's not behind the murder of Faye Duncan. He does work at the hospital."

"Meaning?" Madison asked.

"He could have worn gloves. There were a lot of smudged prints, as well."

"Sure, drop a bomb and run away," Madison said.

"Actually, I have one more thing… I also had a chance to look closer at Zoe's phone and recover her deleted messages. The only ones of interest were ones to and from Ben Dixon, but they just confirm what you already know." Cynthia nodded to them. "I'll keep you posted on what more I find out."

"Thanks," Maddy said, and Cynthia walked away with a wave over her shoulder.

"What are you thinking, Maddy?" Terry asked when they were alone again.

She shook her head. "I'm not quite sure yet." There was that sick feeling again. It was almost overwhelming. Maybe Ben was innocent. Was the killer someone who was closer to Zoe and Faye—Kimberly? Was she back to that theory?

"Ben has told us a lot of lies," Terry said.

"I agree, and you only lie—"

"—when you have something to hide," Terry said, finishing her sentence.

CHAPTER 51

THEY HAD NO CONCRETE PROOF that he was the killer, but Ben was definitely hiding something. What that was Madison didn't yet know, but she hoped they could snake it out of him. She and Terry were outside the interrogation room where Ben was seated. Making suspects wait sometimes served to make them more cooperative. Of course, it could have the opposite effect.

"Ben has motive," she said.

"What are you thinking?"

"What if Zoe had enough of his manipulation and was going to confess the relationship to Elias? Also, Ben stresses quite often how Elias is a doctor. It's like it makes Elias better than other people."

"He puts the man on a pedestal."

"Yes, like that. And it's clear he sees Zoe as far below Elias's league. But what if Ben felt inferior? He could be using his friendship with Elias as a measurement for success, as a bragging right."

"Ben's a male nurse. That comes with a lot of stigma," Terry said.

"Top all this off with Zoe being pregnant."

"But it's not his child."

"He doesn't know that," Madison pointed out.

Terry bobbed his head side to side. "You really think it all ties back to this child?"

"I do. And Ben's alibis for all three murders cannot be verified."

"I hate to point out the obvious…"

She smirked. "Since when?"

"Hardy har," he began, "but we can't place him at the scenes of the murders, either."

She growled.

He held his hands up. "I'm just sayin.'"

"Yeah, I know. It's the truth." Madison paused. "You ever wonder why Zoe was in that alley in the first place?"

"Absolutely."

"Let's see if our 'friend' here can shed any light on this."

"We're going back in?" Terry asked.

"What is it with you and the obvious?" She smiled at him and entered the room.

"I swear I didn't kill anyone." Ben's petitions of innocence started the second the door opened and continued until Madison closed it behind her.

She then took her time sitting. She made eye contact. He had no way of knowing the baby wasn't his, and that could provide another motivation altogether. "What were your thoughts on Zoe having her baby?" she asked.

Ben's Adam's apple heaved. "She told me it was Eli's. Was it mine?"

"So you did know about the baby before we told you?"

No response.

"See, you acted like it was a surprise, and now, apparently, it was Eli's. What do you think of that, Terry?"

"I think he's full of it," Terry said.

"I don't know why I didn't tell you all this," Ben moaned.

"It seems like you hold back a lot," Madison rebuked. "And what you do say are lies."

"She was going to use the baby against Elias. Trust me. For God's sake, she took her clothes off for strangers for a living."

Time to get him off the rant. "Was Zoe going to keep the baby?"

"I think so."

"You *think* or you *know*, Ben? Because there's a huge difference," Madison said.

Terry jingled his change.

Ben ran a hand down his face. "She came to me all upset. Said she was pregnant and swore it was Elias's. She said she had to come clean about us."

"That would have made you angry. You'd lose Elias's friendship."

Ben looked Madison in the eye.

"That's right. We know how important his friendship is to you."

"Well, whatever, none of it will matter now."

"Going back to my first question about how you felt about Zoe having the baby. You were pissed, yes?"

"Yes."

"And Zoe was going to use the baby to extort money from Elias?"

"I think so, yes."

"This has nothing to do with the fact that the baby might have been yours?"

Red bloomed in Ben's cheeks.

"Can you imagine Elias finding out that his best friend slept with his fiancée?" Madison asked, shaking her head. "And, Zoe, well, she was only having sex with you because you bribed her. That had to hurt a little."

Ben shrugged. "Why? She was just a lay to me."

"I think she was more."

"Think what you want."

"She got pregnant and told you she was going to come clean to Elias. You didn't want what you had going to come to an end," Madison said.

He stared blankly ahead. "Zoe told me it was Elias's baby."

"But how could she know that? You said yourself that she slept with anyone."

"Was the baby mine?"

"Maybe she told you why she was keeping the baby." Madison paused, and Ben didn't say anything. "She was keeping the baby because they were going to get married. She might have already known how Elias felt. He does seem like an open book."

Madison made eye contact with Terry. "Can you imagine Elias's reaction when the baby comes out and looks like Ben?" Her gaze leveled back on Ben with her last few words. "But too bad for you because, in the meantime, your child grows up believing Elias is his father."

"Fine, I was pissed. She had no way of knowing whether that baby was mine, Eli's, or any other guy's she was banging. I have no doubt there were more than the two of us."

"Based on what?"

"Gut feeling, lady."

Lady? She'd let it go. This once.

Ben continued. "Besides, Zoe failed to realize she wasn't in any position to call the shots. She didn't want her job as a stripper getting out, either. Elias would have dropped her in a flash."

"Yet, he didn't when you told him. That was whom you were talking to in the parking lot of Club 69. That's what you told us before."

His eyes met hers now. "I don't know why he was so caught up with her. I never got it. And as long as I'm talking… You know that woman? The older one? Zoe's great-aunt? Well, Zoe mentioned that an abortion would devastate her and that she had to keep the baby. Her aunt held a lot of control over her."

First, he hadn't known Faye Duncan, now he did. This man was an habitual liar.

"Sounds like motive to me," Madison said.

"Except I didn't kill them!"

"This is the part we're having a problem with, Ben. If you didn't kill her, who did?"

He raked a hand through his hair. "I have no idea." He glanced at Terry and back to Madison. "Isn't that your job to find out?" He paused. "Have you met Zoe's mother?"

Madison nodded. Where was he going with this?

"She's perfect—at least she wants the world to think so. But she sleeps around like her daughter did," Ben said.

Kimberly had told them her alibi for both murders was that married man she was seeing. Madison recalled that the girls at the club had mentioned Zoe's mother's promiscuity, too.

"Tell us more about the mother." It didn't hurt to hear everything he had to say. She'd sift through his words later to determine which claims were true.

"She was sleeping with a married man, you know. Ask anyone at that hospital."

"Do you always believe rumors?" Terry asked.

Ben glanced over his shoulder to Terry. "When they have a basis of truth to them. I saw her kissing some guy in the parking lot."

Madison shrugged. "It doesn't prove he's married."

"Except I saw his wedding band. He had his hand out the window, in her hair."

All right. Fair enough. Kimberly Bell was seeing a married man, but this wasn't news to them. How could that aspect factor in to three people being dead? As of yet, the pieces weren't fitting together.

If they ever would…

"Tell us why this matters." Madison's tone was dry, and she was certain she gave no impression of being interested in what he had already told them.

"It's just that Zoe had a lot to measure up to, at least from an outward viewpoint. Her mom volunteered and was hot. I mean, for her age, she was a looker. She was always picking on Zoe. They never saw eye to eye, I know that. Zoe got along better with her great-aunt."

"What are you really saying?"

"I'm saying, have you given any real consideration to Kimberly Bell being the killer?"

Chapter 52

They had to let Ben go, and this time it wasn't a decision forced on them by the sarge. There was no evidence to support him killing Zoe, Faye, or Charlie.

"What if Elias wasn't as cool about Zoe being a stripper as Ben had let on? I mean, Elias lied to us, too. He told us he didn't know what Zoe did for a living. But according to Ben, he did," Terry said.

"Assuming he was telling the truth," she pointed out. "He hasn't been exactly forthright so far."

"Do you think he lied about who he was on the phone with?"

"It's possible."

"Then who? Kimberly maybe? He has quite the opinion of her."

Madison shook her head. "No. Nick told us he overheard 'She's not who we thought she was.' It doesn't sound like something he'd say to her. I would think that conversation would go more like, 'Do you want to know what your daughter really does for a living?' The way he extorted sex from Zoe, he probably would have tried that with Kimberly in exchange for the dirt he had on her daughter."

"I see your point."

"We'll have Cynthia check his phone records," Madison said.

"You seem to be forgetting that we released him."

"Yes, because we have no concrete evidence against him."

"How do you suppose we access his phone records, then? Without a warrant?"

She didn't need to answer because some exceptions were necessary. "This case isn't closed until the killer is behind bars, Terry. I'm not going to back down over a technicality."

"A technicality? That's what you call a warrant? Since when?" He gave a derisive laugh.

She shook her head as she pulled out her phone and dialed Cynthia. A few seconds later, the request had been made, and she hung up. "Cynthia said she'd get on it. It might take awhile."

"Okay. Now what?"

Madison's phone rang. She looked at Terry and held the phone up between them with the screen facing her. It was an unknown number. "Let's find out who this is first, shall we?" She accepted the call. "Knight," she answered.

The voice that responded was the last one she had expected. Andrea Fletcher, as in Chief Fletcher.

She spun her back to Terry, longing for more privacy than that would afford. She held up a finger to Terry and headed off to the women's bathroom. He wouldn't be able to follow her in there.

"I'd like to meet for coffee…" Fletcher kept talking, but only a few words were making it through. Madison's mind was still processing why the chief was calling her.

"How about tonight?" Fletcher continued. "Say six?"

Madison flung open the bathroom door and slunk into the corner stall.

"Detective Knight?" The raised pitch of the chief's question told Madison she'd missed responding to something.

"Sorry, Chief, I'm—"

"Andrea, please."

Heat bloomed in her earlobes. Had Troy sent his sister to smooth things over between them?

"I'm not sure that I can make it," Madison said. It was the truth. She was involved with murder investigations that were on the cusp of being solved. She could feel it.

"We could make it another day." There was disappointment in Fletcher's voice.

Was Madison actually considering the chief's invitation? She took a deep breath. "Okay. I'll meet you for coffee. What time?"

"Six at the Starbucks on Main?"

"Sure."

"Great. I'll see you then, Madison."

Madison hung up, realizing how the tone of the call had changed from the start to the end. She went from being addressed as Detective Knight to her first name. Was that a good thing or bad thing?

When she had first found out that a woman was taking over for McAlexandar, she had been thrilled. A female was finally taking the lead in a town where men had held the reins for so long. The memory struck. During her commencement speech, Fletcher had sought her out in the crowd and made a point of smiling at her. Was it out of respect for Madison's reputation or because Fletcher knew about Troy's feelings for her?

Suddenly she knew she had to let Troy go, even if it hurt so badly it stole her breath. She'd be a fool to think she'd stand on her own merit, otherwise, and her career wasn't something she was willing to give up. She had to make the call and sever the tie. But it would have to wait. She had a killer to find.

CHAPTER 53

BEN HAD BEEN RELEASED, but Cynthia's suggestions haunted Madison: he could have worn gloves or his prints could have been smudged. With that in mind, going back to Club 69 seemed like the next logical step. For one, Madison could show Ben Dixon's face to the strippers to see if they recognized him, and two, Madison wanted to hear more of their thoughts on Zoe's mother.

Club 69 was open when she and Terry arrived, and Mario scowled at her the second they entered.

He stood there looking at them, his hands clasped in front of him, standing tall, his shoulders back. "What are you doing here? I've been cooperative. My girls have been cooperative."

It was two o'clock in the afternoon, and a half-naked woman flung herself around the pole. The music had a beat more appropriate for a Saturday night, but the volume was slightly lower. There were about a dozen men spread out around the room, most of them clutching their steins of beer and leering at the woman onstage.

Madison held her phone in Mario's face, the screen toward him. It was a photograph of Ben. "Do you recognize him?"

Mario pushed the cell to the side. "I'd appreciate some respect."

"You want respect? You'll get it when you start talking, because I have a feeling you're not telling us something." Madison lowered the phone but angled it so Mario could still see the image. "So… do you recognize him?"

"Let me see it." Mario fanned out his fingers, and Madison

handed him her phone. He studied the image. "He looks kind of familiar. Don't ask why. A lot of men come through here."

"Do you have somewhere we could talk in private?" Madison asked.

Mario smiled. "Sure do, but we don't need to talk." He winked at her.

"Oh, we need to talk," Terry intercepted.

Something was seriously wrong with this Mario guy. Most of the time he gave her attitude and the next minute he was hitting on her. What was that about?

"Fine. This way." Mario led them through some doors to a hallway with black walls. It made Madison think of the song "Paint it Black."

Mario knocked on a door to the right, and didn't wait on a response before tearing into the room as if Madison and Terry weren't even there.

Some guy said, "Hey, what do you think you're doing?"

"Put the sign up, you stupid bitch," Mario barked. "She'll throw in a free lap dance."

"Hey, you can't do that—"

Mario slammed the door, cutting the girl's protest short. He slid a card out of a holder to the right of the door and flipped it over. OCCUPIED.

Two doors down on the left, Mario opened a door and led Madison and Terry inside.

The room stank of cheap cologne, aftershave, sex, and latex. So much for "outside of the club and on personal time." She swallowed the bile that rose in her mouth. Didn't this man have an office?

Two black—apparently he had an affinity for black—leather sofas were against the wall and butted against each other in an L-shape. Mario sat on one of them, but there was no way Madison would take a seat knowing what went on this room, what was on the surface…

Terry remained standing, too.

"All right, we're someplace private. What is it?" Mario asked, settling in with his arms extended along the top of the sofa.

Madison trained her eye on him. "I want you to tell us what you're holding back." She hadn't lost that nagging suspicion that he knew far more than he let on.

Mario scoffed at them, looked at Terry, and then pointed a finger at Madison. "Is she serious?"

"Always," Terry answered.

"First of all, I'm not holding anything back."

"So that's how you're going to play this? That man's picture that I showed you… You knew him. It was written all over your face."

Mario's eyes snapped to Terry. "She does realize I have a business to protect, doesn't she?"

Terry shrugged his shoulders.

"Fine, I know him, but it doesn't mean any more than that," Mario said.

"Did you see the man in the photo ever confront Zoe?" Madison asked.

"No, but he did ask for a private room. What went on inside was, and is, their business."

So Ben had taken advantage of Zoe and then placed the call revealing her secret anyway. What a piece of work. Add that to the fact that Ben was either a regular customer or he'd done something to stand out to Mario.

"Had you seen Ben before that night?" Madison asked.

"No."

"But you remembered him with all the customers you have? Something must have stood out about him."

"I'm not sure why I remember him."

"I still think there's more to it than that," Madison said.

"You can think what you like. Now, there was a guy who did raise a fuss one night. And, yes, I played stupid before, but I never saw the guy. I only heard about him after the fact." Mario tapped the top of the sofa.

"So this other guy—"

"I never saw him," Mario interrupted.

Madison nodded. "Is there anything else you can tell us? Anyone who stands out in your mind?"

Mario remained silent as if hesitant to talk.

"Tell us what you're thinking. I don't care how stupid it might sound," Madison said.

"Her mother came in here barking at Zoe once. Things got nasty that night, but what was I supposed to do? Kick the woman out?"

Madison's heart raced. Kimberly Bell had confronted her daughter at the club? She brought up a picture of Kimberly on her cell phone and held it out for Ben. "Is this the woman?"

"No." His brow tightened, and he shook his head.

"You're sure?"

"Yeah, I ain't never seen her before. This woman was old, and I remember wondering how in the hell she could be Zoe's mother when she looked old enough to be her grandmother."

Grandmother? Adrenaline was coursing through her, making breathing difficult.

Madison exchanged the photo for one of Della Carpenter. "What about her?"

Mario never leaned forward to look at Della's image. "Not her, either."

Madison shared another picture.

He uncrossed his legs and leaned forward, clasping his hands between his legs. "That's her." He bobbed his head. "She's the one who came here."

Madison's legs weakened, and she almost took a seat—almost. She widened her stance and angled the phone so Terry could see the photo of Faye Duncan.

Back to Mario. "You're positive that's who came here?" Madison asked.

"I swear to God."

"And when was this?"

"A week ago. Last Tuesday."

That was the night before Faye was murdered.

Madison put the phone away. "Why didn't you just tell us

about this the first time we were here?"

Mario shrugged. "Not really sure. I mean, it was her mother, right? I fight with mine all the time."

He must have figured she'd had Zoe later in life, but she found it questionable that he'd accept the age difference. Dismissing that, though, she asked, "So just to be clear, she came here to confront Zoe? Was there any physical contact? Yelling?"

"Raised voices, for sure. I don't think they got physical."

"Then what happened? Did they leave together?" Terry asked.

Mario shook his head. "Nope. The woman left. Zoe's act was up next."

How did Faye Duncan find out that Zoe worked at Club 69? And it was plausible that if Faye knew about the club, she knew about the baby, just as Ben had implied. Did *Zoe* kill Faye? And, if so, how did Zoe end up a victim, too?

CHAPTER 54

THEY SPOKE TO LYNDA AND Vicky before exiting the club. They both said they didn't think Ben was the man fighting with Zoe that night. That news sank in Madison's gut, but she still wasn't releasing her suspicions about him. It just meant there was another man out there who had been angry with Zoe.

"We need to visit Della Carpenter and find out if there's something she's not telling us, too," Madison said as she walked around to the driver's-side door. "Seems to be a trend here."

"Mario said she wasn't the one to confront Zoe." Terry got into the passenger seat and pulled his belt across.

"But why didn't she mention that Zoe and Faye had a falling out?"

"Maybe she didn't know?"

"I'm not so sure about that. We know the two sisters were close. Do you really believe that Faye didn't mention the club and Zoe's 'career choice' to Della?"

"Even if she had, Della might not have thought it tied into their murders," Terry said.

"I'm not sure I buy that, but either way, Faye Duncan came to the club, so maybe she knew something we don't."

Faye Duncan hadn't been the typical sixty-something, especially if she confronted Zoe at Club 69 and not at home in private.

Then it struck her again and nausea seized her gut.

"Faye was making tea just before she died. And she went to the club the day before she died." She turned to face Terry in the passenger seat. "What if she was making it for Zoe? She could have visited her great-aunt the next day to make peace and—"

"You think that—"

Madison nodded. "Zoe could have killed her aunt."

"Okay, but it leaves a lot of unanswered questions. Why? Just because Faye wasn't happy with her lifestyle? If that were motive for murder, more people would be killed by their family members." Terry laughed. "Right?"

"Terry, people have killed for less. I'm just not sure how this all fits together. Cynthia had sent me a message and Zoe's prints didn't match the ones left on the wheelchair. It seems like every path we go down, we hit a fork."

"The important part is that we keep going."

Terry was just as cynical as she could be at times, maybe even more so. Being optimistic wasn't like him at all.

"Are you feeling all right?" she asked.

"Yeah. Why?"

She smiled. "Because you're giving me a pep talk."

"True. And I'm not sure why because if this case is closed by tonight, I'm out eighty dollars. I should be pulling you down." His eyes sparkled with mischief.

She shook her head and pulled out of the club's parking lot, merging into traffic as she headed back to the department. "Let's say Zoe killed Faye. Then who killed Zoe? We still don't know why she'd be in that alley."

"We know her mother volunteered there."

"We've gone over that. And she wasn't there the night of Zoe's murder. Maybe we're thinking too narrow-mindedly." She pulled the car over to the right and turned on the hazard lights.

A van swerved out from behind her, the driver shaking his fist at her.

They were in a department car. Not that it seemed to matter.

Terry's gaze followed the van until it cut in front of them. Surprisingly, he didn't say anything.

"Zoe could have run into the alley to hide from someone," Madison said.

"So her killer pursued her and she sought refuge in a dark alley?" He laughed. "I'm sorry, but if that's what happened, had she never seen a horror movie?"

She glared at him. "It's still a possibility." Madison's eyes widened. "Wait a minute... Zoe might not have counted on the homeless guy being there. Maybe that woman saw something that can help our case. We have to go speak to her."

"The one who did that"—he pointed to her cheek—"to your face?"

"That would be the one."

THE WOMAN WAS SITTING ON a bench at the back of a holding cell, whistling. They were still after her full name. Until that could be found out, they couldn't file the charges.

She stopped the whistling. "You!" Her eyes scanned Madison's face. "I see you."

Madison took a deep breath. She'd had run-ins with crazies before, but this loony tune was overflowing with nuttiness.

The woman rushed to the bars, pressing her nose between two of them, and then she reached out for Madison.

Madison took a step back. There was no way she was going to give this woman another chance to draw blood.

"I need you to be quiet and listen," Madison said.

Her eyes were burning coals. "You."

Certifiable whack job.

"I need to know what you saw in the alley a couple nights ago," Madison said.

"You," she hissed.

Maybe this was a waste of time.

"I wasn't in the alley the other night"—she held up a printed photo of Zoe Bell—"but she was."

"Her." She smacked her lips together a few times in a row. "She was running and screaming. She trespassed."

Madison flicked a glance at Terry.

"She was trespassing?" Madison asked, seeking clarification.

"Yes. Then I see..." Her eyes glazed over.

Madison's heart sped up. Had she discounted this woman prematurely?

The woman remained dazed and silent. Madison jostled the photograph, and the woman's head followed the movement, up, down, up, down.

"She was running away from someone?" Madison tried again.

The woman's eyes fixed on Zoe's face. She nodded.

"Did you see who was following her?" Madison asked.

"I see you!"

"Yes, you see me. I see you, too. Did you *see* who was chasing the girl?"

The woman stepped back and rolled her eyes. "You don't understand."

"Then enlighten me."

"I had a vision. Of you…"

Oh God. This woman wasn't just crazy. Apparently, she was psychic, too.

Madison spun around, putting her back to the cell. This was a waste of time. How could she expect to get anywhere with this woman?

"So you saw the young woman in the picture?" Terry asked, taking over.

Madison couldn't bring herself to turn back toward the woman.

"Yes. And I saw her!"

Madison imagined that a pointing finger accompanied the last statement.

"You said you saw my partner in a vision? We believe you." Terry was playing good cop. He didn't really believe in such hocus-pocus, did he? What was next? Ghosts?

Madison shot Terry a sideways look. If he noticed her glimpse, he didn't let on.

"I did," the crazy woman said. "But first I saw who killed the girl."

Madison whirled around and gripped the bars. The woman's eyes went straight to Madison's hands, and she stepped closer.

Madison moved back.

"You saw who killed her?" Madison asked.

"Yes."

"Who was it? A man or woman?"

"Dark shadows. Evil. Angry."

"Dark shadows? There was more than one?"

Lord, give me the patience to…

"Just evil, angry."

All right, so the woman saw "dark shadows" and she supposedly had visions. The statement might not have anything to do with the number of people who had been chasing Zoe or who had killed her.

The woman shook her head and tsked. "Leonard tried to help."

Leonard? Was that Charlie?

"Who is Leonard?" Madison asked.

"He tried. He failed."

Leonard was Charlie. He had to be.

"What happened then?" Madison asked.

"There was evil. Then you!"

One more ridiculous outburst like this, and Madison would leave this woman for Terry to handle.

Madison let out a deep exhale. "Yes, you've said you saw me numerous times. We want to know if you saw who hurt Leonard and that girl. Did you?"

The woman stared into Madison's eyes. While she seemed to be trying to communicate something, Madison wasn't receiving the message.

"Dark shadows. Evil. Angry," she repeated.

They weren't getting anywhere with a direct approach. "When you saw the girl come into the alley, what happened…before the dark shadows?"

"She was running. She tripped next to me. I said nothing and stayed real still."

"And what happened next?"

"The dark shadows. Evil. Angry."

That was it. Madison was done. She turned to leave.

"You," the woman called out.

Madison wasn't sure why she bothered, but she stopped moving and faced the cell again.

"You are going to bring meaning to their deaths."

Madison managed not to roll her eyes. The woman, however, was being deadly serious. Was she claiming to have *seen* Madison solve the murders? Regardless, Madison had every intention of doing just that.

CHAPTER 55

TERRY TRAILED BEHIND MADISON, but she wasn't going to slow down. She was headed back to her desk and was beyond frustrated. Speaking with the crazy woman hadn't really helped them get any further with the case.

She sat in her chair, and Terry dropped onto his.

"Look at it this way. We have an eyewitness who saw the murders," Terry said.

"You really think a jury's going to believe *her*? She's a kook." Madison scoffed. "She saw me in a vision? Seriously?"

"Well, why not? Some people are clairvoyant."

"Don't tell me… I thought you were just being nice."

"What if I do believe in stuff like that? Is that not my right?"

"I never said it—"

Terry held up a hand. "That's right. It's a personal choice whether you wish to believe it or not."

"Fine." She let her eyes drift to the top of her desk.

Did he really buy into all that? She snuck another glance at him and noticed his resting smile. He was toying with her.

Her mind back on the case, the same question remained, along with a new one. "Why was Zoe in that alley, and who was chasing her?"

There was a pregnant pause.

"I tell you what we have to do is—" She stopped. Her idea was too time-consuming. It would take forever.

"Do what?"

She shook her head. They still had fifty-plus contacts on Zoe's phone. What they really needed to do was find the man who had argued with Zoe at the club. "It's not going to happen. I was going to say hunt down everyone in Zoe's contact list."

"You mean *us*?"

"Yes, Terry, not uniformed officers."

"You don't ask for much."

"Sarcasm, Terry? Three people are dead."

"I'm fully aware. But we need more to justify undertaking that. Didn't you say before that there had to be another way?"

Terry was right. She nodded. "I just wish I had all the answers," she admitted.

"You might as well stop wishing for that. You never will."

"Hey."

Terry laughed. "Relax. That woman said you were going to solve the murders."

"I think what she said was I'm going to 'bring meaning to their deaths.'" Was she really quoting the woman?

"Isn't that the same thing?"

Madison shrugged her shoulders but already knew she'd thought the same thing about what the woman had meant. In many ways, though, giving meaning to a death was better than simply solving it. Motivations sometimes remained enigmas. If she let herself buy into the baloney the woman was trying to sell, then she had to admit that she liked the prediction.

Terry got up from his chair. "I'm calling it a day, Maddy."

"What? It's only"—she checked the time on her phone—"five thirty."

Oh shit! She had that appointment with Fletcher soon! She should probably cancel… Didn't a murder investigation trump chitchat and a coffee?

"Exactly why I'm calling it a night. Maybe more answers will come by tomorrow morning," Terry said.

"Brought to us by the leprechauns?"

Terry angled his head. "Come on, there's no reason to be like that."

She started laughing. "Well…you do believe in psychics. Who

knows what else you believe in? What about fairies? What are your thoughts on those?" Her side was hurting from the laughter between words. She hadn't laughed like this in too long.

"Night, Maddy."

"Night." She watched her partner walk away, wishing she could just head home, too. But she had an appointment to keep, whether she wanted to or not.

MADISON SPOTTED FLETCHER THE SECOND she entered Starbucks. She was in one of two tub chairs positioned kitty-corner with a table between them. She waved and smiled. Madison nodded and gestured to the counter. She'd pick up a caramel cappuccino first and use it to medicate her nerves.

She took a deep breath, her mind racing. Had the chief called this meeting to smooth things out between her and Troy? If so, it was none of her business. Her relationship with Fletcher was to be kept strictly professional. Heck, she couldn't even think of Fletcher by her first name. *Andrea* would be what friends and family called her. Madison was neither.

She placed her order, actually wishing for the barista to take her sweet time. No such luck. In fact, her drink was ready at record speed.

Less than two minutes later, she was approaching Fletcher.

"Hi, Madison." Fletcher smiled. It was a warm expression that had no doubt won many hearts and broken a similar number.

She swallowed, ready to push things away from a personal rapport but nervous, nonetheless. "Good evening, Chief."

Fletcher shifted in her chair, her slender frame taking up only a small portion of the cushion. "I see you prefer to keep our relationship professional."

"I do." Madison took a seat and crossed her leg away from Fletcher.

"I can understand that."

"You can?"

"Of course. I mean, you're dating my brother."

Madison wasn't about to correct her right now, but that

situation may be in the past tense. Really, by her refusing to talk to him and him not pursuing her, it was, in effect, more or less "the talk." So much for Troy's promise about them being a couple unless she really did something to piss him off. Apparently, all it took was for her to have a reaction to him keeping important information from her.

Fletcher took a sip of her drink and continued. "I'd feel the same in your place."

Did the ability to call her out run in the family?

"And how is that?" Madison asked, careful to keep her tone in check. The fact that she cared surprised her. She usually spoke her mind without much thought to such things.

Fletcher set her cup down on the table, then ran her fingers along the leather arm of the chair. "You are a hard-working cop, and you deserve to be where you are. All your accomplishments, well, no one can take them from you, because they're yours." She tossed in a docile smile. It was a flash and then gone. "You probably think that if you're dating the chief's brother, people will talk and I'll go easy on you. And even if I don't—which I have no intention of doing—people will say that I am."

Madison pressed her lips to her cup. Was the woman a mind reader?

"But what other people think doesn't really matter," Fletcher continued. "If I let what others said stop me, I wouldn't be where I am today. I'd probably still be stuck in some meaningless job working out of a cubicle."

"A cubicle?" Madison couldn't imagine Fletcher in such an environment.

Fletcher dismissed her with a wave. "That doesn't matter. What does is that I rose to the challenge, and, God, I love challenges." She met Madison's eyes. "And I know you do, too. I've read your file. You're tenacious and you get the job done. That's what matters to me."

"I won't let anything or anyone stop me from doing what needs to be done, not even Winston. I even stood up to McAlexandar on more than one occasion." Why was she promoting herself as if she were being interviewed?

Fletcher chuckled. "I'm well aware of both things."

"How?"

"I said I've read your file, Maddy. I mean, Detective Knight."

Madison took a deep breath. This woman was good—a politician through to her sinew. She had a way of phrasing things that brought you to her side. Just like her brother—if Madison would have given him a chance.

"So it doesn't bother you that—"

"You are insubordinate at times?" Fletcher interrupted. "It concerns me a little, but you have amazing judgment. Besides, that was then and this is now."

Madison nodded. She picked up on the silent inference—a woman was now in the position of power. There was a stretch of silence, as if Fletcher somehow knew she had won Madison over, but there were a few more things to get off the table. The fact that she'd even considered testing the woman on this subject was crazy.

"Can I ask you something?"

"Of course."

Forget crazy. Her question was careless. But Fletcher's response would give Madison a good gauge on the new chief. "What do you think about Patrick McAlexandar?"

"Are you and I talking as professionals or as friends?"

"Friends." It came out naturally, surprising Madison more than Fletcher.

"Then I'd have to say the man is a piece of shit." Fletcher held eye contact. "And I'm happy to say that I—a woman—" she smirked "—took his place. A nice slap in the face to a man like him if you ask me."

Madison laughed. "If we were drinking wine, I'd toast to that."

Fletcher picked up her cup and nudged it toward Madison's. Madison tapped hers against Fletcher's.

"Next time, though, we do this with a glass of merlot," Fletcher said before taking a sip.

Madison nodded, smiling. *Andrea* was all right.

"Well, I hate to be running off, but the hubby's waiting at home." She threw in a subtle eye roll as she got to her feet.

Madison smiled. "You have him trained well."

Andrea grabbed her purse from the floor and slipped its strap over her shoulder. "Just for the record, Troy didn't send me. I'm older than he is. I send myself."

Madison nodded. She was happy that Andrea had clarified that, but then wondered why she had asked her for coffee in the first place. Was it just to make friends? Still, to hear that Troy hadn't sent her... Maybe it was time for her to put aside her pride.

She dialed the kennel and arranged for Hershey to spend the night.

Chapter 56

Her heart was pounding as she pulled into Troy's driveway behind his Ford Expedition, unsure if she had the willpower to follow through on why she came here.

His house was a Craftsman-style bungalow with olive-green siding and thick wooden columns supporting a front overhang. A picture window accented each side of the entry, and two dormers projected from the roof above those. A double-wide, stamped concrete path cut through the front lawn and led to the door.

She stood there mustering the strength to push the doorbell. Such a simple action had become an arduous task. She wasn't the type who came crawling back with her tail between her legs. In fact, she avoided such situations at all costs. She'd rather cry in private than have it show outwardly that her pride had been hurt. But in this case, it was quite possible that she had responded unfairly. She only hoped that he would forgive her. She'd find out how honest he was when he said it would take a lot for him to end their relationship.

Just do it, Maddy.

She pressed the button. The chimes sounded, and they were *loud*. So much for secretly hoping he wouldn't hear. She'd have no excuse for, and no way of, slinking off undetected.

Footfalls approached the door.

One deep breath. She could handle this. Maybe if she repeated it—

"Madison?" He looked around her, to his lawn, to his drive, to her Mazda. Finally, his green eyes met hers, cool as slate. "What are you doing here?"

"I…" It was hard for her to verbalize the apology, as if by doing so she was admitting to wrongdoing, but wasn't she here to do precisely that?

Troy gripped the top of the door with one hand while the other held on to the frame. With his positioning, he was barring her entrance.

Fine. If he wants to do this in front of his neighbors, then so be it. She coaxed her heartbeat to slow down.

She peered into his eyes. Was that what this was? Love?

"I'd like to talk. May I come in?" she asked.

He didn't say a word as he moved to the side. Once inside, he closed the door. The arm that had extended to shut the door was so close to her, she could feel its heat, and it seemed to stay there longer than necessary. A dull ache formed in her chest when he resumed his distance.

He crossed his arms. He wasn't going to make this easy for her, and she didn't blame him.

The house was silent, not even the hum of a fan or air conditioner or a rushing dishwasher. Nothing.

"I shouldn't have left you at the charity event the other night." Her voice sounded so small. Maybe she should have remained in her comfort zone. She was content being single, wasn't she? Why complicate things with a relationship? But she knew the answer. She wasn't just content with him in her life. No, she was *happy*.

She cleared her throat and then continued. "I'm sorry that I left, and I'm sorry that I didn't talk to you when you wanted to the other day."

Damn! Her eyes burned with tears. She couldn't allow them to fall. She had exposed herself enough by simply coming here. She didn't need to cry, as well. God, he'd think she was weak.

He stood there, his body rigid, peering into her eyes. He must have really bought into the eyes being the window to the soul crap because he executed the investigation—if one wanted to call it that—expertly.

Wasn't he going to say anything? Maybe she had made a mistake coming here and booking Hershey overnight had been presumptuous.

She turned to leave, her hand on the doorknob. "I'm sorry I bothered you."

His strong hand landed on her shoulder and pulled her back toward him, spinning her around to face him. She came to stop against his chest. He seemed to tower over her, but it must have been due to her feeling so vulnerable. She placed a hand on his torso. Was she being too forward? Maybe he was just going to say his piece.

God, his eyes were so hard to read. They were more like a mirror right now, her face reflecting back at her. He delicately traced the cut on her face with the pad of his thumb. Still, he remained silent.

She removed her hand from him, but he took it and kissed her fingertips. Her heart fluttered. Did this mean she was for—

The thought disappeared as he nibbled on the tips of her fingers and drew her closer to him. Their bodies pressed together, and he put a hand behind her head and trailed kisses from the delicate point on her neck beneath the earlobe to the base.

Her eyes rolled back, but she still fought to resist.

"Does this…mean…I'm forgiven?" The question was fragmented by her choppy breath.

He stopped kissing her and pulled back. His eyes narrowed with arousal. His jaw locked and set. His gaze traced over her, starting with her eyes, then lingering on her lips.

He captured her mouth with his, and she let herself go.

THE SEX HAD BEEN HOT, passionate, and on the border of love and lust. It had ended fifteen minutes ago, and her heart still beat rapidly, her body still glistened with sweat.

They were in his bed, about twenty feet down the hall from where it had all started, where she had spoken her apology, where she had laid bare a vulnerability she had buried for years.

She rolled onto her side to face him. He was on his back, and she studied the contours of his body, his sharp, angular facial features. His prominent nose and the dusting of freckles across its bridge. His nest of brown hair that rested against the pillow. His chiseled chest. Strong biceps and shoulder muscles bulging, as if straining to break free of his skin. She reached out and put her fingertips against the one closest to her.

Fingertips…where all this had begun.

He turned his head toward her. His eyes had resumed their normal warmth, and she shimmied against him. He wrapped his arm around her as she tucked her head against his chest, and she ran her hand over his tanned flesh and the spattering of brown curls across his pectorals, down to his six-pack abs. She never got tired of letting her fingers revel in the natural curves of his body. She let her hand go farther down, exploring along his groin line.

"Ready to go again already?" he asked with a soft laugh.

What had she done to get so lucky? And she wasn't referring to sex or even to his body. If she let her heart have its way, she'd accept that Troy Matthews was different from the rest.

She arched back to look at him, positioning herself halfway over his torso and resting there with her hands under her chin. "So you never did answer my question."

He smiled and hitched his brows. "Do you always seek verbal confirmation?"

"It helps for closure."

"Closure? And I thought we were just getting started."

She smirked. "Your stamina is impressive."

"Well, I have been known to—"

She pressed a finger to his lips. Adrenaline rushed through her as her heartbeat thumped in her ears. Was she actually about to speak her feelings out loud?

His green eyes were watching, analyzing, anticipating…

She slowly drew her finger back. "I should go." She wormed to her side of the bed—*her* side?—and got up. She pulled on her underwear and then her jeans as fast as she could move.

Troy got up, too, and came around behind her. Still naked, he kissed her again, in the spot beneath her ear. But its purpose was different from before. It wasn't simply for satisfying carnal hunger…or had she lost it completely?

She turned, shaking the shirt and bra that she held balled in her hand. "I've got to—"

"Go? Yes, as you said. Is it because of Hershey?"

"No. He's in the kennel tonight."

He cupped her shoulders. "Then what's the rush?"

Most women would have a hard time not letting their eyes drift down, but his green eyes held her gaze captive.

"Why not spend the night?"

She licked her lips, savoring his flavor. "I guess I could."

The words came out of their own volition, but her brain wondered if she could trust herself with this man.

Probably not, she realized, but she couldn't resist him any longer.

Chapter 57

Madison accepted Troy's invitation to spend the night and they celebrated with a nightcap, though not the kind Troy had in mind.

They were in his living room, him on the sofa, her on a chair with her legs curled up beneath her. They were both drinking iced coffee—a treat with the benefits of caffeine and sugar. Both of which she'd need.

She might have agreed to spend the night, but it was far from bedtime. It was only about eight thirty. She cradled her glass and sipped it occasionally as she filled him in on the investigations so far and how everything was coming together based on nothing but wishful thinking and the feelings in the pit of her stomach.

"So this woman—the one who scratched your face—said 'dark shadows,' plural? Do you think that means anything?"

Madison shook her head. "She's certifiable."

Troy nodded, sinking further into the couch. "Hmm."

"I'm thinking that the baby's father killed Zoe."

Troy set his empty glass on a side table. "The man might not have been happy about the baby coming."

"Kids have a way of changing a person's life," she said. "Not that I know from firsthand experience," she quickly added. She put her legs down and sat on the edge of the chair. "The girl's mother was seeing a married man. What if Zoe—"

"You're thinking the man had his marriage to lose?"

She met his eyes. "Why not? It would be quite the upset to his lifestyle. Assuming that he's closer to the mother's age, Zoe is not only young—"

"But she could have threatened to tell his wife about their affair, about the baby."

Madison smiled at him. They were finishing each other's sentences again.

Troy continued. "Maybe we're getting too ahead of ourselves. We don't even know the identity of the baby's father or that Zoe was sleeping with her mother's lover."

"And it's quite possible that even once the DNA is run through the databases, nothing will come back in the system. But this is worth exploring, isn't it?"

Troy nodded.

"And if Zoe was pregnant from the married man and her mother found out…"

"She wouldn't be happy, either. It's looking like the killer could be Dear Mom or the man she was sleeping with. Of course, it would carry more weight if Zoe was also involved with him. Do you know who he is?" he asked.

"Yeah, he was Kimberly Bell's alibi. A phone call was made to verify…" Her gut twisted. "He could have lied. We never pulled his background or spoke in person with him." Maybe she had let the ball drop there.

"Maddy, I can see it in your eyes. You're being too hard on yourself. You were looking at the mother, not the man. Cut yourself some slack."

"But still…if he had lied, that means Kimberly did, too." She shook her head as she got up and placed her glass on the table next to Troy's. She'd never said she would stay put in his house for the rest of the evening. She had simply agreed to sleep here.

"Where are you going?"

"I owe it to three victims to provide meaning to their deaths." With the words out, she recognized that she had borrowed them from the kook down at the station. But the summation worked. That was her driving force and always had been.

Troy rushed to her side and hooked her elbow. "That wasn't really an answer to my question."

She looked straight into his eyes when she responded. "I'm going to talk to Donnie Holland."

"The mother's lover?"

"Yes, and if I'm right, also Zoe's."

There was something there, she could feel it. A connection, a motive.

"I'll go with you. Just let me grab my ID and keys." He went to walk away, but she pulled him toward her and kissed his lips. The taste of him, the smell of his sweat, the faint scent of his cologne, all tempted her, but there was work to be done. She had to resist.

For now.

Chapter 58

With the new line of thinking and a lot of conjecture, Donnie Holland made a perfect hypothetical suspect, and that was without a background check.

Madison and Troy were in her Mazda heading to the police station to get that missing piece now. In fact, Troy had insisted that they go into the meeting with Holland armed with knowledge. It must have come from his training for SWAT. She had a similar education, of course, but somewhere along the way, she had taken the reins and acted on impulse a lot of the time. It was one thing that drove Terry nuts. And it was also one aspect that had led to her capture by the Russian Mafia.

If Troy weren't with her tonight, she might have just shown up at Holland's door armed only with the information provided in an online directory.

She slowed for a yellow light and glanced over at Troy. "Holland could have all the motivation in the world. Think about it. First, he's cheating on his wife. Second, he's seeing a girl far younger than he is," she said.

"You're assuming Holland is closer to the mother's age. You said you hadn't conducted a background on him, so you don't know for sure. She could be playing the cougar."

"You're right. But it's just a feeling."

"A feeling? The Bull—"

She silenced him with a glower. "Don't you even think about it."

"Too late."

"But going back to Holland… He gets Zoe pregnant. She refuses to get an abortion. Maybe even threatens to go to the wife," she said.

"All right. And maybe she even tells him it was her great-aunt's idea to keep the kid."

"That would make him angry, right?"

"That it would," he conceded.

"If any of this is what actually happened, he'd have a lot of motive. His very way of life would've been at stake."

She maneuvered around a slower-moving sedan—what was with all the poky drivers lately?—and then signaled right to enter the police lot.

"You passed the guy to turn in front of him?" Troy asked.

"I'm special like that. But the guy was crawling along at twenty."

Troy was shaking his head, giving a low chuckle, when he got out of the car.

They headed to her desk to pull the report on Holland. As soon as his face filled the screen, she had a hard time prying her eyes from it to read his information.

"It's him," she said.

Troy was hunched over her shoulder, resting his hand on the desk beside her. "Him who?"

"Witnesses at Club 69 described a blond man of short stature—" She wrested her eyes from Holland's DMV photo and pointed to his height. "He is five eight with blond hair. The man from the club was said to be midthirties. Holland's thirty-five. Anyway, this man at the club entered the back door and had a heated argument with Zoe. They said there was mention of payback and money. The girls—"

"The girls?"

She turned to Troy. "Other strippers at the club. One thought he was Zoe's pimp and the other a drug dealer. And if I'm right about Holland, we are up to at least a quadruple life for Zoe. First she's a stripper, cheating on her boyfriend with his best friend—" She caught the way his eyes fell. "Sorry…"

He straightened out to full standing position. "There's no reason for you to be sorry. Continue."

"Then she's sleeping with a married man. And, of course, she deceived her great-aunt into thinking she was a sweet girl." She had forgotten to fill Troy in on what Mario had told them about Faye Duncan going to the club and confronting Zoe. She did so now.

"Zoe must have had an exhausting existence trying to balance everything and who she was to everyone."

"I would think so. We've got to speak to this guy." She pointed to Holland's face.

Troy placed a hand on her shoulder. "What else have you got on him? You mentioned the alley where you're certain Zoe was murdered along with the vagrant—"

"Leonard," she corrected.

There was something odd about his expression when she interrupted. She wasn't sure if he appreciated the quirkiness or found it strange. Either way, he didn't comment on it.

"Can you place Holland in the area? Where does he live? Work?"

She clicked around until she got to the screen she was looking for. "He doesn't live near the soup kitchen, but...he works at Peace Liberty Hospital."

"So he had access to both Zoe and her mother...or at least, it's plausible that he did. You had said that the aunt was in for hip surgery a few months back, and the mother volunteered in the abortion clinic, right?"

Madison was nodding. "It's not a far stretch to imagine that Zoe ran into Holland there, either."

"It still doesn't explain why she was in the alley," Troy said. His eyes searched hers for an answer. She didn't have one. Maybe she was trying to find meaning when there wasn't any again.

"Madison?" It was Sovereign's voice.

She rolled her eyes in instinctual response to his presence, clicked the monitor off, and rose to her feet.

Troy stepped back from her but kept the space between them

to a minimum. The stance was very much male and possessive, and she kind of loved it. Not because she wanted to rub anything in Sovereign's face. She just rather liked Troy staking claim to her. She shook her head at the thought. What was happening to her?

"Did you have officers canvass the businesses near the alley?" she asked Sovereign. "And what about the apartment buildings?"

He gave a curt nod. "I did."

Sovereign obviously wasn't feeling too charitable when it came to sharing his findings.

"Did you find anything useful?" she prompted.

"Not really. There were a few occupants in the one building— that run-down one right in the area—that testified to hearing a woman screaming that night. But they either never bothered to look or they didn't see anything."

"Which was it?" Troy asked.

"Which was what?" Sovereign countered.

"They didn't look or they didn't see anything? It can't be both."

Madison tucked her chin to her shoulder, smirking. Sovereign had the tendency to be somewhat vague. When she looked back at the two men, they were squared off, their stances solid and peacocked.

"Both." Bitterness drenched Sovereign's one-word response. "Some looked and didn't see anything. Others didn't bother looking." Sovereign slid his gaze from Troy to Madison. "Do you have a lead on your case?"

"Well, Sovereign," she replied, "I'll be sure to fill you in when we solve all three murders."

"I'm assuming one of those is my case."

"You better get to work then, because I'm about to do your job for you." She turned to Troy, tempted to take his hand but deciding against it. "Let's go."

CHAPTER 59

DONNIE HOLLAND'S HOUSE WAS DARK except for a light on in one front room. Based on the limited illumination and shadows, Madison guessed it was a small study or office.

Two cars were in Holland's driveway—one probably belonged to the missus—but Madison wasn't going to let that stop her. Holland had to answer for his indiscretions and, possibly, the murder of three people.

Troy stood behind Madison on the front step while she rang the doorbell. Troy felt like he was her bodyguard, and she liked thinking of him as her protector.

The door creaked open to a woman who was about the same age as Madison.

Madison held up her badge. "We'd like to speak with Donnie Holland."

The woman's brow wrinkled. "My husband? Why?"

"I'm afraid it's a matter we need to discuss with him privately." It wasn't Madison's place to interfere in their marriage, and it most certainly wasn't her place to disclose her husband's infidelities, despite the temptation. "Is he home?"

She nodded and moved to the side to let Madison and Troy into the house. "I'll get him for you." She eyed them skeptically as she walked away. Seconds later, she returned with a blond man who was slightly shorter than she was.

He let his eyes trace over them. "What is this about?"

"Are you Donnie Holland?" It never hurt to confirm.

"I am. What is this about?"

Madison caught the flickering of light behind him. The couple must've been watching TV somewhere.

She let her gaze go to the woman and then back to him. "We'd like to speak with you in private."

It seemed like he considered protesting the request at first, but then there was a light in his eyes. He must have understood Madison's silent communication. A man like Holland had many tracks to cover, and it was best he not take any chances.

He swallowed roughly, his Adam's apple heaving, and he touched his wife's arm. "Why don't you go back to your TV show? This won't take long."

Her eyes probed Holland's, but she nodded. "Fine."

Madison watched her carefully, wondering if the woman had any inkling as to what kind of man she had married. Did she realize the secret lives he led? The fact that he may have killed three people? Murderers were often people most would never suspect. But the truth was that all killers fell into the category of father, husband, mother, wife, child, or sibling.

Holland's wife left the foyer, and he turned a cold gaze on Madison and Troy. "Come this way." He led them to a small office. It was the room with the light on that she'd noticed when they'd pulled up to the house. He gestured to a love seat. Neither Madison nor Troy took him up on the invitation.

Holland slipped behind an L-shaped desk with a hutch. The surface was stacked with books and papers. He didn't seem self-conscious over the mess.

"What is it that you need to discuss—" he made a dramatic show of checking his watch "—at nine thirty at night?"

"Kimberly Bell." She'd drop the mother's name first and get the basics established.

"What about her?"

"You know her?"

"I do." He settled into his chair. There was no indication of remorse over the affair, no guilt in his expression. Despite his earlier fear of being exposed, he had fine-tuned the art of deception.

"You are having an affair with her."

He shrugged a shoulder. "I'm still not sure why this warrants two cops in my house. A lot of husbands get action on the side." He paused to shoot a sly smile at Troy.

Madison followed Holland's gaze. Troy's jaw drew tight, all hard lines. Yes, Troy was "a keeper," as her grandmother would have said.

"Did you know her daughter, Zoe Bell?" Madison asked.

"It's not like we spend time getting to know each other."

This man nauseated her. She slapped a photograph taken of Zoe at the crime scene down on the desk. On top of it, she placed one of Zoe when she was alive and well.

Holland's gaze lingered on the photographs a little too long.

"You did know her," Madison said.

"It's not what you think—" He picked up the last photo. "You think that I killed her?"

"I think you may have had reason to." She was going to play this cool and calm. Let him hang himself.

"And what would that be?"

"Have you ever been to Club 69?"

Holland looked at Troy as if to communicate that most men have. It was apparent Troy wasn't responding to this guy's attempts at male bonding. Troy was on another level...many tiers above this piece of shit.

"Answer the question," Troy said.

Holland blinked deliberately and paled, indicating that Troy intimidated him. Good. Troy likely intimidated most people with his build and *those* eyes that could see through a person.

"Yes, I've been there," Holland admitted through clenched teeth.

"Were you sleeping with Zoe?" Troy asked.

"Yes." He must have realized there was no point in lying. Again, there was no shame evident in his expression. His justification? Adultery was just something the modern man did. She wanted to hurt the guy.

"Did you ever see Zoe at Club 69?" Madison asked, keeping

her anger in check.

"No."

"Are you sure you don't want to think that answer through? We have witnesses who place you in the club arguing with Zoe," Madison said, stretching their suspicion to truth in search of a reaction.

"If you knew I did then why did you—" Holland stopped talking. "That was a trap."

"Yep, and you fell for it." Madison dropped onto the love seat now and crossed her legs. "Why don't you start telling us the truth now?"

"I had sex with her once."

Madison rolled her hand in a circle toward him. "Continue."

Holland glanced at Troy, who had taken up sentinel to her right, his hands clasped in front of his body, shoulders back, tight, ready to react.

"She told me I got her pregnant," Holland said.

Madison's heart started racing. Had everything truly happened just as she had theorized?

Holland continued. "She threatened to tell Hannah about our affair."

Madison assumed "Hannah" was his wife.

"Did Zoe know that you were sleeping with her mother?" Madison asked.

A cocky grin lit his features. "I think that was part of the appeal for her."

Madison would never be able to wrap her mind around that one. "So why did you confront her at the club? What did you hope to accomplish?"

"She told me that if I gave her five thousand dollars, she'd leave me alone. She even promised to get an abortion."

"But she didn't follow through," Troy said.

Holland shook his head. "She said she was going to keep the baby, that it was the right thing to do. I asked for my money back. Not that it would fix anything. She could always change her mind and come back years from now and destroy my life."

Two things stood out about his statement. First, Zoe hadn't destroyed his life; he had done that himself. In fact, his existence was like a house of cards about to collapse. It was just a matter of time. Second, the girls from the club mentioned they had overheard him *yelling* at Zoe about paying back money.

"This argument got very heated, didn't it?" Madison asked.

"She took the five thousand and spent it! She said she bought a bunch of clothes and it was all gone."

Five thousand wasn't anywhere near enough for Zoe to afford her house and wardrobe. She must have been milking other men for money, as well.

"That must have made you very angry," Madison said.

"You have no idea."

"I think we do. When you realized that Zoe not only took your money but was having your baby, you snapped," she stated.

"The only reason she was even going to keep it was because of her stupid aunt. The woman's stuck in the past."

So he was aware of Faye… It was Madison's turn to play stupid. "What do you mean?"

"She was all about pro-life. Abortions were 'wrong.' She brainwashed Zoe into having the same belief."

"There's a reason for that." She waited until Holland's eyes aligned with hers. "If it weren't for Kimberly's mother standing by her decision to have Kimberly, Zoe wouldn't even be around. Heck, neither would Kimberly."

If what he was saying held truth, Zoe didn't murder Faye. She was going to keep the baby because of her. Their conflict must have been worked out. That would explain why neither Kimberly nor Della had mentioned an argument between Faye and Zoe.

"I didn't really know Zoe, either. I had sex with her once, and she ends up pregnant? I think it was a setup from the start."

"You had a lot to gain from Zoe's death. Heck, you even had a reason to kill her aunt," Madison said.

Holland's face paled even more, and he leaned forward, his hands on his desk. "I didn't kill anyone." Holland's voice was tight, constricted.

"Then you won't have any problem telling us where you were at the time of their murders." She knew that Terry had called Holland and verified that he was with Kimberly Bell, but she was testing him.

"Murders?"

"Yes. Both Zoe and her aunt were killed within the past week." Madison provided him the dates and times.

"A detective already called me, and I told him I was with Kimberly."

"And that's still your story?"

"It's not a story. It's the truth."

"For *all* those hours?"

"Yes," he hissed.

She studied his eyes, his body language. He seemed to be telling the truth. She felt like a deflated balloon—empty.

"One more thing," she began, "when did you last see Zoe?"

"The night we argued at the club."

She nodded. "Don't leave town," she warned, leaving without as much as a good-bye.

BACK IN THE CAR, Madison wanted to be sick. On top of not catching Holland in a lie, she'd embarrassed herself in front of Troy.

Troy touched her shoulder and she looked at him. "Look at it this way," he said. "You found your mystery man."

She slammed a palm into the steering wheel. "I thought we had this bastard. I thought this case was behind me."

He reached over and put his hand on her forearm. "You'll get the killer. I have no doubt."

"Why? Because I'm a bulldog?"

He flashed one of those rare smiles. "Something like that."

She balled up her fist and punched his shoulder lightly.

"Hey, what was that for?" He rubbed where she hit him.

"It means I like you."

They made eye contact. It was almost as if he was waiting until she looked into his eyes before he spoke.

"I love you, too."

Chapter 60

Madison had left Troy's bed at about six that morning. She'd tried to do it as stealthily as possible, but the man was too attuned to his surroundings. She supposed it went with his training and had benefited him numerous times in the field. It likely meant the difference between life and death on several occasions—for him, those serving under him, and innocent civilians.

He had put on a pot of coffee and made her an omelet before sending her on her way. She smiled fondly at the memory as she drove to work, the way his eyes had brightened when he'd told her to have a great day. The coolness from when they were fighting had melted away completely. The three words he'd said the night before had changed the dynamics of their relationship.

She had yet to say *I love you* back to him, but he obviously got the message. Wasn't that enough?

Her heart pounded just thinking about verbalizing her emotions. Feeling love for him was one thing, but to put it into words was like taking a proverbial leap from a tower. It made things real.

He had an easier time exposing his heart with their relationship, and she admired his courage to do so, especially when his love life had been far from easy, too. For Madison, it had been a cheating fiancé, but for him it had been his wife. Vows spoken. Vows broken. That had to hurt much worse.

It was almost eight thirty when Madison got to the station. There was no need to stop at Starbucks this morning. She had drunk enough caffeine before leaving Troy's to tide her over for the day.

As she passed by her desk, Terry wasn't there and it didn't look like he had been in yet. She instantly thought of Annabelle and pulled out her phone. No text messages or voice mails. Hopefully everything was all right. She'd give him until nine and then call him if she hadn't heard anything.

She entered the lab in search of Cynthia, hoping that she'd have more results to share by now. Ben's phone records, a DNA match for the fetus…anything that could help with this case. She still had one person in mind to visit, too: Della Carpenter. She needed to know if Della had been aware of Zoe's lifestyle and that she and Faye had a falling out, even a short-lived one.

Madison heard giggling as she entered the lab, but it wasn't Cynthia's voice. Tucked into the corner of the room, Lou and Samantha were standing close to each other, laughing. When they saw her, they jumped apart.

What the hell?

She flashed back to that look they'd given each other in the alley. And now they were huddled together all alone?

"What's going on, guys? And you better not dream of bullshitting me." There was no way she'd stand by while Lou cheated on her best friend. She'd protect Cynthia until her dying breath, and if there was an afterlife, she'd do it then, too.

Lou hooked his thumbs on the waist of his pants and then tucked them into his pockets. "There's nothing going on." He pulled one hand out.

"Nothing? I did say no—"

"It's not bullshit, Maddy!" Samantha protested.

"I suggest you shut the—"

Lou tugged on Madison's arm and hauled her to the other side of the room.

"Get your hands off me." She tried to yank out of his grip and finally wriggled free.

Samantha came toward them, but Madison's glare grounded the technician's steps to a halt.

"It's not what you think." Lou gestured toward Samantha.

Madison crossed her arms. "And what do I think this is?"

"Knowing you, you're thinking I'm messing around on Cyn."

Madison pressed her lips and remained silent.

"Well, I'm not."

"We're planning an engagement party," Samantha said. Her voice was small, cautious.

"A party?" She analyzed their eyes, their postures, and gave their defense consideration. They were telling the truth. Then the betrayal that she thought would be Lou's became hers. "I'm her maid of honor. Aren't I supposed to organize that?"

Her stomach swirled. Had she let Cynthia down? Was she a bad friend because the thought to arrange an engagement party had never crossed her mind?

"I didn't think it would be something you'd enjoy doing," Lou said.

"It seems there are a lot of assumptions going around. I'm the maid of honor."

"See, I told you, Lou," Samantha said.

Lou shot her a glare, and Samantha blushed.

"You're right. I should have at least went to you first," he said.

Any hurt morphed to anger. "Damn straight you should've."

"I'm sorry."

She sighed and nodded. She knew his apology was sincere. "I'll give you the benefit of the doubt next time."

He chuckled. "That would be nice. Can I call you later? We"—he bobbed his head toward Samantha to include her, as well—"can meet up someplace and brainstorm the party. Who to invite, where to hold it. All the details."

She had been wrong to assume the worst about Lou Stanford. He loved Cynthia. He was marrying her, and he was one of the few men who was going to mean his vows when he spoke them.

"Sure. Just remember, like me, she doesn't like surprises. We'll have to be up-front once it's planned," Madison said.

"That's right. See, I should have partnered with you on this from the start. You know her better than anyone."

Madison felt bad for Samantha. "I'm sure Sam would have

done a great job planning it with you. But, yeah, now I'm on board, the three of us are going to rock it." She didn't know the first thing about throwing an engagement party, but she'd figure it out. That's what Google was for.

The lab door swung open, and Cynthia entered. "What are you three going to rock?"

Madison didn't respond.

Cynthia's gaze went to Lou, then Samantha, who quickly excused herself.

"We're going to rock this case," Madison said.

"What case? Aren't you and Lou enemies or something on these investigations?" Cynthia chuckled. "He *is* paired with Sovereign."

"Eh, I won't hold that against him," Madison said.

"I've got to go. We'll talk later, baby." Lou kissed Cynthia and left the lab.

Cynthia jacked a thumb after him and spoke to Madison. "He's acting so strange lately." She shrugged her shoulders and snapped on a pair of gloves.

"Do you have any updates for me?" Madison asked, moving to more comfortable territory. "Please tell me you have something."

"I have a DNA match for the fetus."

"Well, don't keep me waiting in suspense."

"Mario Cohen."

"That's the one owner of Club 69 where Zoe worked."

"Well, he was the father of Zoe's baby."

Elias had mentioned Zoe saying she liked her boss. "But why would he have killed her?"

"That's your job to figure out."

"Wow, thanks ever so." Madison smirked at her.

Mario's house was nowhere near the alley. Madison considered further motive. Mario would have lost a stripper, and depending on how Zoe played things, she might have been extorting him, too.

"What about Ben Dixon's phone records?" Madison asked.

"You're never satisfied, are you?"

"I'm *tenacious*."

"Uh-huh. You must really think Ben's lying about who he called in that parking lot."

She shrugged. "He's given me no reason to trust him."

"Well, you'll have to leave and wait on those findings. I didn't end up getting the records by the end of yesterday. I'm hoping they will come in first thing today."

"Can you call to follow up with the company?"

Cynthia held the eye contact and let out a staggered breath. "For you, I can do that."

CHAPTER 61

TERRY HAD SHOWN UP JUST after Madison had gotten their lead. He essentially entered the lab and then backed up his steps, and they got in their department sedan and sped off.

"Mario Cohen is the father? I can't say that surprises me," Terry said from the passenger seat.

She had just parked in the lot of Club 69.

"He's the father, but Zoe still had sex with Ben before she died. It's probably the real reason Mario recognized him. He was likely aware of their sleeping together," she responded. She then filled Terry in on her visit with Donnie Holland, and he was grateful that she hadn't pulled him away from Annabelle.

"Going back to Mario. He's a proud man, but he doesn't really strike me as the jealous type," Terry said.

"Okay, this might be a long shot, but remember when we spoke to Ken? He'd said that Zoe had sex with everyone but him? Well, he did sound jealous. What if he found out that Zoe was pregnant, possibly even with Mario's baby—"

"He'd be pissed."

"But enough to kill?" She held eye contact with Terry.

"Well, I guess we'll find out."

The front door of the club was locked, but the plates on the two vehicles in the lot came back to Mario and Ken.

"Let's go around back," Madison said, leading Terry to the dancers' entrance.

The back door was unlocked, but the second she cracked it open she heard yelling. Madison held her finger to her lips, and

Terry nodded.

Their voices were familiar.

"Mario and Ken," she whispered to Terry.

"You are a stupid shit!" Mario shouted.

"We've been through this—"

"You're no damn good at keeping quiet. And the cops are sniffing around. I'm not going down with you!"

Something toppled over inside, and there was a loud crash. The sound of shattering glass cracked as loud as a thunderbolt and then rained down for a moment longer.

Madison pulled her gun from her holster, and Terry did the same. They headed in the direction of the noise.

More banging and thumping. The men were definitely in a scuffle.

"You killed her!" It was Mario's voice again.

Something seemed to smack into the wall on the other side of where Madison stood in the hallway. A barstool? A table?

Based on the layout of the club, it would be a wall within one of the private rooms, she reasoned.

She and Terry carefully cleared their way through the club until they were outside of the room.

She banged on the door. "Stiles PD!"

All movement inside stopped.

"Put your hands up in the air. We're coming in," she called out.

She made eye contact with Terry to make sure he was ready. A slight bob of his head and she breached the door. It was an office and storage room.

"Stiles PD!" she repeated for the sake of protocol. "Hands up!"

"Put them on the top of your head and interlace your fingers," Terry added.

"We're not armed. And he killed Zoe." Mario pointed at Ken.

"Hands on your head!" Madison shouted.

Mario followed the directive.

She went behind him, holstered her gun, and cuffed Mario while Terry did the same with Ken.

"Now, tell us what the hell's going on." Madison demanded.

"He killed Zoe," Mario repeated.

"And why would he do that?" Terry asked.

"Because she wouldn't give him the time of day!"

"Fuck you, Mario. She had sex with me the night she…" Ken's words trailed off, his eyes going from Mario to Madison.

She tried to recall Ken's home address, but it wasn't coming to her. Did he live near that alley, or were he and Zoe in the area for another reason?

"You had sex with her the night she died?" Madison asked Ken.

Ken stared at Mario when he answered, jaw clenched. "Yes," he ground out.

There was only evidence of one man having slept with Zoe in the days before she died. Ken must have used a condom. "Did you use protection?"

His brow furrowed, obviously unsure why it mattered, but he answered, anyway. "Yes."

"Did you kill Zoe?" Madison asked directly.

Ken bit his lip for a moment. "I-I didn't mean for it to happen."

"You didn't mean for *what* to happen? You hit her in the head and then killed an innocent homeless man," Madison said.

"He wasn't innocent! He saw!"

"You stripped him and put his clothes on Zoe," Madison continued. "Doesn't seem like an accident to me. What did you do with her clothes?"

There was a subtle diversion of his eyes, and she followed the direction of his gaze.

"It's in a drawer?" Madison motioned for Terry to check out the desk. She kept her attention locked on Ken while glancing to Terry.

He moved behind the desk, gloved up, and pulled out the top drawer, then the bottom. He came out with a plastic grocery bag. He opened it and looked inside. "It appears to be women's clothing—" he pulled out a shirt "—and about Zoe's size."

"You stupid shit, you brought that in here!" Mario yelled.

Madison grabbed Ken at the wrists where his arms were linked together and tugged Mario in the direction of the door. "That's it. We're going downtown. You have a lot to exp—"

"Wait," Terry interrupted. "There's something else in here." He dug around in the drawer and came out with another bag. He pulled out a towel with something wrapped up inside it.

"What is it?" she asked.

Terry shot her a quick look, scolding her for her impatience. He unraveled the fabric and came out with something. A ladle? It was strange looking and oval shaped. In one hand, he held it up, and in the other, he held up the towel and the bag. The white cotton was stained red.

"Bag it and bring it with us," she said, tightening her grip on Ken and Mario.

"But I didn't do anything," Mario pleaded.

Terry worked to get the items back in the bags and then took over with Mario.

"Oh, I think you did," Madison said. There was still the matter of Faye and the fact that Zoe had been carrying his baby. She had always felt Mario was hiding something, and she still did. If he had known Ken killed Zoe, why hadn't he come clean? "It wasn't all Ken, was it?"

Mario's eyes snapped to hers.

She continued. "The two of you killed three—"

Ken's feet ground into the floor. She couldn't move him. "Three? I confessed to killing Zoe."

"And I never killed anyone." Mario's body was shaking, and his face was red.

"And the homeless person. He had a name by the way. Leonard. And you killed a sixty-eight-year-old woman."

"No. No. I didn't kill them. I didn't." Ken was shaking his head violently now.

"You just said that the homeless man saw everything and wasn't innocent."

"*I* didn't kill him." Ken turned his head, and his gaze went to Mario.

The kook's words came to mind. *Evil shadows.* Plural. Two

people had been in that alley.

"I'm not going down for what you did," Mario said.

"But you were there," Ken screamed. "You didn't...didn't stop me. You helped me dress her!"

CHAPTER 62

"Why did you kill Zoe?" Madison was seated across from Ken in an interrogation room.

"I didn't mean for it to happen, but she…she…" Ken's head slumped forward.

Madison let the silence ride out for a while.

"We were in the Paradise Motel."

Paradise Motel was one of the crappy establishments near the alley that rented out by the hour. And here, he had told them the first time they spoke that Zoe 'opened her legs' for everyone else but him.

"All right, and then what happened?" Madison prompted as she leaned on the table.

"Everything turned to shit." Anger contorted his expression. Tears streamed down his face and his one hand formed into a fist. "She told me—" he wiped a hand across his face "—that Mario was the father of her baby. All I saw was red."

Sadly, Zoe would've had no way of knowing who the father of her baby had been. Ken, obviously prone to jealousy, hadn't thought that part through.

Madison clasped her hands and spoke calmly. "Then what happened?"

"She knew I was angry and ran out of the room. I chased her." He paused, his eyes glazing over. "She went into that alley. And I-I just picked up that—ladle?" He looked at her.

"Yes." It turned out to be a Japanese serving ladle.

"And I hit her on the head with it. I didn't really mean for her to die." Ken covered his face with his hands and sobbed.

There were pieces that still weren't fitting together. She let him cry it out for about a minute.

"You said Mario helped you dress Zoe in the vagrant's clothing? Why was Mario in the alley in the first place and why was he protecting your secret?" Madison asked.

Ken chewed on the inside of his cheek. "I did him a favor when we were younger. Some girl accused him of rape. I testified that he couldn't have done it as he was with me."

Madison's earlobes heated from anger. "You lied under oath?"

No response.

She took that as a confession. She wondered if Mario had any idea that returning the favor would mean covering up a murder.

"It seems you're pretty good at lying," Madison said, baiting Ken.

"What do you mean?"

"You told us at the club, when we first met you, that you never slept with Zoe."

"I panicked."

"Is that what you did when you saw that homeless man and knew he witnessed you kill Zoe?" Madison raised her voice with each word. "He saw—maybe he even tried to intervene—and you killed him. You panicked then, too?"

"No, no, that's not what happened."

"Then by all means, enlighten us."

Terry jingled his change and had Ken turning around to look at him.

Madison smacked the table with her palm. "Tell. Us. What. Happened."

"Fine. Mario said we had no choice."

"Mario?"

"Yeah. He's the one who killed him."

MARIO SEEMED COMFORTABLE IN AN interrogation room like it was a second home for him.

"Ken said that you killed the homeless man."

"That shit." Mario rolled his eyes.

"So you're not denying the accusation? Tell us what happened."

"And why should I do that?" His eyes were cold and distant.

"Your prison sentence might be lighter. If we get everything from Ken—"

"Bullshit! But fine. Zoe was already dead. Ken called me and I went to him. We were talking about what to do with Zoe's body when I saw him watching me from beneath a blue tarp. The ladle was on the ground next to me"—he shrugged—"I did what I had to do."

"Which was?" She needed him to be precise so his confession couldn't be twisted by a skilled defense attorney.

"I picked it up and I hit him in the head."

That didn't necessarily fit, as Mario was taller than Ken. "Are you sure of that?"

"You don't believe me?" Mario glanced back at Terry.

"Don't tell me, tell her," Terry said.

"I thought from the standpoint of covering my ass, so I crouched lower so that I was closer to Ken's height. I don't understand why the big deal. Nobody's gonna miss a bum."

Adrenaline fused through Madison's core and had her hands shaking, her arms chilled. "That *bum* was a living human being."

"Well, he's not now." Nonchalant, as if taking a life had no consequence.

She jumped up from her chair, its legs scraping against the linoleum. She was ready to have into him when she caught Terry's eye to keep her cool. She steadied her breath and sat back down, knowing there were more questions to ask.

"Why did you dress Zoe in his clothing?" she asked.

"Isn't that obvious? We didn't want her identified."

"But then you position her on a street corner."

"She should have felt at home there."

The guy's attitude was beyond appalling. He discarded life the same way he did garbage. She swallowed roughly. "Was Zoe a prostitute? Is that what you're saying?"

"Nope. She just slept around and then the stupid bitch wound up pregnant. Go figure."

Terry pounced next to Mario.

Mario splayed his palms. "What?"

Terry had a rapid pulse in his cheek.

That's it. They had enough.

"Let's go, Detective Grant." She already had the door open, Terry had gone through, and an officer was entering the room when she heard Mario say, "Hey, what about me?" She couldn't bring herself to tell him that Zoe had been carrying his baby.

MADISON HEADED STRAIGHT TO THE LAB. Cynthia was at her desk reading through the contents of a folder.

"Speak to me," Madison said.

Cynthia looked up. "Neither Ken nor Mario were a match to the cigarettes found next to Faye or in her backyard."

"And?"

"*And*, Ken's car was processed and forensics place Zoe in his vehicle. I also sent Mark and Samantha over to the men's residences to see if they could gather anything that might help, but it's not looking like they were involved with Faye's death. Maybe Zoe had killed her aunt?"

Madison ruminated on that possibility again, but it didn't seem quite as plausible as it had before. She recalled images of seeing Zoe for the first time, the sincere grief in her eyes...

"Maddy, are you all right?"

"Yeah, of course. Anything else?"

"Actually, yes. I received Ben's phone records and had a chance to go through them. Now, he did call Elias that night outside the club, but he called Faye Duncan the day before she died."

"Faye? Are you sure?"

Cynthia licked her lips and nodded.

None of this was fitting together.

"Why would Ben call Faye?" Madison asked. Then she remembered how Ben had mentioned covering for Zoe's lifestyle, including hiding it from her family as long as she paid him off with sex. Then all became clear.

"You'll have to ask him that," Cynthia said.

"Ben had lied about a lot of things, and people only lie when they have something to hide." She dialed dispatch and requested Ben be brought in immediately for questioning.

Terry and Cynthia were watching her as she lowered her phone.

"What?" she asked.

"Maddy, there's more," Cynthia began. "The blood found in the alley wasn't a match to either cigarette found, nor to Ken or Mario. It might have been there from another time. The clothing you retrieved from the club's office definitely belonged to Zoe Bell, and blood pulled from the ladle was Zoe's and Leonard's. There's no doubt Ken and Mario killed them," Cynthia summarized.

"But we still don't know who killed Faye Duncan," Madison finished.

Two out of three cases wasn't good enough. And technically, only one of those cases was hers.

CHAPTER 63

MADISON WAS DOING THIS INTERROGATION by herself. She slammed the door to the room behind her. Ben was seated at the table.

"Why did you call Faye Duncan two Tuesdays ago?" She slapped a color print of Faye dead in the wheelchair on the table in front of Ben. "Don't even think about telling me another lie."

He chewed his bottom lip. "Remember how I said that I told Zoe I'd tell on her if she didn't sleep with me?"

"Yes." But she wished she could forget.

"Well, she wasn't being as cooperative as she had been at first."

"So you snitched on her to her great-aunt? How did you even know how to reach Faye?" Madison asked.

"An online directory. It wasn't hard. Zoe was always blabbing about the woman."

"All right. So you called Faye. Then what happened?"

"She was a scary old bat. When I told her about Zoe, she was screaming as if her house were on fire. She freaked me out."

"Then what? You killed her?"

"I didn't kill her. I've given you my alibis."

"Oh, that's right. You were at home 'sleeping.'"

"I had no reason to kill her or Zoe."

"We know you didn't kill Zoe."

He straightened up. "Then you know I didn't kill Faye. Why am I here?"

"Not so fast," she said. "We don't know who killed Faye."

He crossed his arms over his chest. "Well, I'd have no reason to kill Faye."

Madison wasn't sure if it was the words or way he had said them, but the fact sank in. He really *didn't* have a reason to kill the woman.

Son of a bitch!

She needed to think everything through again. Faye had been making her guest tea around the time of her death. The bruises on her arms indicated a struggle. But by some unfortunate stroke of fate, she hadn't drawn any epithelium from her assailant.

Think, Madison, think.

Neighbors had told canvassing police officers that the only people they saw around Faye's house were family members.

Family. The killer was right in front of her all along.

She ran from the interrogation room.

"Can I go now?" Ben called out.

"Watch him," she directed an officer outside the door.

She was out of breath by the time she reached the lab. "Cynthia, what kind of tea had Faye Duncan been making?"

"Just a second." Cynthia went over to her computer and brought up the evidence log. "Rose hip."

"What does that smell like?"

Cynthia hitched a shoulder. "Um, kind of like olive oil with a bit of a nutty aroma?"

"It's not really a common flavor, is it?"

"I wouldn't say so."

"Son of a bitch. She did it."

"What? Who?"

"What do we know about Della Carpenter?" Madison asked.

"What do you mean?"

"I'm thinking that she killed her sister. Neighbors would think nothing of seeing her wheeling Faye down the street. They may have seen her pushing Faye during the time she was recovering from her surgery."

"Oh, God." Cynthia went over to her computer and pulled up a background on Della. "She was married once, had one child—"

"All right, we know all that. Give me something useful."

Cynthia tapped the frame of the monitor with one hand as she scrolled the mouse with the other.

"Stop!" Madison pointed to the screen. "There's motive right there." She was already to the door when Cynthia called out to her.

"Terry left. Annabelle's in labor."

She had run away from the interview room so quickly she hadn't noticed her partner wasn't in the observation room. Madison's heart raced even faster.

DELLA OPENED THE DOOR. Her face was stoic, as if she'd been expecting Madison. "You know?"

Madison nodded. When she went to Della's house to find Zoe, the girl had handed her a cup of tea—rose hip tea.

"Why did you kill your sister?"

"She was so self-righteous." Della's tone was cold. "I was at her house for a visit, and things got out of control."

"What got out of control?" It was obvious the situation had, and adrenaline must have helped Della load Faye's dead body into the wheelchair.

"All of it. Doesn't matter now. She's dead." There was a hard killer lurking behind those eyes.

"How? What happened?"

"We were arguing about Zoe. Faye found out that Zoe stripped at some club, that she was pregnant, and that Zoe didn't know who the father was. She told me how she received a call from some guy telling her all about it. But all her life my sister had it *so* easy."

"So you were arguing, and…" Madison prompted.

"She gripped at her chest and yelled at me to call nine-one-one and that she was having a heart attack. I don't know why, but I was frozen. I couldn't move. I watched her drop to the floor. Then I got a wheelchair from the hospital and…you know the rest." Della's eyes misted but not one tear fell. "Faye was loved. She could do no wrong. You know that I got pregnant as a teen and ran away? Those people would have taken my baby from me or made me kill her! Now, if it had been Faye, they would have welcomed the baby with open arms."

"Is that because you weren't really theirs?" Madison knew the answer—it was included in the detailed background check—but she wanted to draw Della out more.

Della's eyes were a blend of fire and ice, but she remained silent.

"That's right, I know. You were adopted." Madison expelled a breath. "You felt inferior to Faye from the very beginning. It had built up in you over the years and to hear her talking about Zoe's life choices, well, it just made you snap." Madison snapped her fingers along with her words.

"She had it all. She was Miss Goody Two-shoes. That's why I wheeled her out there with no ID. No one was supposed to find out."

Madison recalled their first meeting. Della had said Faye "was loved by everyone who met her" and with hindsight, she recognized a buried disdain. And when Della had commented on Faye being found outside the hospital "where the protests happened," Madison had wrongly accepted that as an obvious conclusion based on the context of their conversation. Now, all was clear.

"It doesn't work like that," Madison said. "You killed your own sister out of jealousy."

Della's nostrils flared, and tears pooled in her eyes. "You have no idea what it's like to hit the road at sixteen, pregnant and alone, with nowhere to go. I was so scared. I had no one. My family abandoned their girl when she needed them the most."

Della was separating herself from what had happened by referring to her younger self as "their girl."

Madison softened her voice when she spoke again. "Why wait so long?"

"To kill her?"

Madison nodded.

Della's jaw twitched and Madison wasn't quite sure if it was with rage or regret. "She always had the past over me. She got to grow up with parents while I was alone."

"That's still not an answer."

"It built up over the years, I guess, as you said. But when I heard her start into Zoe's choices in life, well, I couldn't handle it. She obviously judged me back then…back when I was a teen. I thought she just followed their lead."

"*Their* lead?"

"Her mom and dad. But when Faye found out Zoe was pregnant and wouldn't let it rest, well, I lost it. She took a stand for pro-life while condemning my granddaughter. She was livid that Zoe was pregnant out of wedlock—and to top it off, that she didn't know who the father was. Faye's two standpoints don't jibe in my book. She was a hypocrite."

Madison tempered her response. "She didn't feel that way about you. In fact, Faye was proud of your strength. It's the main reason she protested abortion."

Della's eyes met Madison's, incredulous. "Huh."

"I swear, Della. Her fellow protesters told us that. She was so proud of you. You had the courage to stand up for yourself, for Kimberly."

Della started crying. Her entire body heaved with the intensity of the sobs. "I killed my sister!"

CHAPTER 64

DELLA CARPENTER WAS BOOKED FOR the murder of Faye Duncan, and then Madison went down to visit Cynthia in the lab. There was still no word from Terry, but she'd grab Cynthia and they'd head over to the hospital together and try this a second time.

"There's one thing that wasn't resolved. The cigarette next to Faye body's I can see being anyone's, but what about the one found in Faye's backyard?" Madison asked.

"Oh, I have the answer to that now. Della Carpenter. Now that we have her DNA and fingerprints, I was able to run them against the evidence," Cynthia said.

"I wasn't under the impression the woman even smoked. And let me guess: she matched the prints left on the chair?"

Cynthia nodded.

"Guess you never know. God, she never gave me any reason to suspect her. Outwardly, the woman was the sweetest little thing." It really was impossible to tell who a person was strictly based on appearance. If these investigations had taught her anything, it was that. Della had hidden well below suspicion too—maybe in too plain of sight. "What about the third blood profile on the newspaper?"

"No hits." Cynthia paused for a few seconds. "Well, shall we go to the hospital and see how Annabelle and Terry are making out?"

"I think so." Madison smiled as Cynthia wrapped her arm around her shoulders.

ANNABELLE WAS IN LABOR WHEN they arrived, and Terry was in the delivery room with her. He was a brave man, watching a baby come into this world. All the bodily fluids, the blood, the—

She shuddered. She couldn't think about the *how* of it all right now.

Madison and Cynthia waited in silence until Terry walked into the waiting room, a somber look on his face.

Madison ran over to him, Cynthia on her heels. Tears threatened to fall.

The baby's health…

She stopped just shy of her shoes touching her partner's. "Is everything all right?" Her question remained out there for a few seconds. "Terry?" Her voice quaked just saying his name.

His serious expression made way for a huge grin. "She's healthy!"

"You had a girl!" Madison jumped and then hugged Terry. "Congratulations!"

"Yes, congratulations!" Cynthia added. "What did you name her?"

"Well, I thought for sure the baby was going to be a boy. We had the name picked out and every—"

Madison stepped to the side to let Cynthia hug Terry.

"We were going to call our son Daniel. So our daughter's name is Dani." Tears filled his eyes as he smiled. He was such a proud papa. Madison felt her own eyes growing wet.

"How big is she? How is Annabelle?" The questions were pouring out of Cynthia, and Terry was all too happy to answer them. And Madison didn't blame him. He had everything worth celebrating. A healthy, eight-pound-six-ounce baby girl and a wife who was doing spectacular considering she had just birthed an eight-pound-six-ounce baby. Madison found herself smiling along with him.

She extended an envelope to Terry and he hitched his brows.

"Your eighty dollars."

And just when she didn't think his grin could become larger, he proved her wrong. "I'm going to enjoy spending every cent."

She narrowed her eyes at him. "You might want to hold on to some of it for our next case."

"Uh-huh."

He didn't ask who killed Zoe and she didn't tell him. There would be plenty of time to discuss work. They never did get the results on Faye's or Zoe's tox screens, but they always took time, and it didn't really matter now that they had their confessions.

The balance of life was delicate. In one moment, someone died while another came into the world. This *now* would never come again.

"Madison, did you hear me?" Terry asked.

She shook her head. "Sorry…"

"I asked if you wanted to come see the baby and Annabelle."

"I sure do." And she did, but her legs wouldn't move. There was something she had to do that couldn't wait. "I just have to make a quick call."

Was she actually going to do this?

"Okay. It's room three-twelve." He touched her arm and then headed down the hall with Cynthia.

Madison pulled out her cell phone and pressed Troy's name in her Favorites section. When he answered, she figured it was best to say it right away, before she changed her mind. "I love you, too."

Read on for an exciting preview of Carolyn Arnold's thrilling FBI series featuring Brandon Fisher

ELEVEN

CHAPTER 1

NOTHING IN THE TWENTY WEEKS at Quantico prepared me for this.

A Crime Scene Investigator, who had identified himself as Earl Royster when we first arrived, came out of a room and addressed FBI Supervisory Special Agent Jack Harper. "All of the victims were buried—" He held up a finger, his eyes squeezed shut, and he sneezed. "Sorry 'bout that. My allergies don't like it down here. They were all buried the same way."

This was my first case with the FBI Behavioral Analysis Unit, and it took us to Salt Lick, Kentucky. The discovery was made this morning, and we were briefed and flown out from Quantico to the Louisville field office where we picked up a couple of SUVs. We drove from there and got here about four in the afternoon.

We were in a bunker illuminated by portable lights brought in by the local investigative team. A series of four tunnels spread out as a root system beneath a house the size of a mobile trailer and extended under an abandoned cornfield.

A doorway in the cellar of the house led down eleven feet to a main hub from which the tunnels fed off. The walls were packed dirt and an electrical cord ran along the ceiling with pigtail fixtures attached every few feet.

We were standing in the hub which was fifteen and a quarter feet wide and arched out to a depth of seven and half feet. The tunnels were only about three feet wide, and the height clearance was about the same as here, six and a half feet. The bulbs dangled down from the fixtures another eight inches.

I pulled out on the collar of my shirt wishing for a smaller frame than my six foot two. As it was, the three of us could have reached out and touched each other if we were inclined.

"It's believed each victim had the same cuts inflicted," Royster said. "Although most of the remains are skeletal so it's not as easy to know for sure, but based on burial method this guy obviously had a ritual. The most recent victim is only a few years old and was preserved by the soil. The oldest remains are estimated to date back twenty-five to thirty years. Bingham moved in twenty-six years ago."

Lance Bingham was the property owner, age sixty-two and was currently serving three to five years in a correctional facility for killing two cows and assaulting a neighbor. If he moved in twenty-six years ago, that would put Bingham at thirty-six. The statistical age for a serial killer to start out is early to mid-thirties.

The CSI continued to relay more information about how the tunnels branched out in various directions and the ends came to a bulbous tip.

"There are eleven rooms and only ten bodies." Jack rushed the briefing along as he pulled a cigarette out of a shirt pocket. He didn't light up, but his lips suctioned around it as if it was a life supply.

Royster's eyes went from the cigarette to Jack's face. "Yes. There's one tunnel that leads to a dead end and there's one empty grave."

"What do you make of it?" Jack spoke with the cigarette bobbing in his mouth and turned to me.

"Of the empty grave?"

Jack's smile slanted higher on the right, his eyes pinched, and he removed the cigarette from his mouth. "That and the latest victim."

Bingham had been in prison for the last three years. The elaborate tunnel system he had going would have taken years to plan and dig, and it would have taken strength, leaning toward Bingham not working alone. "He had help. Someone followed behind him."

Jack perched the unlit smoke back in his lips. "Hmm."

"Anyway, you'll want to see it for yourself. I haven't seen anything like it," Royster continued.

Jack's eyes narrowed, and his brows compressed.

"Come—" The back of a wrist came to his nose in an instant. The spray of sneeze only somewhat diverted. More sniffles. "Sorry 'bout that. Anyway, this way."

Jack motioned for me to go ahead of him.

My thoughts were on the width of the tunnel. I took a deep breath, careful to stagger it so that he wouldn't notice.

Tight space.

I pulled out on my collar again. Sweat dripped down my back.

"Go ahead, Kid."

Both Jack and the CSI were watching me.

The CSI said, "We'll look at the most recent victim first. Now as you know the victims alternated male and female. The tenth victim was female so we believe the next is going to be—"

"Let me guess, male," Jack interrupted him.

"Yeah." Royster took off down the third tunnel that fed off from the bottom right of the hub.

I followed behind him, tracing the walls with my hands. My heart palpitated. I ducked to miss the bulbs just as I knew I'd have to and worked at focusing on the positive. Above ground the humidity sucked air from the lungs; down here the air was cool.

Another heart palpitation.

I counted my paces—five, six. The further we went the heavier my chest became, making the next breath even more expectant and less taken for granted.

But, this was my first case. I had to be strong. The rumor was you either survived Jack and the two years of probationary service and became a certified Special Agent or your new job would be security detail at a mall.

Five more paces and we entered an offshoot from the main tunnel. According to Royster, three burial chambers were in this tunnel. He described these as branches on a tree. Each branch came off the main trunk for the length of about ten feet and ended in a circular space of about eleven feet in diameter. The idea of more space seemed welcoming until we reached it.

A circular grave took up most of the space and was a couple of feet deep. Chicken wire rimmed the grave to help retain its shape. With her wrists and feet tied to metal stakes, her arms and legs formed the human equivalence of a star. As her body had dried from decomposition, the constraints had kept her positioned in the manner the killer had intended.

"And what made them dig?" Jack asked the CSI.

Jack was searching for specifics. We knew Bingham had entrusted his financials to his sister, but when she passed away a year ago, the back taxes built up to the point the county had come to reclaim the property.

Royster answered, "X marked the spot." Neither Jack nor I displayed any amusement. The CSI continued. "He etched into the dirt, probably with a stick."

"Why assume a stick?" Jack asked the question, and it resulted in an awkward silence.

My eyes settled on the body of the female who was estimated to be in her early twenties. It's not that I had an aversion to a dead body, but looking at her made my stomach toss. She still had flesh on her bones. As the CSI had said, *preserved by the soil.*

Her torso had eleven incisions. They were marked in the linear way to keep count. Two sets of four vertical cuts with one horizontal slashed on an angle through each of them. The eleventh cut was the largest and was above the belly button.

"You realize the number eleven is believed to be a sign of purity?"

My chest compressed further knowing another person was going to share the limited space. Zachery Miles was a member of our team, but unlike Jack's his reputation hadn't preceded him. I had read his file and he had a flawless service record and the IQ of a genius. He was eight years older than I was.

Jack stuck the cigarette he had been sucking on back into his shirt pocket. "Purity, huh?"

I looked down at the body of the woman in the shallow grave

beside me. Nothing seemed too pure about any of this.

"I'm going to go." Royster excused himself.

"Without getting into the numerology and spiritualistic element," Zachery continued, not acknowledging the CSI.

Jack stretched his neck side to side and looked at me. "I hate it when he gets into that shit." He pointed a bony index finger at me. "Don't let me catch you talking about it either."

I just nodded. I guess I had been told, not that he needed to treat me like a child. I possessed no interest in things I had no reason to know about. I believed in God and angels despite the evil in the world, but beyond that I had no desire for more insight into the spiritualistic realm.

"The primary understanding is the number one is that of new beginnings and purity."

My eyes scanned Zachery. While his intelligence scoring revealed a genius, physically, he was just an average guy. If anything, he was slightly taller than Jack and me, probably coming in at about six-four. His hair was dark and trimmed short. He had a high brow line.

"Zachery here reads something once—" Jack tapped his head. "—It's there."

JACK AND I SPENT THE next few hours making our way to every room where Jack insisted on standing beside all the bodies. He took pause studying each of them carefully, even if only part of their remains had been uncovered. I'd pass him glances, but he seemed oblivious to my presence. We ended up back beside the last victim where we stayed for twenty minutes, not moving, not talking, just standing.

And I understood what he saw. There was a different feel to this room, nothing quantifiable, but it was discernible. The killer had a lot to say. He was organized and immaculate. He was precise and disciplined. He acted with a purpose, and like most killers he had a message to relay. We were looking for a controlled, highly intelligent unsub.

Nine victims had their intestines removed, but Doctor Jones, the coroner, wouldn't conclude it as the cause of death before conducting more tests. The last victim's intestines were intact. And, even though, COD needed confirmation, the talk that permeated the corridors of the bunker was the men who did this were scary sons of bitches.

Zachery entered the room. "I find it fascinating he would bury his victims in circular graves."

I looked up at him more from a need to break from the body than from curiosity. *Fascinating?* I turned to Jack when I heard the flick of a lighter.

He held out his hands as if to say he wouldn't light up inside the burial chamber. His craving was getting desperate, though, which meant he'd be getting cranky. He said, "Continue, Zachery, by all means. The kid wants to hear."

"By combining both the number eleven and the circle, it makes me think of the coinherence symbol. Even the way the victims are laid out."

"Elaborate," Jack directed.

"It's a circle which combines a total of eleven inner points to complete it. As eleven means purity so the coinherence symbol is related to religious traditions—at minimum thirteen. But some people can discern more, and each symbol is understood in different ways. The circle itself stands for completion and can symbolize eternity."

I cocked my head to the side. Zachery noticed.

"We have a skeptic here, Jack."

Jack faced me and spoke with the unlit cigarette perched back in his lips. "What do you make of it?"

Was this a trap? "You want to know what I think?"

"By all means, Slingshot."

And there it was, the other dreaded nickname, no doubt his way of reminding me that I didn't score perfectly on handguns at the academy. "Makes me think of the medical symbol. Maybe our guy has a background in medicine. It could explain the incisions being deep enough to inflict pain but not deep enough to cause them to bleed out. It would explain how he managed to take out their intestines." *Was this what I signed up for?*

"Hmm." Jack mumbled. Zachery remained silent. Seconds later, Jack said, "You're assuming they didn't bleed out. Continue."

"The murders happened over a period of time. This one—" I gestured to the woman, and for a moment realized how this job transferred the life of a person into an object. "—She's recent. Bingham's been in prison for about three years now."

Jack flicked the lighter again. "So you're saying he had an apprentice?"

Zachery's lips lifted upward, and his eyes read, *like Star Wars.*

I got it. I was the youngest on the team, twenty-nine this August, next month, and I was the new guy. But I didn't make it through four years of university studying mechanics and endure twenty weeks of the academy, coming out at the top of the class, to be treated like a child. "Not like an apprentice."

"Like what then—"

"Jack, the Sheriff wants to speak with you." Paige Dawson, another member of our team came into the burial chamber. She came to Quantico from the New York field office claiming she wanted out of the big city. I met her when she was an instructor at the academy.

I pulled out on the neck of my shirt. Four of us were in here now. Dust caused me to cough and warranted a judgmental glare from Jack.

"How did you make out with the guy who discovered everything?"

"He's clean. I mean we had his background already, and he lives up to it. I really don't think he's involved at all."

Jack nodded and left the room.

I turned to Zachery. "I think he hates me."

"If he hated you, you'd know it." Zachery followed behind Jack.

Chapter 2

Salt Lick, Kentucky was right in the middle of nowhere and had a population shy of three-fifty. And just as the name implied, underground mineral deposits were the craving of livestock, and due to this it attracted farmers to the area. Honestly, I was surprised the village was large enough to boast a Journey's End Lodge and a Frosty Freeze.

I stepped into the main hub to see Jack in a heated conversation with Sheriff Harris. From an earlier meeting with him I knew he covered all of Bath County, which included three municipalities and a combined population of about twelve thousand.

"Ah, I'm doing the best I can agent. But, um, we've never seen the likes of this before." A born and raised Kentucky man, the Sheriff was in his mid-fifties, had a bald head and carried about an extra sixty pounds that came to rest on his front. Both of his hands were braced on his hips, a stance of confidence, but the flicking up and down of his right index finger gave his insecurities away.

"It has nothing to do with what you've seen before, Sheriff. What matters is catching the unsub."

"Well, the property owner is in p-pri, prison," the Kentucky accent broke through.

"The bodies date back two to three decades with the newest one being within the last few years."

Harris's face brightened a reddish hue as he took a deep breath and exhaled loud enough to hear.

I think Jack had the ability to make a lot of people nervous.

His dark hair, which was dusted with silver at the sideburns, gave him the look of distinction, but deeply etched creases in his facial features exposed his trying past.

Harris shook his head. "So much violence. And it's tourist season 'round here." Harris paused. His eyes read, *you city folks wouldn't understand.* "Cave Run Lake is manmade but set in the middle of nature. People love coming here to get away. The word gets out about this, there go the tourists."

"Ten people have been murdered and you're worried about tourists?"

"Course not, but—"

"It sounds like you were."

"Then you misunderstood agent. Besides the counties around here are peaceful, law-abidin' citizens."

"Church goers?" Zachery came up from a tunnel.

"Well, ah, I wouldn't necessarily say that. There are probably about thirty churches or so throughout the county, and right here in Salt Lick there are three."

"That's quite a few considering the population here."

"S'pose so."

"Sheriff." A deputy came up to the group of them and pulled up on his pants.

"Yes, White."

The deputy's face was the shade of his name. "The in-investigators found somethin' you should see." He passed glances among all of us.

Jack held out a hand as if to say, *by all means.*

We followed the deputy up the ramp that led to the cellar. With each step taking me closer to the surface, my chest expanded allowing for more satisfying breaths. Jack glanced over at me. I guessed he was wondering if I was going to make it.

"Tis' way, sir."

I could hear the deputy speaking from the front of the line, as he kept moving. His boots hit the wooden stairs that led above ground from the cellar.

I took a deep inhale as I came through the opening into the

confined space Bingham had at one time called home. Sunlight made its way through tattered sheets that served as curtains, even though, the time of day was now seven, and the sun would be sinking in the sky.

The deputy led us to Bingham's bedroom where there were two CSIs. I heard footsteps behind me. Paige. She smiled at me, but it quickly faded.

"They found it in the closet," the deputy said, pointing our focus in its direction.

The investigators moved aside, exposing an empty space. A shelf that ran the width of the closet sat perched at a forty-five-degree angle. The inside had been painted white at one time but now resembled an antiqued paint pattern the modern age went for. It was what I saw when my eyes followed the walls to the floor that held more interest.

Jack stepped in front of me; Zachery came up behind him and gave me a look that said, *pull up the rear Pending*.

"We found it when we noticed the loose floorboard," one of the CSIs said. He held a clipboard wedged between an arm and his chest. The other hand held a pen, which he clicked the top of repeatedly. Jack looked at it, and the man stopped. "Really it's what's inside that's, well, what nightmares are made of."

I didn't know the man. In fact, I never saw him before, but the reflection in his eyes told me he had witnessed something that even paled the gruesome find in the bunkers.

"You first, Kid." Jack stepped back.

Floorboards were hinged back and exposed a hole about two and a half feet square. My stomach tossed thinking of the CSI's words, *what nightmares are made of*.

"Come on, Brandon. I'll follow behind you." Paige's soft voice of encouragement was accompanied by a strategically placed hand on my right shoulder.

I glanced over at her. I could do this. *God, I hated small spaces*. But I had wanted to be an FBI Special Agent and, well, that wish had been granted. Maybe the saying held merit, *be careful what you wish for, it might come true*.

I hunched over and looked into the hole. A wooden ladder went down at least twenty feet. The space below was lit.

Maybe if I just took it one step at a time.

"What are you waiting for, Pending?" Zachery taunted me. I didn't look at him but picked up on the amusement in his voice.

I took a deep breath and lowered myself down. My feet got a firm hold on the ladder rung and I worked on getting my torso the rest of the way into the space.

Jack never said a word, but I could feel his energy. He didn't think I was ready for this, but I would prove him wrong—somehow. The claustrophobia I had experienced in the underground passageways was nothing compared to the anxiety easing in on my chest now. At least the tunnels were the width of three feet. Here four sides of packed earth hugged me. It felt as if a substantial inhale would expand me to the confines of the space.

"I'm coming." Again, Paige's soft voice had a way of soothing me despite the tight quarters threatening to take my last breath and smother me alive.

I looked up. Paige's face filled the aperture, and her red wavy hair framed her face. It was replaced by the bottom of her shoes.

I kept moving, one rung at a time, slowly, methodically. I tried to place myself somewhere else, but no images came despite my best efforts to conjure them. And what did I have waiting for me at the bottom? Only *what nightmares are made of.*

Minutes had passed before my shoes reached the soil. I took a deep breath and looked around. The confines on my chest eased as I realized the height down here was about seven feet. The room was about five by five, and there was a doorway at the backside.

One pigtail fixture with a light bulb dangled from an electrical wire. It must have fed to the same circuit as the underground passageways and been connected to the power generator as it cast dim light, creating darkened shadows in the corners.

I looked up the ladder. Paige was about halfway down. There was movement behind her, and it was likely Jack and Zachery following behind her.

"You're almost there," I coached them.

By the time the rest of the team made it to the bottom, and the deputy along with a CSI, I had caught my breath.

Paige was the first to head around the bend in the wall.

"The Sheriff is going to stay up there an' take care of things." The deputy pointed in the direction Paige went. "What they found is in here."

Jack and Zachery had already headed around the bend. I followed behind.

Inside the room, Paige raised her hand to cover her mouth. It dropped when she noticed us.

A stainless steel table about the length of ten feet and three feet wide was placed against the back wall. A commercial meat grinder sat on the table. Everything was pristine and light from a bulb refracted off the surfaces.

To the left of the table was a freezer, plain white, one owned by the average consumer. I had one similar, but it was the smaller version because it was only Deb and me.

My stomach tossed thinking about the contents of this one. Paige's feet were planted to where she first entered the room. Zachery's eyes fixed on Jack, who moved toward the freezer and with a gloved hand opened the lid.

Paige gasped, and Jack turned to face her. Disappointment was manifested in the way his eyes narrowed. "It's empty." Jack patted his shirt pocket again.

"If you're thinking we found people's remains in there, we haven't," the CSI said. "But tests have shown positive for human blood."

"So he chopped up his victim's intestines? Put them in the freezer? But where are they?" Paige wrapped her arms around her torso and bent over to look into the opening of the grinder.

"There are many cultures, The Korowai tribe of Papua New Guinea, for example, who have been reported to practice cannibalism even in this modern day," Zachery said. "It can also be involved in religious rituals."

Maybe my eyes should have been fixed on the freezer, on the horror that transpired underground in Salt Lick of Bath County, Kentucky. Instead, I found my training allowing me to focus, analyze, and be objective. In order to benefit the investigation, it would demand these three things, and I wouldn't disappoint. My attention was on the size of the table, the size of the meat grinder, and the size of the freezer. "Anyone think to ask how this all got down here in the first place?"

All five of them faced me.

"The opening down here is only, what, two feet square at the most? Now maybe the meat grinder would fit down, hoisted on a rope, but the table and the freezer? No way."

"What are you saying, Slingshot?"

My eyes darted to Jack's. "I'm saying there has to be another way in." I addressed the CSI, "Did you look for any other hidden passageways? I mean the guy obviously had a thing for them."

"We didn't find anything."

"Well, that doesn't make sense. Where are the burial sites in relation to here?"

"It would be that way." Zachery pointed at the freezer.

We connected eyes, and both of us moved toward it. It slid easily. As we shoved it to the side, it revealed an opening behind it. I looked down into it. Another light bulb spawned eerie shadows. I rose to full height. This find should at least garner some praise from Jack Harper.

"Nothing like Hogan's Alley is it, Kid?"

Chapter 3

Hogan's Alley originally named after a comic strip from the late 1800s is a mock town used by the FBI in Quantico, Virginia as a training ground for future special agents. Placed on ten plus acres, the government built it with the aid of Hollywood set designers. The fact that Jack mentioned it by comparison rendered me silent.

I latched eyes with him before studying the size of the hole. It was just large enough to fit the freezer through if turned and taken in lengthwise.

"This guy did a lot of planning," Paige said. She moved closer to the tunnel entrance. "He definitely didn't want to get caught and probably never thought he would. That could be the elevated thinking of a narcissist."

Jack watched her speak, and something about the way his eyes fell, tracing to her lips, made me wonder about the nature of their relationship.

"Well, I'd definitely peg him as a psychotic too. Narcissists usually only kill if it's the result of a personal affront. But this man gutted his victims and grinded their intestines. Who knows if he ate them?" A visible shiver ran through Paige, and for some reason gauging her reaction intensified the severity of the situation.

For the last while, the training had taken over. I had cataloged the victims as fictional, not once living and breathing individuals. With the snap back to reality, I became aware of the presence of death and the way it hung in the air like a suffocating blanket.

My stomach tightened and I felt sick.

"Question is, did these people threaten him in some way? Were they random? Or were these planned kills? The patience he seemed to execute with the cutting and burial indicates he was very organized. I'd almost lean to believe that they were planned, not random," Zachery said.

"It could be they reminded him of one person who wronged him. That's not uncommon," Paige offered.

I was frozen in place, unable to move and incapable of thinking clearly.

The CSI hunched over and shone a flashlight into the opening. "It spreads out after a few feet. It almost looks as high as it does in here."

"I want to know what happened to the intestines." Jack made the blank statement. "Slingshot, any ideas?"

"The guy knew he was going to prison and had them cleaned up?"

"But why?"

I wanted to say, *what do you mean why?* I thought the answer was obvious, the question rhetorical. But I reasoned on the two words Jack spoke. There was little risk that this room would be discovered even if the bodies were. And if the bodies were, what was a little ground-up human intestine? Another toss of my stomach brought bile into the back of my throat. "I'm not sure."

An ominous silence enveloped the room as if we were all absorbed in contemplating our mortality. The human reaction to death and uncertainty, of wanting to know but not wanting the answers, of sympathy for those lost yet relief that it wasn't us.

The CSI made his way through the opening. His flashlight cast more light in the dimly lit space. I followed and heard the rest of them shuffle in behind me.

After a few feet, I was able to stand to full height.

The CSI looked up at the lit bulb. "The guy thought of everything."

The electricity that had been run down here was basic and minimal. A band of wire ran from the *meat room* to here. But it wasn't so much the electrical that garnered my attention.

To the side of the room, there was a stretcher with metal straps and stirrups. Beside it was a stainless steel tray with a single knife lying on it. Just like the table and meat grinder, light refracted off it. A tube of plastic sheeting stood vertically beside the bed.

"This just keeps getting creepier." Paige took up position beside me.

"Say that again," Deputy White said. "'Cuse me." A hand snapped up to cover his mouth.

Jack was the last to come through the tunnel. I swear even he paused when his eyes settled on the items in the room. "What do you make of it, Kid?"

I put both hands on my hips. The one near the gun wanted to pull it on the man, but my control won out. *Why was it only me who needed to provide the answers?*

"He killed them here." I pointed back to where we came from. "Ground up their intestines in there." I felt sick.

"Whoa nicely put, Pending," Zachery said.

"And how did he get them down here?"

"Well, there's got to be another way in. The freezer alone discloses that, and I mean obviously he wouldn't be able to make the victims go down the ladder, past the meat grinder." I took a deep breath. *Tell me this is the worst we will ever have to deal with.* I wanted to say the words audibly but knew it would be construed as a weakness. "There has to be another way in here, a passageway that connects to the burial sites."

Paige said, "Bingham—"

"You assume," Jack corrected her. "Maybe he worked with someone from the start. They picked the victims and brought them here."

She disregarded him. "Bingham brought them down through the passageway that comes off the cellar. Maybe he drugged them or held them at gunpoint—"

"Or knife point."

Paige rolled her eyes.

I looked forward to the day I could express myself in that

manner to the *Supervisory Special Agent*.

"Whatever. The point is he had a system worked out. Bring them down, bring them in here, cut them, kill them, gut them—"

"You're assuming he didn't gut them while alive."

The deputy tightened the placement of his hand over his mouth and swiveled his hips to the right.

"You said kill them, and then gut them?" Jack asked.

"Either way." A large exhale moved her hair briefly upward. "Gut them to kill them. There you happy? He's one sick son of a bitch either way."

"And he just went away on a fluke charge, killing cows and assaulting a neighbor." I knew once the words came out I should have thought them through. Deputy White looked capable of hauling me to the field and flogging me.

"Cattle are a v-very important investment 'round here. Farmin' is what we people do. It's to be respected an' so is the livestock."

The hint of a smirk dusted Jack's lips. My discomfort brought him happiness. I felt my earlobes heat with anger.

"I didn't mean it like that."

"Then what did you mean?" Both the Kentucky-bred deputy and the local CSI kept their eyes on me.

"He has ten bodies buried underneath his property. Ten *human* bodies. There's a freezer which seems to have been used to hold the unspeakable." My arms pointed in both directions. "Numerous passageways, all the secrecy. Who was this guy really? And don't say a killer. Because I think he was more than that."

"What are you saying, Slingshot?"

"He didn't kill them like this for no reason." I gestured toward Zachery. "Maybe it's something to do with that coinherence symbol of his, or maybe it has something to do with the health profession, but whatever it is, it was for a reason. This guy had something to say."

Zachery stepped toward me. I moved back. He said, "The killers always have something to say."

"Well, I believe this one has more to say than most." All of them watched me as if I were about to shed light on the case. I wish I were.

CAROLYN ARNOLD is the international best-selling and award-winning author of the Madison Knight, Brandon Fisher, and McKinley Mystery series. She is the only author with POLICE PROCEDURALS RESPECTED BY LAW ENFORCEMENT.™

Carolyn was born in a small town, but that doesn't keep her from dreaming big. And on par with her large dreams is her overactive imagination that conjures up killers and cases to solve. She currently lives in a city near Toronto with her husband and two beagles, Max and Chelsea. She is also a member of Crime Writers of Canada.

CONNECT ONLINE

carolynarnold.net
facebook.com/authorcarolynarnold
twitter.com/carolyn_arnold

And don't forget to sign up for her newsletter for up-to-date information on release and special offers at
carolynarnold.net/newsletters.

Made in the USA
Charleston, SC
16 December 2015